DUKE OF MANHATTAN

LOUISE BAY
USA TODAY BESTSELLING AUTHOR

Published by Louise Bay 2017

ISBN - 978-1-910747-46-9

CHAPTER ONE

RYDER

Everything was better on a private plane. Flying private wasn't something the British aristocracy did. My family would consider it too frivolous—*nouveau riche*, as they described it. It wasn't the first or the last thing my family and I disagreed on—I loved everything about the experience. The way the leather seats hugged my ass. The fact that flight attendants' skirts looked shorter and legs looked longer. Even their attention was more flirtatious.

The blonde beauty assigned to this flight dipped low to pour my water and give me a look down her blouse at her high, rounded breasts.

I appreciated the courtesy.

If I'd been going back to London under better circumstances, I might have considered seeing if her attention to detail extended to the bedroom. I liked luxuriating in a blow job and I had the feeling Melanie would be happy to make it last as long as I wanted.

But even gripping this beautiful woman's neck as she buried her face in my lap wasn't going to improve my day.

I glanced at my watch.

"Thirty minutes to landing, sir," Melanie said. It was a shame I'd miss out on her. I didn't normally deprive myself, but I wasn't in the right head space. "Can I get you anything else?"

"No. I'm going to make a quick call." I needed to tell my sister I was about an hour away.

I unclenched my fingers from the soft, cream leather on the arm of the seat. It had been six hours since I'd learned of my grandfather's fall. I didn't often miss being in London but it was times like these where I wished New York was a forty-five-minute drive away from my family.

I had to keep telling myself that there was nothing I could do for my grandfather whether I was sitting next to him by his bed or here in the air.

"Have you landed?" Darcy asked as she answered my call.

"Thirty minutes."

"So you'll be here in a little over an hour. Message me just before you arrive and I'll come down and meet you."

"Why? Is there something you're not telling me?" Had my grandfather's condition deteriorated since I'd last spoken to her?

"No. This hospital is just hard to navigate." She sounded tired, like she'd been up all night. I'd be able to relieve her burden a little when I arrived.

"Is he conscious?" I asked, still unconvinced she was telling me the whole story.

"Yes. He says he's never felt better, but clearly breaking your hip at eighty-two isn't good." Her voice was tight. She was holding herself together. Keeping a stiff upper lip.

"He's going to be fine." This time. "Have you had the results of the CT yet?"

"No. You know it took them a couple of hours to

convince him to have it done." The corners of my mouth tried to tug into a smile without my permission. Darcy would hear the amusement in my voice and be furious with me for taking his side. Grandfather was an indomitable character and there was little anyone could persuade him to do if he didn't want to. And vice versa, when people told him he couldn't do something, he found a way. We were a lot alike in that way. He was my hero when I was young. And more of a parent to Darcy and me than our own feckless mother and father. Our father had run off with a waitress before I could remember him and our mother had never recovered and spent most of her time seeking spiritual enlightenment at various places in Asia. Our grandfather was the man who had soothed us when we were upset, who had come to school plays—who we *still* turned to for advice.

"He hates people fussing," I said.

"I know, but after the stroke, we can't take any chances."

My grandfather's stroke two years ago had been a shock to us all. Luckily for us, he was a fighter and he'd regained most of his speech and movement. But he was frail and weak on his left side, which made him vulnerable to falls. "I know. Still it's going to be fine," I said with as much authority as I could muster, but if his fall had created a bleed in his brain . . . I took a deep breath and tried to steady my rising heart rate.

"Victoria called," Darcy said, her words clipped and tight.

I clenched my jaw and didn't reply. I couldn't bear to hear about my cousin's selfish wife.

"No doubt she wanted to know if they could start counting the silver," Darcy said.

I took a deep breath. I had to keep it together or I'd upset my sister.

My grandfather's title passed to the next married male heir. As I was oldest, it should have been me. But as one woman had never been enough for me, my cousin Frederick, and his wife, Victoria would be the next Duke and Duchess of Fairfax.

It wasn't like I needed the money. I'd made more for myself than my grandfather was worth, and I certainly didn't care about the title. I'd never wanted to be the Duke of Fairfax. Frankly, I'd never understood why my sister being a woman precluded her from being next in line. She should get the title, the money and the estate—and all the headaches that went with it.

Frederick and I had never been close, although as he was heir to Woolton and my grandfather's grandson, I saw more of him than I would have liked. He was jealous and mean-spirited as a child and he'd never grown out of it. He seemed to envy everything I ever had—toys, friends and later women. Despite the fact my sister and I had to live with our grandfather because our parents didn't want us, Frederick hated that we lived at Woolton and he didn't. He never missed an opportunity to criticize what Darcy was doing for the estate. And constantly made comments about me *running away* to America. Insults I could have coped with. What I didn't like was the fact that when I called him to tell him of our grandfather's stroke, instead of asking which hospital he was in or about the prognosis, the first thing he did was tell me he'd call me back when he'd spoken to his lawyer.

There was no going back for us after that.

"Well, tell Victoria to speak to me in future. I'll have no

problem in telling her to fuck off." The fact was, as soon as my grandfather was dead, the silver would be hers to count. And although I didn't have the same pull toward our family's history as Darcy did, it still didn't seem fair.

"We need to talk when you get here. Properly."

I knew what was coming. We were going to discuss how me getting married would change everything. "Of course."

"I mean about Aurora," she said.

Darcy had hinted that our childhood friend would be a willing wife a number of times. This time she sounded more determined. But I'd have to be clear that Aurora wasn't someone I was going to marry. "I'm going to see the lawyers about things while I'm in London, too." I was still hopeful that we'd find a legal solution to Frederick inheriting the estate.

A couple of beats of silence passed. "You know how I feel about that," she said.

"I don't want to fight over grandfather's estate," I replied. Darcy hated the idea that there would be a battle over our grandfather's assets, because it seemed to somehow taint the importance of our love for the man. However, knowing how he wanted my sister to inherit, I knew he would welcome a solution. "But what's our alternative?"

"I really want you to consider an arrangement with Aurora—she cares about our family, and she'd make an excellent wife."

"I don't want to get married." Certainly not to someone who only wanted me for the title I'd inherit. And the alternative—that she'd want a real husband—was worse. Aurora and I had known each other as kids, first crushes, but she didn't know me now, not as an adult.

"I'm sure most men feel like that. And it's not like you have to . . . you know . . . *live* like husband and wife."

"That's not the point, Darce." *Fucking* Aurora would be the least of my problems. She'd always been attractive. I'd have slept with her before now if I hadn't thought she'd read all kinds of meaning into us having sex. But I knew myself well enough to know I could never be faithful to one woman. There were too many beautiful girls in the world. I preferred the ones I didn't know. It was less complicated.

"It's not like we're talking about the rest of your life." I really wanted to make this better for my sister, but she'd see that I could buy her another property, really similar to Woolton Hall. I knew it wouldn't be exactly the same, there wouldn't be that emotional investment she had in Woolton, but her life wouldn't change significantly. The thing was she was married to the estate—it had been her whole life since we were kids. After university, when Darcy said she was going to work full time on the estate, I urged her to find her own path in the world. But working at Woolton was the only thing she wanted to do. She loved the place.

"I have thought about it. A lot." We'd been talking about this for *years*. My grandfather's stroke had only escalated things. "You know Aurora isn't the right woman for me."

"She's as good as anyone. She'd let you do your own thing."

I wasn't the kind of guy who cheated on his wife. Marriage was a commitment, a promise to be faithful, and I didn't break my promises so I didn't make any that I couldn't keep—I wasn't about to become my parents. I wanted to look back at my life and be proud of the man my grandfather had brought up. I wanted to do my grandfather's sacrifices justice.

"Let's talk when you get here. Whether we like it or not, Grandfather is eighty-two. You're running out of time to think about this. You need to act quickly or it will be too late."

She thought she could convince me. As much as I hated to disappoint my sister, it wasn't going to happen.

Fucking was my favorite sport, and I'd gone pro a long time ago. I wasn't about to leave the field a moment before the whistle was blown. And I was determined the game would last as long as I had blood in my veins. Besides, who was I to deprive the women of Manhattan?

I tried not to shudder as I opened the door to my grandfather's room. I hated that very particular smell you got in hospitals. I wasn't sure if they all used the same cleaning products or whether death and disease carried their own fragrance.

"What the hell are you doing here?" Grandfather bellowed at me from his bed as I stepped inside.

I chuckled. "Now that's not a very nice welcome. I hope you're being slightly more charming to the nurses." I winked at a girl in her early twenties who was checking blood pressure readings.

"Everyone is making such a bloody-awful fuss, Ryder. I've been falling over for eighty-two years. I'm not sure why everyone's acting like I'm on my death bed."

I shook my head. "You broke your hip, Grandfather. Did you expect no one to care?"

"They're talking about surgery," Darcy said from behind me.

I spun around. "Surgery? What for?"

My sister looked pale as I pulled her into a hug.

"The hip. They're saying he needs a partial replacement," she mumbled against my shirt.

I squeezed and released her. "He's going to be fine. I'll speak to the doctors."

"I already did. They said surgery almost always follows a fall like this."

"Stop fussing," Grandfather called from his bed.

I laughed. If sheer force of will could keep someone alive, Grandfather would live forever.

"You look good." I patted my grandfather on the shoulder.

He shrugged off my hand. "How's business?" he asked, always ready to live vicariously through me and my life in New York. His whole life had been managing the family's holdings, which included Woolton Hall, a large, stately home outside London, the surrounding land and nearby village, which was rented out to villagers, and a townhouse in London. I never asked him if he resented the responsibility that came with the title, or if he might have done something else, had he been given a choice over his future. But he was a man of honor and commitment, a man to be admired. The person I aspired to be.

"It's good," I replied. "I'm trying to buy a small luxury fragrance business at the moment."

"Fragrance? Doesn't really seem like your thing."

"My thing is anything that makes money." I had an eye for spotting growing businesses and buying them just before their loans were called in or their lack of cash flow paralyzed them. "It's a solid business that needs investment to take a step up."

"And you're going to give them what they need?" he asked, pointing his finger at me.

I shrugged. "I'm a generous guy. You know that."

Darcy rolled her eyes. "No doubt there'll be more in it for you than them."

I nodded. "But there'll still be *something* in it for them. And that's the point. I don't screw them. I'm just shrewd." I was excited about the company I was targeting at the moment. The business hadn't been up and running very long and yet they'd done incredibly well. Retail wasn't my sweet spot but this business was worth stretching myself for.

"How are things back at the house?" I asked as I pulled a chair up to my grandfather's bed.

"The stables need a new roof," Darcy replied. "And frankly so does most of the west wing."

"She doesn't know what she's talking about," my grandfather replied.

My sister had taken over the majority of the running of the estate in the last couple of years. She'd worked side by side with my grandfather since graduating and he'd carefully passed down all that he knew.

"Grandfather, Darcy always knows exactly what she's talking about."

He growled and looked out of the large windows onto the Thames. His lack of argument was as much of an admission as we were going to get.

"I'm going to make a phone call," Darcy said. "Do you want anything while I'm gone?"

I squeezed her hand. I knew what running the estate took out of her, especially as she knew eventually she'd have to walk away from everything she'd done. I'd never understood why she didn't leave, find something of her own to put all of her energy into.

She twisted her hand free and shot me a tired smile.

"We need to talk," my grandfather said as soon as Darcy had gone. I never liked those words coming from anyone's mouth. Bad news always followed.

I leaned back into the chair, ready to take on whatever it was that he had to say.

"I'm getting older, Ryder."

Christ, had Darcy been on at him about me marrying Aurora? We'd agreed to keep Grandfather out of it. I didn't want him to worry that he was leaving behind a big mess for Darcy and me when he died.

My stomach turned over and I leaned forward. "If you're worried about the hip surgery, don't be. You heard Darcy; it's perfectly normal after a break. You're going to be fine."

"I need to tell you something before I go in to surgery." His eyes fixed on mine just like they had when I was a child and I was in trouble. I hated to disappoint him. What had happened? "It's about my investment in Westbury Group."

"Your investment?" My grandfather had given me a couple of thousand pounds when I started up and in return he'd taken a special share. But he'd always refused to take any dividends from the company and he'd never shown any interest in the day-to-day operations. I'd almost forgotten about it.

"We should have sorted this out a long time ago. I guess I just liked the idea of being an investor in your success."

"What are you talking about?" He sounded defeated, and that wasn't the man I knew and loved. "Do you need money for the repairs Darcy mentioned?"

He chuckled and patted the hand I had resting on the side of the bed. I'd never question my grandfather's love, but he didn't show it through hugs and declarations. Darcy and I just knew from the way he was always around, making sure we never needed anything, weren't in trouble, alone or forgotten. He was our anchor.

"No, I don't want your money." He glanced at our hands before nodding. "I'm afraid if your cousin gets his hands on my share, he might have a different view."

I squinted as the early morning sun reflected off the windows and into the room. "I'm not following you. What's my business got to do with Frederick?"

He took a deep breath and began to cough. Jesus, I hated to see him so frail. I poured him some water from the plastic jug on his side table but he waved me away. "I'm fine," he said, wheezing.

"You need to take it easy."

"I said I'm fine." He inhaled and his breathing evened out. I sat back in the chair, trying to look more relaxed than I felt. "Do you remember when I invested in Westbury Group? I took that special share so you wouldn't have the burden of a loan?"

"Yeah, of course." I scanned his face, wanting to get to the crux of what he was saying.

"Well, the money came from the estate, and so the share is in the estate's name."

"I remember," I replied.

"Well, a year or so ago I went to Giles to see if there was anything we could do about this blasted succession thing. It's not right that you should have to be married to inherit. The estate, Woolton, the title. It's all rightfully yours."

I'd been to see our family lawyer and estate trustee to

discuss the future, but I'd never had a conversation about it with Grandfather. I didn't like to be reminded that one day he wouldn't be around to keep me in line.

"You know that it's not important to me. I have my own money and I can more than look after Darcy." I hated talking about what happened after. The thought of a world that my grandfather wasn't a part of wasn't something I wanted to think about.

"Well, that's the point. I'm not sure it *will* be yours."

Had I heard him correctly? "What do you mean?"

"The terms of the trust set out that I can't alter or sell any of the assets of the trust after I turned eighty." My grandfather may be the Duke of Fairfax and heir of the Woolton estate, but everything was managed through a trust that governed exactly what could and couldn't be done in order to preserve the estate for future generations.

"Right. I'm not following you." I glanced over at the door, expecting Darcy to return at any minute. Perhaps she'd understand what grandfather was trying to say.

"So I can't transfer that share back to you. You can't buy me out," he said.

I shrugged. "So. Your investment hasn't affected the way I run the business at all. Keep the share."

"But it's not mine. It belongs to the trust. Which means when I die"—I winced as he said the words—"it passes to Frederick."

I still wasn't understanding. I studied his face, trying to work out exactly what he was saying. "So he'll have a minor share. So what?"

"Have you looked at the paperwork we put in place at the time?" he asked, shifting on the bed.

I couldn't remember any of the nuts and bolts of what we'd done. I'd been too excited to get my business off the ground to care. I'd found a small biotech firm in Cambridge I'd wanted to invest in, an opportunity that wouldn't have lasted long. And it had been one of the best decisions I'd made. It had made me a fortune, and opened the door to new opportunities. It was from that investment that all my success had come and I'd finally felt as if I deserved my place in the world. A much as I loved my grandfather, as I child, I still lived with the reality that I wasn't enough for my parents. Westbury Group helped me feel grounded. It was *mine*. And it wasn't going anywhere. "I can't remember the details. But everything has worked out fine. What's the problem?"

"In order to give you the money from the trust, the share needed to have certain powers. So, if I don't like the way you're running the group, I can take control of the company."

"That's never been an issue, though." There was no one in the world who I trusted more than my grandfather to go into business with.

"But when the share transfers to Frederick . . ."

The scrape of my chair echoed around the room as I stood abruptly. I shoved my hands in my pockets, trying to keep calm. "Are you telling me that Frederick is going to be able to take control of my company?" My grandfather was the person I could trust most in the world. Frederick was the person who I trusted least. "That he could take everything I've worked for all these years?"

"I'm sorry, my boy. I never meant for it to be like this."

I paced up and down by his bed. "So we change the paperwork, right? Can't we pass a resolution that changes the rights of that share?" I stopped and gripped the cream metal bar at the foot of the bed, waiting for my grandfather's response. That had to be the solution, right? "I still own the majority of the company."

He shook his head. "I wish it were that simple. Once I turned eighty, no changes to investments can be made. I'm so sorry, I had no idea my investment in your company, in your future, could affect you like this."

My knuckles whitened as my grip on the bed tightened. "This isn't your fault."

"I should have had Giles do a full review of our assets much sooner, but . . ." But the stroke had happened and all we'd cared about was his health.

"Don't think about it." I didn't want my grandfather to worry about it. I could do that for both of us. Westbury Group was everything I'd worked for my whole life. It meant I never had to rely on anyone—it was my independence. Westbury Group ensured I didn't have to be reliant on anyone for anything.

"I'd like to think that Frederick will do the right thing, but . . ."

I sighed. We both knew that would never happen. If Frederick got the chance to ruin me, he'd grab it with both hands. He'd been waiting his whole life to prove to me he was the bigger man. He wouldn't pass up the opportunity.

I had to make this right.

"We'll find a solution. I'll speak to Giles about it."

I might not be the next Duke of Fairfax, but I would do everything within my power to make sure that Frederick didn't end up destroying everything I'd ever worked for.

CHAPTER TWO
SCARLETT

Dating in New York City was the worst.

I was following all the advice the internet had to offer—not being too available, not having sex too early and not putting all my eggs in one basket. But I just lurched from one disappointment to another disaster. I'd thought the guy last Thursday was super cute in complimenting my shoes until he confessed he liked to dress up in women's clothes at the weekend and would like to see if my pink suede five-inch heels came in his size. Maybe I was being too picky, but I just didn't want to fight with my boyfriend over who wore what when we went for dinner.

And then there was the guy who looked like he'd never had a haircut and didn't look me in the eye once during our entire date. And how could I forget the forty-something, sweaty man who told our waitress she had a nice rack?

I swiped across the screen of my phone to see a text from Andrew—so far no disaster with him. We'd only had one date, and besides getting the feeling he was a neat freak, he seemed relatively normal. I wasn't attracted to him exactly. And he hadn't made me laugh. But he didn't have me wanting to stab him in the eye with a fork after twenty minutes, so I'd agreed to date number two.

Looking forward to seeing you tonight.

I pulled up my calendar and found an entry that said, "*Dinner with Peter.*" I looked back at my phone. Had I gotten the contacts confused? Peter was the one who wore plaid and had a cat. I'd agreed to a third date with dinner because on our second date, he'd tipped our waitress really well, even though it was clear he didn't earn very much. I wasn't exactly attracted to Peter either.

I scrolled through the messaging history. No, the text was definitely from Andrew.

Shit.

I'd double-booked.

The door to my office swung open and my business partner, Cecily, poked her head of corkscrew curls around the door. "Are you free?" she asked.

"Sure, if you can help me solve my dating dilemma." I'd been sharing dating dilemmas with Cecily since college. Roommates our sophomore year, we'd bonded as soon as we'd unpacked our copies of *The Notebook* and abandoned the day for a few hours with Ryan Gosling. I'd been a finance major and her sweet spot had been marketing. It made for the perfect business pairing.

"That sounds like fun. Being married is so boring sometimes." She took a seat in the chair opposite my desk.

I'd never thought that marriage was boring. I'd loved my husband, had looked forward to going home in the evening and hanging out with him. Over two years after our divorce, and I still missed him. Missed having a partner in crime. Missed my best friend. I forced a smile. "That's what Marcus said." Apparently, being in Connecticut with me wasn't enough for my ex-husband. It was the reason I was here looking over the Hudson and living in a one-bedroom apartment in downtown Manhattan with 90 percent of my belongings in storage. As a married woman I'd lived in a beautiful four-bedroom, clapboard house in Connecticut with incredible views of the water and a fifteen-minute commute to my office. The change was still like a knife to the stomach sometimes. Still in my twenties, I should be embracing living in the city that never slept.

Maybe I *was* boring.

When he left me, he told me he hated the idea his life was mapped out for him, but me? I'd been happy. Content. With Marcus by my side, everything had been as I had always imagined my life would be from a little girl. I hadn't thought to wish for anything more.

"I'm sorry. I wasn't trying to be insensitive."

I smiled. "It's fine. It was a long time ago." Except it didn't feel like it on days like today. I didn't want to be dating. I'd much prefer to go home and snuggle into bed with a book than go to some fancy restaurant and try to be engaging and funny.

Dating was exhausting.

"So what's your dilemma? I'll share mine if you'll share yours?" she asked as she took a seat on the other side of my desk from me.

"You have a dating dilemma? Does your husband know?" I said, grinning.

"I'm discreet," she said with a wink. "Come on, spill."

"I'm just double-booked, that's all. I made dinner plans with Andrew and Peter tonight."

"Again?" She cocked her head to one side. "Isn't that the second double-booking in the last couple of weeks?"

Yeah. And exactly how had I let this happen *again*?

"Well I guess it means you're wanting to see them."

The exact opposite, actually. Andrew and Peter were both nice enough, but I couldn't see a future with them. Neither of them were my soulmate.

"It's no big deal. I'll just cancel one of them." Or both of them and have a date with my e-reader. "I assume your dilemma's not a dating one."

Cecily's curls bounced as she laughed. "No such luck, and it's not just my dilemma, either. It's yours too." She widened her eyes. "We've had another approach from Westbury."

Westbury was by far the most enthusiastic investment company we'd been speaking to about stepping in to pay off our loans that were about to become due. But it was also the least flexible in its terms.

"I'm so sorry we're in this situation," Cecily said.

"Don't apologize. We had to have that money and we didn't have any other offers." Cecily Fragrance had become successful almost too quickly and a year ago we had needed a lot of money, fast, to be able to fulfill the orders we were getting. Cecily might have signed the loan documentation because I'd been out of town, but it was as much my decision as it had been hers. "We knew it was a short term thing. Who knew we'd be this successful?" The loans were due to be paid back but we had to keep any cash we had to continue to invest in the inventory. We needed the loans replaced. Next month. If we didn't get them our cash flow would disappear. "And Westbury hasn't changed its offer?"

"It's still all or nothing. They take the whole business, they hire us as employees and we lose our shareholding."

Westbury had a reputation for being shrewd and successful. "The money's better though," she said, sounding more positive.

Most investors were happy to take a minority stake in the company, but Westbury Group wanted the lot. Cecily and I had started this business. We'd handpicked each one of our employees. Hell, I'd even chosen the coffee machine. We didn't want to just walk away. But was Cecily wavering? Was she on the ropes?

"What do you mean, better?"

Her eyes flickered over the surface of my desk. "Enough to pay all the shareholders what we'd hoped to get at the end of year three."

I snapped my mouth shut. That was a *lot* of money.

Cecily and I *could* start again. But I loved Cecily Fragrance. It had become something I never thought a job could be—a passion.

It had provided distraction while I was grieving the loss of my marriage. I'd never understood it when my friends talked about their work like it was a hobby until Cecily and I started our business. It never felt like work for me. I loved it. And Cecily Fragrance had been the only good in my life since my divorce. I had needed a change, to not just see the hole where my husband had been wherever I looked. Marcus walking out had rocked my world, but a drive to prove he'd made the wrong decision had lit a fire in me. It was proof to my husband that I wasn't as predictable, boring and safe as he thought I was —he'd no doubt expected me to stay in a corporate job at an investment bank with a steady monthly salary for the rest of my career. Setting up my own business, with no structure and process unless I created it and taking a chance on getting paid every month was something he never would have thought I was capable of. And not something I'd ever imagined for myself. But when your world is on its ass, sometimes, you'll try anything. I might not have been able to save my marriage, but I wasn't ready to give Cecily Fragrance up.

"What do you think? You want to walk away? Give up everything we've worked so hard on and let someone else reap all the success and rewards?" *Say no. Please say no.*

She winced. "Well, not when you put it like that. But I'm not sure we have a choice. None of the other offers pay off our loans in full."

Had she given in so easily?

I certainly hadn't. My brother was a wealthy guy and would want to help us out if I told him the situation. But I knew his company had taken over a rival recently and he didn't have a lot of cash at the moment. Besides, I wanted to do this on my own. I didn't want my brother to have to save me.

"I understand that you'd rather see Cecily Fragrance continue without you than fail with you." I didn't think it would have to come to that. I knew we could make this work. We'd brought it this far.

As the face of the company, Cecily handled all the major business meetings, while I concentrated on keeping the wheels turning on the day-to-day operations. I'd heard plenty of horror stories of management getting distracted with new investment and I was determined not to let that happen. I'd not dealt with the investors but if Cecily was being beaten down, it was my turn to step into the ring. "We may still get other offers, might even be able to use those to increase some of the offers we've already had."

She picked lint from her skirt. "Maybe. I just really don't want us to go under and we'd still have jobs."

"How about I meet with all the bidders and try to negotiate?" I suggested. "I worked for an investment bank. I might have learned a couple of things on the way." Surely there was a way Cecily and I could keep running this business with the loans replaced.

"You think you might change their minds?" she asked.

I shrugged. "Who knows? But it's worth a try, isn't it? We still have some fight left in us, don't we?" I wanted to know I hadn't lost hers.

"The next instalment on the loans is due in a month—we don't have long."

I nodded, trying to ignore the twitch under my eye telling me it was an almost-impossible task. "We can't give up, Cecily. This is our baby."

She smiled half-heartedly. "It's taken so much energy to get this far, I'm not sure I have enough to finish the race."

"Well, that's why I'm here. I'm going to get us both over the finish line. Whatever it takes."

I was going to save Cecily Fragrance.

And I was going to cancel on Andrew *and* Peter and call my sister, Violet, for drinks. I wanted to have the evening I wanted to have, rather than the one I thought I should have as a twentysomething in Manhattan.

"I hope to God you're banging them both. And at the same time every Tuesday," Violet said as I explained to her about my double-booking. My sister told me nothing but the truth, and she believed in me more than anyone I knew. If I was going to fight Westbury Group to retain a shareholding, then

Violet was the perfect pre-match pep squad.

"Shhhh," I said, glancing around to check if anyone had heard her.

The bar, one of my favorites, felt like a private member's club from the fifties with its low lighting, Chesterfield sofas and American standards coming from the grand piano in the corner. It represented how I'd imagined Manhattan would be rather than the realities of dating, long hours and traffic that weren't quite so glamorous.

"Well, really, what were you doing bringing me to a place like this?" she asked.

She was right. This was the sort of place Harper and I came with our best friend Grace. Violet and I normally ended up going for burgers in midtown. "I like it."

"So?" Violet asked. "Are you banging them both? I know it's too much to hope that you're doing them at the same time." She squinted at a party of suits across the bar who I'd noticed had checked her out as she'd wafted in earlier. "I think I'd like to try a three-way before I'm old. Two men, though," she clarified. "I did the two girls and a guy thing in college and it didn't work for me."

I spluttered into my glass, half choking. "Violet. Please. Save me from death by embarrassment. At least for tonight."

"Well if you answer my question, I'll stop over-sharing."

"No, I'm not *banging* them—certainly not both at once."

"Urgh," Violet said. "I might have known. Tell me you've fucked *someone* since your divorce. Please. Tell me your vibrator isn't the only thing to have given you an orgasm in the last two years."

Violet may be teasing, but the way she said it, I felt slightly ashamed that I'd still not managed to take that step of first-time sex after divorce. My sister was so . . . liberal with her relationships with men; I knew she'd find it difficult to understand why I'd not slept with any of the guys I'd dated. I didn't even understand it myself. But none of them had seemed quite what I was looking for. They hadn't been special. I'd dated plenty of men since Marcus, gotten myself back out there. I just hadn't taken that final step.

I'd even dated guys exclusively. Well one guy. For about a week until it became clear that there was no way I was going to be able to avoid sleeping with him, so I ended things.

Violet grabbed my hand. "I know I've said this all along, but what you need is a one-night stand. You're overthinking the sex thing. It's just sex. Like brushing your teeth or exercising. It's a fact of life."

"It's difficult." I understood and I agreed with Violet—sex wasn't such a huge deal. But sex after marriage was terrifying. Perhaps because I'd finally be accepting that my marriage was over and also because sex was a precursor to a relationship—a threshold that I had to step over. If I kept on this side, then I was safe. And when things ended, no one could say the relationship was a failure if it didn't exist in the first place. I didn't want to go through life leaving a trail of disappointment and broken relationships behind me.

"It's really not. And frankly, if you're really nervous you can just lie there while he does all the work. It won't be as good but if that's all you can manage, with your banging body and beautiful face, you don't need to do anything to get a guy off."

"Are we *really* having this conversation?" I wasn't nervous. I missed sex. I just didn't want a relationship that was doomed to failure.

Violet reached out and patted my hand. "We're going to keep having this conversation until you get over this issue you have around your first time, first love thing. Your life isn't a Coke commercial. No one's life is a Coke commercial. And Marcus has gone and he's not coming back. Anyway, you know he's fucking Cindy Cremantes now."

I'd heard that particular rumor last time I was at my brother's house in Connecticut. Cindy was still working at the pharmacy in Westchester as she had since school. I wasn't sure why she was so much more exciting than I was.

"I don't think my life is a Coke commercial."

"I beg to differ. I understand that Marcus is the only guy you ever slept with, but despite this décor, we're not actually in the fifties." She circled her finger in the air. "You're not a housewife. You don't have to pretend you don't like sex. That's not what life is like in the modern world."

"I like sex plenty. I'm not frigid."

Violet sighed. "Marcus didn't leave you because you're boring in bed. You don't have to be afraid."

"Yeah, I know." Marcus wasn't boring in the bedroom, and I enjoyed sex with him. But I would have been open to something . . . new, more. I didn't want to throw our car keys into a bowl at the next country club dinner or anything but maybe he could have fucked me on the kitchen floor or talked a little dirty to me once in a while. Once, when we were newlyweds, I'd interrupted his shower and dropped to my knees all ready to give him a blow job when he awkwardly told me he didn't have time because he was running late for work. "I'm just not ready for a relationship."

"Sex isn't a relationship. You're waiting to see if these

guys you're dating are Mr. Right until you fuck them?" she asked, drawing her brows together as if it was the most ludicrous thing she'd ever heard.

I shrugged. "More that I'm avoiding a relationship by not having sex."

She nodded. "Okay. Got it. But you're missing out— having sex with someone doesn't mean you're having a relationship with them. Not always. What you need is sex with a stranger."

I'd never picked up a guy before—barely even flirted with someone who wasn't my husband. Marcus and I had been dating since high school. "So how would this one-night stand thing go? If, in theory, I was prepared to do something like that."

Violet swallowed her sip of vodka before breaking into a huge grin. "Pick a guy." She nodded toward a man sitting at the bar, swirling his drink and staring at the bottom of his glass like he had a lot on his mind. "He's hot. No wedding ring. Get it done."

Get it done? It wasn't highlights or a run around the park.

"Don't be stupid. I can't just pick up a guy." From what I could see the man at the bar *was* attractive—a strong jaw, a nicely cut suit you could tell was handmade. But he could still live at home with his mom or have a fetish for peeing on women . . . or men. I was prepared to push at my boundaries, but there were limits.

"You keep telling me you want to be more adventurous. Now, I think you've got no worries on that score—you've just let dipshit Marcus get in your head. But in theory, if you did want to have a one-night stand, he would be perfect."

She lifted her chin toward the hot guy at the bar.

"Just find someone to fuck. Someone you'll never see again and then when you find someone you really like, you can have a relationship *and* the sex."

"I liked Andrew. And Peter, for that matter."

"Maybe you did. But not enough. Maybe it's all the pressure. With a stranger, there's no expectation—apart from that you're both gonna get laid."

Maybe that was it. Maybe I just didn't need to think about it—about anything.

"You're doing that thing," Violet said, frowning at me.

"What thing?"

"The thing where you tap your index finger. It's annoying."

"You're annoying."

She just shrugged as if the idea didn't bother her at all. Violet was always so sure of herself and everything around her. It was almost as if she were wearing super-strength glasses with a prescription straight out of science fiction— she saw things differently, more clearly than I did. Usually, she was right.

"In theory—because there's no way I'm ever going to do it—if I *wanted* to pick up the guy at the bar, what would I do?"

"In theory?" Violet asked.

I nodded while taking the two tiny black straws sticking out of my cocktail into my mouth.

"You wouldn't have to do much. Just find a reason to go to the bar."

"Why would I need to go to the bar? They have table service."

Violet exhaled loudly. "I said *find* a reason. It doesn't matter what it is. Just go to the bar and order an unusual drink." She paused, her mouth slightly open as if she were midway through a word. "A French 75."

"That's a cocktail?" It sounded more like a paint color or a dog breed.

"A French 75 is *the* cocktail. How do you live in New York City and not know these things?" she asked. "It's not on the menu, which makes you look cool and sophisticated. And it's a talking point."

"So, I go to the bar, order the drink. And then what? I ask him to fuck me?"

"Shhh, this is a nice place," Violet said giggling. "Just go over, stand close to him. Be open to it. Maybe glance sideways at him. In that dress, it's all you'll have to do."

I glanced down at my dress. It was my red one. I'd worn it for work. It couldn't be that sexy.

"Maybe after I finish my drink."

Violet rolled her eyes. "Maybe my ass. You'll never do it."

I kept being told what I wouldn't do. What I wasn't. By Marcus, by recruitment consultants who'd said I'd never be a finance director after working in treasury, by my brother who said I'd never move to the city.

Well fuck it.

I'd done all those things. I could walk up to a bar and order a damn drink.

"Two French 75s coming right up." I slid out of the booth and didn't glance back to see if I'd shocked Violet. I didn't want to lose my nerve. It wasn't like I had to talk to the guy at the bar. If anything, it would be better if I didn't. I could prove to Violet that picking up a man wasn't as easy as she thought it was.

My red patent heels clipped on the wooden parquet floor, out of sync with the heartbeat pounding in my chest. The guy Violet had pointed out was sitting at the corner of the bar, so rather than slide in next to him, I went to the corner, that way I could check to make sure it wasn't just his profile that was handsome.

I placed my hands flat on the shiny mahogany, deliberately not looking to my right. The barman wasn't behind the bar.

"I think he went out back for a second," the handsome guy said with an accent I couldn't place. I glanced over. Nope, his profile wasn't the only thing handsome about him. As soon as I looked at him, it was as if my eyes were glued to his. He grinned. "Hi."

I sucked in a breath and smiled, curling my fingers under my hands and squeezing my nails into my palms. "Hi." His eyes, a deep chocolate brown, watched me as if I was the only thing in the room.

"Ryder," he said.

"Oh. Scarlett." I nodded, still smiling. "My name that is. I mean, my name is Scarlett."

Get it the fuck together, Scarlett. He's just a man.

Except, he wasn't *just* anything. He certainly didn't look like any man I'd ever met. He looked like a movie star. Even sitting down, I could tell he was tall—taller than Marcus who stood at five eleven. His skin was tan and his hair a shiny chestnut brown. One large hand gripped his glass and the other stroked down his jaw.

He raised his eyebrows. "Scarlett? As in O'Hara?"

"No, as in *King*."

The corners of his lips curled up into a half smile and he nodded. "Scarlett King. I like that."

I like that, I repeated in my head, trying to sound like he did. And then I got it. He was British.

His full, pouting lips.

His almost smile.

His accent.

Wow.

If either Peter or Andrew had been like this guy, I wasn't sure I would have been able to stop myself from sleeping with them, whatever my concerns. But they weren't. They hadn't made the hairs on the back of my neck stand on end. Hadn't gotten me to push my shoulders back and my chest forward. Hadn't made me think about what they'd look like naked.

"Sorry to keep you waiting," a man said to my left. I tried to turn my gaze back to the bartender, but Ryder had captured it.

"Scarlett and her friend over there would like a drink. Put it on my bill," Ryder said.

"That's a bit risky. What if I said I was ordering a bottle of Cristal?" I asked.

"I'd say they don't offer it here but the twenty-o-one Krug is excellent. And put it on my bill."

I didn't know how to reply.

"Martin. The Krug," Ryder said to the barman. He sounded so authoritative. Perhaps it was just the way each word he said was a little clipped because of his accent.

Shit. I didn't want to look like one of those girls that was just after the most expensive drinks she could get. "Oh, no! You don't have—I really just came over for a couple cocktails. The same again if you don't mind," I told the barman. I'd forgotten the name that Violet had given me.

"You're turning down Krug?" Ryder asked with a frown.

"Yeah, this way, I can talk to you without you thinking you bought your time."

Ryder raised his eyebrows. "Now that I can live with. So where shall we start?"

Shit, I had no idea what came next. I'd only gotten as far as ordering a cocktail when talking it through with Violet. He tilted his head slightly and I waited for him to decide. "Tell me what you're discussing so conspiratorially about over there with your friend," he said. "You looked like two girls who didn't want to be interrupted."

Weren't we supposed to start with the basics? What I did for work? Did I live in New York? Something in the way he looked at me told me this guy wanted my soul straight out the gate.

"You first," I said. "Why are you here? Drowning your sorrows? Bad breakup? Lost a trillion dollars?"

He chuckled. "Nothing like that," he said, taking a sip of his drink. "Trying to keep myself awake so I wake up tomorrow without jet lag. I flew in from London earlier today."

London. Interesting.

"You're here on business?" I asked, leaning against the barstool, letting myself relax a little.

"I'm based here and my business is here too. You live in the city?"

I nodded. "So you were just visiting London?"

"Yeah, my grandfather had a fall and so I flew back to check on him."

I rolled my eyes. What a cheeseball. "You were visiting

your sick grandfather?" I stood up and looked to see if our cocktails were ready. "Does any girl believe it when you tell them that?"

He laughed. "You're right. That sounded like a line. But it's true. Luckily he's fine and you haven't hurt my feelings." I didn't know if he was playing with me.

"Well, if your grandfather is sick, then I'm sorry."

His eyes seemed to sparkle as he watched me, giving me lots of time to finish what I was thinking. "Thank you," he said finally. "If I was wanting to be cheesy, I'd ask you to tell me something about yourself that no one else knows."

"That's cheesy? I think it's kinda nice-cheesy. Rather than sleazy-cheesy."

"Well it's good to know which box I'm in." His sparkle was back. His eyelashes were so long, I had to look closely to check he wasn't wearing mascara. The city was full of metrosexuals, but I wasn't about to go to bed with a man who wore makeup. I liked a guy who thought anything other than shower gel and shampoo was strictly for people with vaginas.

But Ryder's lashes were bare of any enhancement.

"So, why don't *you* tell *me* something that no one else knows? Something real," I said.

He narrowed his eyes as he looked at me as if he was trying to figure out whether he could be honest. "Sometimes I can't sleep at night because I worry I won't get it all done before I die," he said, looking away and into his drink.

The sparkle left his eyes when he'd spoken and I reached for him but didn't want to touch, didn't know where that would lead, so left my hand resting on the wood next to his drink. "Get what done?" Maybe he was back from visiting his grandfather and contemplating his place in the world.

"Everything I'm here to do." He stared at my hand and I pulled it away. "You never think about it? What's left at the end?"

His expression was so sad, I wanted to make it better.

"Not on a Tuesday," I replied in a matter-of-fact way.

He looked back at me, grinning. "That's a good strategy. I'm going to try it. Now, your turn."

"Something no one else knows?" My family knew me very well and Marcus knew me inside and out. "I'm not sure there's anything *no one* else knows."

"Liar," he whispered.

I was pretty sure this conversation wasn't the sort that led to bed. It certainly didn't feel like foreplay.

"Okay, one thing no one else knows," I said, pulling my shoulders back and picking up the two cocktails the barman set down in front of me. "I think you're a sexy guy."

And before I could catch his expression, I turned back to Violet with our drinks.

Had I just said that? Well, it was true. And no one else knew it except me. I mean, I'm sure plenty of people told him he was a sexy guy. But *I* hadn't told anyone. Not until I'd told him. I wanted to let out a squeal. I couldn't believe I'd actually said it. I was pretty sure Violet would approve.

"Why did you leave him? It looked like it was going well," Violet complained as I sat back down opposite her.

"What did you expect? That he'd flip me over the bar and fuck me in public?"

"Maybe," she replied.

I chuckled. I'd not gotten his full name. And he'd not asked for my number. But it had been fun. And not as scary as I'd expected.

"Well at least you've lightened up. Just think how much lighter you'd be if you'd fucked him."

"Sex isn't the answer to *everything*." It wouldn't save my company or pay the mortgage.

"Yeah but *good* sex makes everything a little bit better," Violet said.

"I couldn't agree more," a man said from beside us.

I snapped my head around to find Ryder standing over our table. How much had he heard?

"I think *you're* sexy," he said, staring straight at me. "And I want your number."

"I'm just leaving," Violet said, grabbing her purse and scooting out of the booth.

"Wait, I'll come with you." It had suddenly gotten very hot in here and I needed some air.

"No you won't," Ryder said. "You're staying here for a little while. With me. I want to get to know you a little better."

Violet's mouth widened in a bright smile. "You heard the man with the accent. Call me later. I love you." And before I had another chance to argue she'd disappeared and I was left sitting opposite the sexiest British guy I'd ever met, who didn't seem to find me boring at all.

Chapter Three
Ryder

I hadn't planned on fucking anyone tonight. I'd only gone to the bar to avoid falling asleep in my apartment. I'd left London at noon and if I could stay awake until midnight Eastern, I wouldn't be plagued by jet lag.

But jet lag was the last thing on my mind now.

Even if I didn't go home with her and fuck her into the early hours, the beautiful woman in front of me was going to keep me awake all night. The memory of her raven-black hair and the way she kept trying to swallow her smiles would keep me bright, alert and hard.

"You live in Manhattan?" I asked.

She nodded. "I have a small place in SoHo. I moved from Connecticut just less than two years ago."

"Connecticut?"

"Yeah. I grew up there. Got married there. Stayed until my divorce . . ." She trailed off at the end as if she didn't want me to hear.

Interesting. She didn't look old enough. "Were you married long?"

She slid the napkin that sat underneath her drink to the left. "Long enough."

She wasn't giving much away. She was hot. And feisty.

And had more than a little Scarlett O'Hara in her. But I didn't have Rhett's patience. Sex was an escape. It wasn't about emotions or opening up or any of the shit that women thought it was. It was release—mindless oblivion.

I took a sip of my Negroni.

"Have you been married?" she asked.

I almost choked on my drink. As if. I hammered on my chest with my fist, trying not to look like a total dick.

Married? Well wouldn't that make everything easier? I'd managed to lock it away in the back of my mind for a few hours. And there it was back in a flash—the thought of losing Westbury Group to Frederick. Or Fred-a-dick as we used to call him as kids.

"No, never been married."

"Come close?" she asked.

Didn't she get it? We weren't on a date. We were just passing some time until it was acceptable to leave and fuck.

Did I want to get in deep? In her? Yes. Emotionally? Hell no.

"I've known a lot of amazing women."

She tapped her index finger against her glass. I couldn't tell if it was nerves or disapproval. "I imagine you have."

I leaned forward and whispered, "You seem pretty amazing."

She tried to bite back that half smile again as she shook her head. "You're a cheeseball."

"Because I give you a compliment?" I asked, a little confused. Women ordinarily thought I was smooth. Or so I thought.

"No, because you can't possibly know whether I'm amazing. But I get it. You're trying to get me into bed."

It was almost as if I was hearing exactly what she was thinking. And it was refreshing and a little bit uncomfortable. "Well, you're right about me trying to seduce you. But I'm not confessing to the cheeseball thing."

She gave me a full smile and my stomach roiled. Talk about a weapon of mass distraction. "What happens if you're successful and I come home with you and it ends up a disaster?" She put her hand up to stop me from answering. And I was grateful because I had no idea what to say. "Never mind," she said. "Let's go."

"Go?"

"Your place. I take it you live nearby?"

I hadn't expected it to be that easy. I thought she'd take a little more time, require a little more attention. But I wasn't about to argue. "But you're just in SoHo."

She raised her eyebrows. "But you don't have an invitation to mine."

Most women preferred to go back to their place. If they lived out of the city, I took them to a hotel. Usually the Regent, which was two blocks from my apartment, so I didn't have far to go when we were done.

"You changed your mind?" she asked, lightly, like it wouldn't bother her at all.

"Sorry, I was thinking."

"About where you live? Did you forget?"

I chuckled. This girl might have banter. I didn't encounter that much in the women of New York. I took out my wallet and flipped it open. "You think you're funny?" I asked as I pulled out a fistful of twenty dollar bills.

"Sometimes," she said with a laugh.

"Well, I'm going to fuck the funny right out of you."

Without checking her reaction, I slid the money onto the table and led her out of the bar.

Stepping out into the crisp Manhattan air, I took a deep breath as I placed my hand in the small of Scarlett's back, guiding her toward my building. So what if I took her home? She didn't seem like the stalker type and it meant I could just roll over and go to sleep without having to scramble for my boxers afterward.

"It's not far," I said. "Just on the next block." She hadn't looked at me or said a word since we'd left the bar. She'd shoved her hands in her pockets and studied the sidewalk.

"Would you prefer to get a cab?" I asked. I never normally tried to fill silences, but it seemed like Scarlett was a little nervous. She didn't need to be, but I was pretty certain that reassuring her I wouldn't cut her into tiny pieces wasn't going to help the situation. She'd soon relax under my tongue.

"No, I like to walk. It's my thing. Except normally in flats."

"Yes, those don't look like they're made for walking." I glanced down at the red, fuck-me shoes she was wearing.

She laughed. "They don't feel like they are either." But she took off ahead of me as the sign flashed *walk* and she began to cross the road. I caught up in two long strides.

"That's disappointing. I'd hoped you wouldn't want to kick those off as soon as we got inside." I smoothed my hand up her back.

She glanced sideways at me and just nodded. I was hoping for a little more . . . encouragement. I dipped my head to whisper into her ear. "I'll see if you can be convinced."

She took a breath as if she were about to speak but didn't say anything.

"We're here," I said, grateful my apartment was so close.

She pulled out her mobile. "Okay. Stand there," she said, pushing on my shoulder so I stood with my back against the wall to my building. I thought maybe she was going to kiss me but her touch wasn't one of desire.

Before I had a chance to ask her what she was doing, she'd taken my picture. "What's your apartment number?" she asked.

"It's the penthouse. Why?"

She glanced up from her phone and narrowed her eyes as if she were assessing whether I was telling the truth or not. "I'm sending it to Violet."

"Violet?"

She nodded as she tapped on her mobile. "My sister. You met her earlier."

"Well, had I known you were sending it to a family member, I would have worked harder on my pose," I said.

She laughed. "Oh you would? Well, knock yourself out," she said, holding up the phone again.

I scrunched up my face and poked out my tongue.

"I thought you were going to go all Zoolander on me," she said, laughing. "I might have changed my mind about coming up to your apartment now, if you've given me a glimpse into what you look like in the morning."

I shook my head and slung my arm around her shoulders. "Well I better get you inside quickly, then."

Scarlett continued to concentrate on her phone as we rode the elevator up. "There. She got the message."

"We're talking about Violet?" I asked.

"Yep. So we're all good. If I die tonight, this is the first place they'll look for you."

I chuckled as I glanced at her. She was clearly practical.

"I'm just a little nervous." Her voice was muted. "This isn't really my thing. Not sex. Sex is my thing. Totally. Love it. Just. You know. With you. I'm not sure how this goes." She winced and took a breath. "I'm going to put myself on mute now. I'm ridiculous."

"Okay," I replied, not quite sure how to react. New York was full of uber-sophisticated women. Scarlett looked like one of them but she was fresh and unsullied somehow. She just said exactly what she was thinking, without second guesses. I liked it. "You're fine. Don't mute on my account."

She looked up at me and smiled and made a motion to zip or unzip her lips, I wasn't sure.

"We're going to enjoy our evening together," I said, trying to be reassuring.

"I hope so."

I knew so.

"After you," I said as the elevator doors opened.

"The elevator opens right into your apartment?"

"Sure." I shrugged off my coat and left it on the chair by the console table where my housekeeper had left my mail.

I shuffled through the envelopes as I made my way into the living space.

"Wow," Scarlett said from behind me.

"Scarlett, I want you to take off your clothes," I said, walking down the two marble steps toward the sofa as I began to open an envelope.

"Excuse me?"

I glanced up at her and held her gaze. "You heard me. You want this to be good. So you have to trust me to tell you what we both need."

Her eyebrows pulled together but she didn't ask again.

This was the moment I knew whether or not the sex would be good.

Would she do as she was told?

Would she mind undressing in the lit room?

Would she want to please me?

It felt like hours passed as we stared at each other. Eventually she reached behind her to unzip her dress.

Nice. I didn't have to ask her twice.

She peeled the red fabric off her shoulders, pulling it forward to reveal a black lace bra. Her breasts weren't huge but they were generous and suited her frame. Wiggling her hips one way and then the other, she slid the dress over her ass and it fell onto the floor.

"Keep the heels on." Blood rushed to my cock as I said it. I'd enjoy fucking her in those things.

She didn't smile, didn't break eye contact. She just reached behind her and unsnapped the clasp of her bra.

I nodded in encouragement as she hooked her thumbs through the straps and took it off.

I looked away first. I couldn't help it. The sharp points of her nipples were a perfect pink, and begging to be sucked.

But not yet.

As she leaned forward to take off her panties, her breasts swung deliciously. She was still watching me, her mouth slightly open—I had to stifle a groan at the thought of those lips around my cock.

She stepped out of her underwear and stood tall, pulling her shoulders back.

Gorgeous.

Her waist was small and her hips flared out in perfect proportion to her shoulders. My fingertips buzzed at the thought of pushing against that warm, soft flesh around her ass. Her black hair, which had looked so great against the red of her dress, contrasted even more sharply against the white of her skin. I wanted to gather it up and pull her head back so she could look only at me.

"You're beautiful," I said.

She rolled her hips, enjoying my attention.

"Now sit down and open your legs."

She paused for just a second, looked behind her and sank onto the sofa, letting her knees fall open.

"Bring your bottom forward." I said. "And wider. I want to look at you."

She placed her palms on the inside of her thighs and pulled them apart. I swear, this woman could make me come without a single touch. So compliant, so confident, so beautiful.

I tossed my mail, vaguely aware of it skidding across the floor, and stalked toward her. Standing over her, I shrugged off my jacket.

It wasn't just the fact that she wanted to please me that got me hard—that was what normally did it for me. With Scarlett, it was the way the woman who'd nervously chattered on our way here was so fucking confident about her body.

About my desire.

And she had every right to be confident. On both counts.

"Anyone ever tell you how pretty your pussy is?" I asked, kneeling between her thighs.

She was trimmed into a neat triangle but I appreciated

that she wasn't bare. I liked to fuck women—real women. Her back arched in response. I'd take that as a no.

I wanted to dive straight into her but I would resist. I would ratchet up her need for me a little more.

"Wider," I whispered.

What a view. Those breasts. That pussy. That perfectly flat stomach. Those deep brown eyes.

To think I might have missed out on this if I'd stayed in this evening.

"I want you to keep your hands on your knees until I tell you to move them, you hear me?"

She rolled her lips together and nodded.

"I need to hear your answer."

"Yes. I'll keep them there."

"I'm going to lick and suck and make you come—but you're not to move your hands."

Her belly quivered and she let out a breathless, "Yes."

Perfect. It was like her desire was neutralizing the nerves.

My cock pressed against the fabric of my pants, but it was going to have to be patient.

I took off my cufflinks. Then slowly rolled up my shirt sleeves. She squirmed in front of me but made no attempt to urge me on; it was as if she was enjoying the buildup as much as I was.

I glanced at her again, checking that she wasn't out of her depth. Her sleepy eyes told me she was hazy with lust. I focused back on her pussy. She was wet already. I could see it. Smell it. Leaning forward, I hooked my arms under her legs, and blew.

I trailed my tongue over her slit, not wanting to hit her clit straight away; my strokes grew deeper, longer, like she was pulling me in.

She let out a short, sharp huff of breath just a split second before I reached her clit. As I circled and pressed she let out a long, loud moan that connected straight to my already straining cock.

Oh yes. I liked women loud.

Her wetness grew and I couldn't stop imagining it coating my dick. All that heat. I was going to have to make her come quickly so I could get down to the business of fucking her.

But she tasted so good. And she was behaving so well. Her hands exactly where I'd told her to put them. I wanted to keep sucking, licking—giving and taking.

Her body started to judder and fractured sentences tumbled from her mouth.

"Oh God, no—"

"Oh Jesus I—"

"Just like—"

"Fuck—"

"I'm—"

My fingers tightened, trying to keep her in place as she bucked against me before she gasped. Her hips pushed off the couch and her pussy contracted as I sat back and watched her juices slip between her ass cheeks. Fuck. I pulled off my tie and removed my shirt in record time.

She'd been almost too quick but I was grateful. I needed to be inside her. Normally I liked a blow job to get nice and hard for the first stroke.

Not tonight. Not with Scarlett.

Her breasts were still heaving as her breathing leveled out. Her eyes were tightly screwed shut.

"Scarlett, look at me."

Immediately, she opened her soft, hazy eyes.

I tried not to smile too wide.

"You ever tasted yourself?" I hadn't kissed her. Hadn't had the urge before now.

She frowned as if she didn't understand the question.

Without breaking eye contact, I took her hands from her thighs and clasped my fingers through hers. I leaned over her, hovering to see if she'd resist.

She lifted her chin and I took her mouth with mine. My tongue met hers in a tangle of hot and wet, soft and needy.

She tasted divine. Her pussy, her mouth. I wanted it all.

Her tongue was as eager as the rest of her body. I growled against her, my cock reminding me with a twitch that I wanted to be inside her.

I broke off our kiss and twisted my hands free from hers.

Standing, I stripped down, grasping for my wallet as I did. Jesus, I needed to calm down. She wasn't going anywhere.

I found a condom and stuck it between my teeth as I pulled off my underwear and stepped back toward the couch.

She fixated on my dick. I got that a lot. Mother Nature had been good to me.

She frowned. "Be careful with that thing, will you?"

"Careful?" I asked with a grin.

She pushed up on her hands, the movement of her breasts completely captivating. "I think it might break me in two," she replied.

"I hope so." I wanted in her so deep.

"I'm serious. I'm not used to . . ."

She was on the verge of making a confession I didn't want to hear. I just wanted to bury myself in her.

"I'll make it good." I stood over her as I stroked my cock up, rounded the crown and slid my hand back down to the root. *So good.*

How would I have her first? As I rolled on the condom, I considered my options.

Flip her over, go deep? No, I wanted to look at her as I pushed in the first time.

Have her ride me? No. I wanted to control the timing and the pace.

Without asking she leaned back and spread her legs. Her long, dark hair streamed down her front, her nipples poking out, still wanting an audience.

Yes, that would do nicely.

I lay my palm flat on her stomach, guiding my cock with the other hand. I stroked the tip up her folds to her clit and down to her entrance.

"Relax," I whispered.

"Make it good," she said, a plea I couldn't ignore.

I wanted it to be good. It would be good for us both. Sex might be a sport to me but I made sure there was never a losing side.

I inched in. "Breathe," I instructed.

Her muscles under me relaxed and I pushed in farther.

She let go of her knees and grabbed at my elbows, her eyes opening wide. She didn't ask me to stop, but I wasn't sure what she wanted. "You okay?"

She nodded. "Yes." Her breathy answer seemed to channel the blood to my dick.

Slowly, she let me in. Holy fuck, she was tight.

"Jesus, beautiful," I said as I was as deep as I could go. "You're perfect."

She took a breath. "You're big. I wasn't sure if you'd . . ."

"Feel good?" I asked.

She rolled her lips together. I released the base of my cock and pressed my thumb against her clit.

"No, don't. I'm—"

I paused. "No?"

"It's just, I'm so full. And if you . . . I'm going to come again."

Oh wow. Yeah, I liked this woman.

I moved my thumb back and forth as her breathing became heavier, more labored. I wasn't moving my cock at all. It just stayed sunk in her, feeling every contraction of her pussy. Sitting there getting my dick milked by her, not using anything other than my thumb, if I didn't think of something else, I might very well be coming with her.

I wanted to draw this out, make it last.

Her hands left my arms and grabbed the sofa cushions either side of her as she arched her back and screamed.

The sensation of her orgasming around me dissolved my ability to hold back and I began to move. Small slow movements, pulling in and pushing out, watching her as she floated down to earth.

Her head turned one way and the other. "So good," she mumbled.

It was all the encouragement I needed, and I picked up the pace.

I liked to see women from every angle. Liked lots of different positions. But tonight I was content to just watch her pleasure trickle across her face, feel her body shudder as I plunged into her.

She pushed to her elbows, glancing down at where we joined. I leaned forward to kiss her, and she thread her fingers through my hair, pushing her breasts against my chest.

I groaned, the tips of her nipples grazing against my skin.

"You feel so good," she said, pulling away from my mouth.

I reached behind and under her ass. "Back at you."

I'd begun to pant. The change in angle, the press of her skin against mine, the way she looked at me as if she trusted me—it was all pushing me forward, upward. "You thought I wouldn't fit." I licked up her neck. "But you got so wet for me."

She met my thrust, and I could feel the end of her.

She wrapped her arms around me, her nails digging in to the skin of my back.

She let out a long, drawn-out vowel sound. But I wanted to hear her say my name.

"Tell me what you want," I said, pressing my thumbs into the soft flesh beneath her hips and rocking her toward me.

"I want to come again."

I pulled her closer. I wanted to come so badly, but I wanted to make this last forever. "Ask me nicely," I choked out.

Her voice started in a rumble. "Please, Ryder, make me come again."

My name on her lips was all it took. She braced her hand against my chest, throwing her head back as her orgasm claimed her.

The sheen of her skin, the heave of her chest—the squeeze of her coming around my dick. It was all I could think of as my need for release, my need for her, took over and I gripped tighter, pushed harder—slammed into her again and again.

As I glanced down, her wide eyes and half-open mouth ripped my climax from me.

I grunted as I poured into her.

Her body relaxed against me and instead of extracting myself from her touch, I pulled her close, our heartbeats running next to each other.

She trailed her index finger across my inner elbow and I had to concentrate so I didn't shudder.

I needed to move, lie down. I slipped my hands back under her ass and lifted her up. I pulled off the condom and discarded it. Swooping to grab the two unopened packets that lay scattered on the couch, I headed to my bedroom. Her legs fit snugly around my waist, her breath on my neck making my cock jump even as I walked.

I flipped on the bedside lights and sat down on the bed, Scarlett's legs on either side of me. I lay back, pulling her with me.

"You've exhausted me," I said.

She rolled to my side, sweeping her hand across my chest. "Really?" she asked as she trailed her nails gently up my cock —dangerous and just what I wanted. Fuck, she was wicked. She sat up and leaned across my body to take me in her mouth. I don't know what possessed me—I rarely said no to a woman's lips around my cock—but I pulled her up and rolled her to her side, facing away from me. My fingers found her clit and without me having to ask, she reached back and fisted my dick.

Her grip was perfect.

I moved my hips, pushing through her tight hand as I swept her hair from her neck and pressed my lips just above her shoulder. I wanted to taste every inch of her body. I sucked and she cried out, renewed wetness coating my fingers. We rocked backward and forward, until I was overcome with that same urge to be inside her.

I grabbed the condom packet and ripped it open. Rolling onto my back, I slid the latex on. I glanced back at her. She'd moved to her stomach, her rounded ass leading down to her swollen pussy.

She really was the perfect fuck.

I reached between her legs, circling her entrance before prizing open her cheeks and trailing my fingers up to her asshole. She groaned and I couldn't wait a second longer. I straddled her and pushed my dick into her pussy, watching her ass squeeze and release under my fingers. I increased the pressure and she whimpered as she swallowed the tip of my thumb.

"Oh God," she mumbled into the mattress, squeezing my cock and my thumb so hard I thought I'd explode. I clenched my jaw and tried to focus on my breathing, pushing my body deeper into hers.

She reached behind her, trying to bat my hand away, then pushed herself up on the bed. "Please, Ryder. I can't handle—I think I'll pass out if you don't move your hand. I mean I'd die happy but fuck, it's too much all at once."

I chuckled and relented, removing my hand and shifting us until I was on my knees and she sat impaled on my cock facing away from me, her legs on either side of mine. It was better—having more of her touching more of me.

She surrounded every part of my dick and her head tipped back onto my shoulder, her mouth on my jaw. The rhythm was just right, her sounds as loud as I'd hoped, and I let myself enjoy her and that moment hoping I could draw it out—make it last forever. It might have been seconds or days but it was perfect. She was just perfect.

Her whispers were just what I needed to hear. "Oh, God, Ryder, yes." She made me forget everything.

We were both wound so tight we were about to snap. She broke first, whimpering into my mouth, stretching her body against mine as I felt her begin to fall. I couldn't wait a moment longer and I pushed up, erupting into her.

Fuck. Me.

Yes.

She fell forward, collapsing onto my pillows, her wild black hair spreading across her body.

A second later I was next to her.

"I can't move," she said.

I knew the feeling. "Then don't."

Blood pounded in my ears and I wasn't sure if it was her panting or mine that filled the room.

"I need to pee," she said, eventually.

"Yeah, you better get up, that is *not* my kink."

She giggled and I smiled. I liked that I made her laugh for some reason. Maybe because her smile was so beautiful. I liked that I could induce it.

She pulled herself up, and made her way to the bathroom. "Hey, Scarlett, the door." She hadn't shut it, but she ignored me.

The toilet flushed and the faucet squeaked and she reappeared. "Those things we just did, and you're worried about me shutting the bathroom door?" She smiled and shook her head.

Well, when she put it like that . . . It was just that I wasn't used to people being in my space. It was weird to see someone padding around my bedroom, peeing in my bathroom. She climbed back onto the bed and collapsed in the same spot she'd just left—on her side, facing me.

She mumbled as I covered us both with a blanket.

"What did you say?" It sounded like more than thank you.

She lifted her head from the pillow. "Violet was right."

This was why I didn't have sleepovers. I wasn't good at small talk with women. "She was?"

Her eyes slid shut as she nodded. "She said it wouldn't be as bad as I thought. And it wasn't."

I scooted down the bed so I was mirroring her. "What wasn't bad?"

She let out a sigh as she spoke. "The sex."

"What?" I pushed up onto my hand. Had I heard her right?

Scarlett's eyes opened, wide and startled. "What?"

"You expected sex with me to be bad?"

She grinned and shut her eyes. "Shhh. No, silly."

Had I missed something? I lay back down, tempted to ask her what she meant but not wanting to share anything more. I already knew more about Scarlett than I did most of the women I fucked.

She took a deep breath and then said, "First sex after the divorce. She said I just needed to get it done."

That pinched more than it should have. She'd just been getting it done with me? It wasn't that bad? Jesus, maybe I was losing my touch—I thought we'd been phenomenal.

She shuffled closer and put her hand on my chest. Instinctively, I placed my palm over hers. Normally, I'd have left by now. I wouldn't have stuck around to hear the reasons a woman had slept with me. I guess I'd always assumed it was my charm and good looks—that it was me that they wanted to sleep with rather than just someone. Maybe I was the asshole that John said I was.

Well, I'd prove that we were more than just getting it done. Soon, I'd be ready for the next round and I was determined I would stop her thinking about anything other than how good I made her feel.

CHAPTER FOUR

RYDER

I had far too many plates spinning.

A night of a lot of phenomenal sex and not much sleep left my brain a little fuzzy.

I liked a full workload. But things were getting out of control. Despite numerous phone calls with lawyers and trustees, at the moment, Frederick was likely to end up my boss if my grandfather died. I needed to find new office space and Cecily Fragrance was pushing back on our offer, even though it was more than generous.

And then there was last night and Scarlett.

"What's got you in such a bitchy mood?" John, my finance director, highest paid employee and best friend since college, asked as he stood in front of my desk, while I was trying to find a file I couldn't even remember the name of.

"You're the finance guy; you're supposed to know everything. You figure it out," I snapped as he took a seat opposite me.

It was true what they say about the more powerful and successful you are, the less people tell you the truth. And I'd seen how many businesses that destroyed. Employing John was one of the first things I'd done, and he'd given me shit from the moment he started.

I loved him for it. Mostly.

No matter how big the Westbury Group got, or how much money I made, John always told me the truth.

I slumped into my office chair, a stack of papers on my desk spilling onto the floor. John raised his eyebrows. He was right. I was in a bitchy mood.

"I think I got used for sex last night."

John covered his mouth as he guffawed like a teenager discovering porn in his dad's closet.

I sighed so deep I wheezed. "Fuck you."

"No, apparently, you're the one getting fucked these days."

I shrugged. "I think I was like the first sex after her divorce or something." She'd told me as much and I'd lain awake most of the night, thinking up questions that I never asked her.

Had she ever cheated on her husband?

Was Violet her only sister?

Why did she get divorced?

Was she still sleeping with her husband up until the divorce?

How did he compare with me?

I mean, she came like a train. But maybe she had with him too. For some reason, this girl had gotten under my skin. Maybe it was because she'd seemed nervous before we'd gotten to my apartment but almost overfamiliar in the way she peed with the door open and seemed to tell me everything she was thinking.

"You mean you actually spoke to this one?" John asked, still grinning.

I narrowed my eyes at him. But he was right. Not that I

never spoke to the women I fucked, because of course I did. How else would I get them into bed? It took more than my pretty face.

I just never really listened to what women said, never thought about their motivation. I was getting what I wanted, after all.

And my focus was always right there, in the moment. Not just on me. I wasn't a completely selfish dickhead. I wanted the women I fucked to have a good time, too. But I guess their enjoyment fed my ego too. But I didn't think beyond that room, beyond that moment. I didn't think about the before or the after. Scarlett had pushed me out of my carefully constructed reality. Just a little.

"Has it ever happened to you?" I asked.

Scarlett had gotten up halfway through the night and headed out. I'd pretended to be asleep.

"Been used for sex?" John asked. "I can only hope so. Why do you care that these women stupidly sleep with you?"

I'd always assumed the women I seduced wanted to fuck *me*, but now I wondered if anyone would have been enough for Miss King. Was I simply the service provider? A glorified town car?

Wasn't that one step away from male prostitution?

"I can see your imagination setting off fireworks. Are you seriously wound up by this girl?" he asked.

"Not wound up, no. Just . . . " How did I feel? Irritated? No, that wasn't it. More a little thrown off balance, a little intrigued by her.

"Call her. See if she agrees to a date. Then you'll know if she was just using you for your body."

Yeah, maybe I'd call her. Ask her a couple of questions.

"Seriously, man, you're getting a little doughy around the middle. I don't think it was your abs."

I glanced down at my stomach and then back up to find John chuckling. "You wish you had a body like mine," I said. I put in the work and I got the results I wanted. It was the same with most things in life. The gym was no different.

"Now, enough with the girl talk." He stuck his hands behind his head. "Tell me you're going to close Cecily Fragrance this week."

Fuck. That was the file I was looking for. I'd had our researcher do some comparable valuations that I could put in front of the owners at our meeting this afternoon. I spotted the file half hanging off the edge of the desk and grabbed it. "I'm going to settle it at this meeting."

"You going to up the offer?"

I hadn't quite decided that yet. "I need to convince the two major shareholders to walk away. I just haven't found a way to make that compelling for them. They're being emotional."

I got the feeling it wasn't about the money for Cecily. I was going to make her a very rich woman, an extra twenty thousand dollars wouldn't make the difference. No, I think she wanted to retain a stake in the business. And that just wasn't going to happen. She'd hate what I'd want to do. Instead of staying with a few product lines in very high-end stores and boutiques, I'd expand and go into as many department stores as possible.

And it wouldn't be me doing it. I'd parachute a new president in. Cecily wouldn't like that either. This was personal, and that was her weakness. I'd find a way to get her to accept my offer this afternoon.

"You want me to come with you?"

"No, thank you. I don't need a nursemaid."

"Well, you seem a little off your game. Maybe it's the jet lag."

"I told you, I—"

"Don't get jet lag. I know. Maybe it's this woman." He slapped his hands down on the arms of the chair and stood up. "Maybe you just need a break. I know you're close to your grandfather—why don't you take this meeting with Cecily Fragrance and then fly back to England? Take some time with him?"

Little did he know that my grandfather in hospital was only the tip of a very large iceberg. As much as I wanted to close Cecily Fragrance, what I really needed was to keep control of Westbury Group.

I needed to stop thinking about last night and focus on my future.

CHAPTER FIVE
SCARLETT

I'd prepared thoroughly for my meeting with the Westbury Group. I had all the arguments about retaining a stake in Cecily Fragrance memorized. I closed my notes on my iPad and took a deep breath. I'd found a place I loved to work and I was going to fight to keep it. This was personal for me and no one could trump personal.

The people from the Westbury Group would arrive any minute. I took out my compact from the top drawer of my desk and checked my makeup. If I hadn't taken Violet's advice last night, I wouldn't have had to put so much concealer under my eyes this morning. My best preparation would have been a good night's sleep. But I guess if I'd have done the sensible thing, I wouldn't have had the most amazing sex *ever*.

How was it possible for last night to have been so different from the sex I'd had with my ex-husband? I'd been nervous until I'd actually gotten into the apartment with Ryder, and then he completely took control and it took all my reticence and nerves with it. Violet had been right; I'd been equating sex with a relationship and become paralyzed. Ryder somehow had just unburdened me of all that. Marcus had always been so cautious with me, so worried I was enjoying it. Ryder took what he wanted from me—apparently that was exactly what I'd wanted from *him*.

The knock on my office door jolted me back into the moment.

"Hey, the guys from the Westbury Group are here," Karen, my financial controller, said. She was going to join me for the meeting so she could take notes and be an extra set of ears. I didn't want to miss a thing.

"Are you ready?" I asked, picking up my notepad, tablet and business cards.

Karen nodded—her movements jittery.

"Don't be nervous," I said, trying to reassure her. "Like we said yesterday, just write me a note if you think I'm missing anything and you don't want to speak up."

I knew what it was like to be across the table from a bunch of overconfident suits. What Karen didn't realize was these guys would be as full of shit as anyone. They just dressed well and had a lot of money. "Remember, they still have to use toilet paper, just the same as the rest of us." My dad had always encouraged Max, Violet and me not to be intimidated in the boardroom. He told us office life was just a game and to remember if you worked hard and lost, it just meant the other players understood the rules better. You had to dust yourself off and start fresh for the next game. I hadn't realized how right he was until I'd started my corporate career.

I had to pretend this was just another game. But this was the first time I was going into a meeting where losing would be personal. "Right, I think I have everything," I said as I headed toward her.

"They're in the boardroom," Karen said as we walked

side by side down the corridor lined with gray carpet tiles.

Boardroom made the room sound grander than it was. It was just the bigger of the two meeting rooms we had.

It's just a game.

"How many came?"

"Two," Karen said. "There's Mr. Westbury, who you were expecting, and his assistant who looks like he just started shaving."

I could do this.

I clasped my hand around the cool metal handle of the conference room door, took a deep breath and entered.

"Gentleman." My smile froze as I took in the face of the man standing in front of me.

It was the man who had made me come three times last night.

The man whose fingers I still felt digging into my ass.

The man's whose cock had split me in two and filled me with pleasure.

His eyebrows raised and he smirked as he held out his hand. It wasn't just my smile that had frozen, I was blocking the door and Karen was behind me. I shook off my surprise and took his hand.

"Ryder Westbury," he said, his index finger making a small circle on the inside of my wrist. "Good to see you."

I pulled my hand away. "Scarlett King, Finance Director," I replied. "And this is my colleague Karen Chung."

I knew Ryder's assistant was speaking but I couldn't hear what he was saying through the booming in my ears. I was putting all my energy into not screaming *How the fuck did this happen?* at the top of my voice.

"We were expecting Cecily. Is she coming?" Ryder asked.

That accent. No wonder it was him that I decided to end my period of celibacy for.

We took our seats on opposite sides of the oval table that was almost too big for the room.

"Cecily asked me to take this meeting. We're equal shareholders, after all," I said as I opened my tablet and began tapping and swiping, trying to appear engaged.

How was I meant to negotiate against a man who'd seen me naked?

Watched me come?

I glanced at Karen. Should I admit I knew Ryder? But then I'd have to explain how. *I picked him up at a bar last night. He's the second man I've ever had sex with. And he's incredible in bed. Right, let's negotiate.*

No, I couldn't say anything. But I'd have to tell Cecily after this meeting.

Jesus, wasn't the whole point of a one-night stand that you'd never have to see the guy again?

"Where do you want to start?" Ryder asked. He smoothed his hand down his tie and I couldn't not think of the hard abs beneath his fingers. The man looked like he spent most of his life in the gym, so where did he find the time to run the Westbury Group? "I've brought some comparative analysis to help you understand our offer."

To help us . . . ? Who in the hell did he think he was dealing with?

I leaned back in my chair. He thought we didn't get it? Maybe he thought we were just women fucking about with girlie products.

"What is it, Mr. Westbury, that you think we don't understand, exactly?"

He glanced at me, then at Karen and then back at me. "I just wanted to make sure you had some context. Wanted you to see the valuations that this type of business is going for in the current market."

"You think we haven't done our research? I'm happy to run through our process if that would make you feel more comfortable." I smiled. Sarcasm was always a core skill of mine. "We've compared your offer with other valuations in the marketplace. We've conducted a discounted cash flow analysis. We've also examined key economic data for the strength of this sector over the next five years. We understand what the business is worth."

Ryder grinned and sat back in his chair, mirroring my position. "I'm just trying to be helpful."

The way he said it, with the authority of his English voice, I *almost* believed him. "Well, we appreciate it," I replied. "But we can work out the context of your offer just fine."

"That's great. As I said, just trying to be helpful."

Trying to be helpful, my ass.

"And as *I* said, we appreciate it. But your offer doesn't work for us. We have a vision for the company and we believe we're the right people to execute it."

"I understand," Ryder said. Last night he'd looked at me as if I was the only thing in the universe—I hadn't remembered how dark his eyes were. "And that's why we want you both to stay on."

"As employees," I said.

He nodded, drawing my attention to the angle of his jaw, enhanced by the light that was coming in from the window behind him. God, he was good looking. I wasn't sure if it was because I didn't know him well, but compared to my ex-husband, he seemed more masculine, more sexual. Even sitting across from me fully clothed, all I could think was how the contours of his body looked under his suit.

I glanced up to find his eyes trailing down my body. Was he imagining me naked, just as I was imagining him?

"Well, as you know, Cecily doesn't want to give up the entirety of her shareholding and neither do I. As founding partners, we believe the business will be well served by us retaining an equity stake." I raised my eyebrows as Ryder slid his gaze back to mine and realized he'd been caught out staring at me.

Instead of being embarrassed, he just grinned. What a player.

"And it makes sense for you, because it will keep us motivated as we will have real incentive to ensure that Cecily Fragrance has the best possible future."

The silence that followed was uncomfortable but I wasn't in the business of making Ryder feel good. Not this morning anyway. Last night had been a different story.

"I'm going to be honest with you," Ryder announced as he shifted in his chair.

My heart began to thunder. He wasn't going to say anything personal, was he? I'd kick his ass if he mentioned last night.

"In my experience, it doesn't work to have the founders of a business retain an equity share. They don't understand that they aren't the ultimate decision-maker. There's not enough of a shift in stature. And that leads to an unhappy relationship between the founders and the investors that takes up time and energy better directed toward the future of the business."

The way the words tumbled out of his mouth, gravelly and considered, made me shudder. Each syllable he spoke seemed to be said with care and attention and made American accents seem dismissive and lazy. He was good at what he did.

"So, I'm going to make a very good offer. And it will be as far as I can go." He took no notice of Karen. All his focus was on me and every atom of my body pulsed in response. "I'm willing to pay you both a very generous salary to remain with the business, but ultimately, if you want to walk away, I understand and can accept that."

That was his concession? That we didn't have to stay? That was exactly the opposite of what we wanted. We wanted more involvement, not less.

Before I had a chance to speak, he continued. "I think you should talk to Cecily and think about it carefully. It's very generous, as is the cash offer. And I know that the loan repayment is due shortly and that the other offer you have is considerably less attractive than the one I've presented. So please, take some time to think about it."

His chair scraped across the carpet as he stood. That was it? Our meeting was over? No discussion?

The four of us stood. And Ryder pulled out a business card. "Call me when you're ready to agree." He held my gaze as I snatched the card from his hand.

"We're very disappointed this is the position you're taking—"

"Brett," Ryder interrupted me and turned to his assistant. "Please will you excuse us? Karen, perhaps you could show Brett to the lobby?"

What an arrogant piece of work. The last thing I wanted

was to be alone with him. I was keen to forget I knew him outside of this meeting.

We stood opposite each other as Karen and Brett left the room. "Scarlett," he said as the door closed; his voice was soft. Personal.

I stared out the window but didn't reply.

"It's good to see you again."

How did I respond to that? It was *too* good to see him. But not like this. Not when he wanted to take my company away from me.

"I had a really good time last night."

Really? He was being so inappropriate.

I looked him in the eye. "Ryder, you're here on business. Let's keep this professional," I snapped.

"Please, just give me a few minutes."

"Professional," I reminded him.

"Okay," he said. "Let's talk business."

I slumped into my chair. "I thought you'd said all you had to say."

"I want to level with you." He leaned forward, his forearms against the table, his hands clasped together. "Cecily Fragrance isn't going to get a better offer. If you don't take it, those loans will be called in and you could lose the entire business."

I tilted my head. "Thanks for the explanation of our financial situation. You know, some of us know what we're doing around here. I'm not stupid and neither is Cecily."

"I know you're not stupid. But you're bound to be emotional about this business. You helped found it. It's understandable. You built it into a great brand," he said in a cool, even and oh-so-sexy voice I could bathe in. But I needed to stop focusing on his accent and timbre and understand the words. "I need you to be rational. To understand that this is a really good offer for you both. You need to take it."

I didn't want to take the deal. But it wasn't because I wasn't rational. It was no accident that Cecily and I had created a thriving business. We were good at this. We just had a cash flow problem which was an issue for lots of rapidly expanding businesses. On top of this, I loved my job and it was daily evidence that I was more than my ex-husband thought I was—more adventurous, more entrepreneurial, more risk taking. He never thought I'd be running my own business.

"What's the alternative?" Ryder asked. "You go under?"

"I told you, we have other offers," I said. None of them would pay off our loans in full, which we had to do. The Westbury Group's offer was the only viable one.

"But they're not as good as mine."

"How do you know?" Christ this man was a piece of work. I supposed there had to be a downside to being hung like a horse.

"It's my business to know, Scarlett. I know a lot of people in this town."

He was bluffing. There's no way he knew the terms of the other offers we had.

"I know enough to know that mine is the best offer."

"If you're right that we're being emotional, then you can't solve that with cash. You need to let us retain a stake."

He was shaking his head before I'd even finished my sentence. None of the signs looked good. There didn't seem to be any room for us to keep shares.

Fuck.

"Your offer shows that you know this business is a good investment. So, pay off the loan. Take a minority shareholding with new loans and we can repay your investment at a more reasonable rate of interest. Cecily and I created this business. We know what we're doing."

He was still shaking his head. "It requires a different approach to take it to the next level. We'd have to completely change the way you distribute and what the company should be aiming for."

"Fuck you," I said. "You have no idea what I'm capable of. Think about it and then call Cecily."

"You don't want to deal with me?" he asked, pulling back in his chair.

I flipped shut the cover of my tablet. "I can't negotiate with you. It's not right. You should deal with her."

"Because of last night?"

I nodded and the edges of his mouth began to curl up. "I'm crazy from lack of sleep today," he said.

I rolled my lips together, determined not to grin. "Yeah. Me, too."

"But it was totally worth it," he said.

"That's because this is just another deal for you. For me it's my whole life."

"Your whole life?" he asked.

Was I being over-dramatic? I loved Cecily Fragrance. I'd been so used to my marriage being the center of everything that the divorce had left a huge hole. My job had taken that slot. I loved the people I worked with. It felt like I was hanging out with friends all day. And having such direct responsibility for all these people's livelihoods was rewarding. I hadn't realized work could be so much fun.

I drew a circle on the table with my index finger. "It's important to me. That's all." It felt like a life raft I was clinging to.

"I like that passion in you. But you'll still have a job."

"It's not enough." I stood and he followed my lead.

I looked up at him from under my lashes. Jesus, did he have to be so goddamn handsome? "I won't change my mind, Scarlett. My terms are my terms. I want all of Cecily Fragrance or none of it."

"We won't change our minds either," I replied.

His arm twitched as if he was about to reach for me. Perhaps then he'd tell me to open my legs. My cheeks heated at the memory. Last night, I'd just done it and it had been such a relief. It felt good to give up some control.

His eyes were hooded and his gaze heavy as it wandered down to my chest and then back up. What was he thinking?

He shoved his hands into his pocket. "I have to go. You're making me hard." He stalked over to the door.

Had I heard him right? Was I really capable of making a man like him lose focus like that?

"It's been good to see you," I said, ignoring his confession. There was a part of me that wanted to suggest we see each other again. Maybe a cocktail after work.

I resisted.

I wasn't about to be turned down twice by him.

CHAPTER SIX

RYDER

"Did you close the Cecily Fragrance deal?" John asked, coming toward me as I walked through the glass doors into the reception area at Westbury Group. My meeting with Cecily Fragrance hadn't turned out how I'd expected. Not least because I'd run into Scarlett.

"Do I not give you enough to do that you have time to greet me as I come back from my meetings?" I wasn't about to admit to the entire company that I still hadn't closed Cecily Fragrance.

"I was going to the restroom, you dick, but I take it that's a no."

"Well, careful you don't piss away the rest of your IQ. Come find me when you're done." I marched past him toward my office.

I wouldn't normally have been affected if someone I'd fucked sat across me at a business meeting, but it had only been a few hours. I could still feel Scarlett's soft ass under my fingers, still had her scent in my hair.

I'd frozen when I'd seen her enter the room. It took me a few seconds to work out what was going on.

Normally I passed out and slept like a baby after a great lay. But despite being the best since I could remember,

Scarlett had kept me awake. And it wasn't just because she was in my bed. Even after she'd gone I'd not been able to sleep. I'd been thinking about her and her contradictory mix of nerves and familiarity. I'd vowed at five thirty this morning that the next woman I slept with, I'd only fuck if I knew nothing about her. Scarlett had left too many unanswered questions. I'd rather know nothing.

Even seeing Scarlett again hadn't allowed me to ask the questions I wanted answers to. Instead it just raised new ones. Why did she like her job so much? Where had she worked before? Where had she gone to college? Had she been a good student?

I closed the door to my office and emptied my pockets—my mobile, my wallet and my keys—onto my desk. My phone lit up as it clunked against the wood showing three missed calls. I swiped it open. It was my grandfather's lawyer. He was working with me to try to find a solution to the biggest problem in my world at that moment—Frederick's inheritance of my company.

I hoped he'd found a way out.

I dialed him back immediately.

"Ryder, thanks for calling me back," Giles said.

"No problem. You have good news for me, I hope."

A fraction of a second too long passed for it to be good news.

"I did warn you." More silence. *Fuck.* "I've spoken to the top barristers. The trust is very clear. I'm sorry."

"There must be something we're missing," I snapped.

"But I think there is a very simple solution."

My heartbeat spluttered against my chest. *I knew it.* There was no way I was going to lose control of Westbury Group.

"You need to find yourself a wife," Giles said.

I groaned and rested against the side of my desk. "Well, unfortunately, life's just not that simple."

Even when all my friends from college and I were playing the field in our twenties, they'd all given themselves a deadline of thirty or thirty-two—thirty-seven in Jim Hassleback's case—to settle down, get married and have kids.

I'd never given myself a deadline.

Never seen a wife and kids in my future. I knew I liked women too much to limit myself to one. Last night had been a reminder. Scarlett had been unexpected. I'd not been looking for anything and it had been incredible. Imagine if I'd had a wife back at home? I couldn't deny myself a beautiful woman like Scarlett. And I wasn't a man who would cheat on his wife. I kept my promises.

"Darcy mentioned she thought Aurora would be willing," he said. Jesus, there was no escaping my sister's interfering. Aurora was sweet and attractive and no doubt she'd make a wonderful wife but that wasn't what I wanted.

"Aurora's not an option," I replied.

"Well, you need to find yourself an option. You're a rich, handsome man, Ryder. If you don't like Aurora, I'm sure you can find someone you do."

"It's not like I can look through a catalog," I said, although that would help explain how Jim Hassleback got his wife.

What kind of woman would get married for money? No one I'd want anything to do with. Aurora might have been an option, but she wanted too much. And the whole reason she wanted to marry me was to *be married to me*. A divorce a year later wouldn't suit her at all.

"Well you have to decide what you want more—to remain a bachelor or retain your company."

My stomach twisted at his stark declaration, but I couldn't argue.

"I suppose there's always the small chance that Frederick won't interfere and will just be a silent partner like your grandfather was," Giles said.

"I think we know that's unlikely." Frederick's jealousy had pervaded our whole lives. He hated that I got to go to boarding school in New York while he'd been sent to the far north of Scotland. He hated that my friends didn't like him. That girls didn't like him. In his head, he'd made it all my fault.

Frederick would see taking over Westbury Group as payback. Simple as that. And I couldn't let him do it.

"It's bad enough that he's going to get the title and the estate. Isn't that enough for him?" I asked.

"I'm afraid to say it, but I don't think anything will ever be enough for him."

Frederick had a chip on his shoulder the size of Canada. It wasn't just me who thought so.

"I want you to think about marriage—if not Aurora then I'm sure if we put our heads together we could find someone else. The sister of a friend or someone."

"What, and I pay them a ton of money, we have some registry office service and then we divorce?" Could I really do that?

"Well, it's not quite that simple. The marriage has to last until you inherit," Giles said.

Jesus.

"And you can't give Frederick a reason to challenge it.

The terms of the trust say that it must be a genuine marriage."

"What does that mean?" I asked.

"You'll have to live together as man and wife. Go to events together. On holiday. You need to have a marriage."

I blew out a huff of air. This would be more than an arrangement. I was going to have to have a relationship with a woman, even if it wasn't sexual.

"Is there anyone you can think of who would respond to a generous payment that I know you'd be prepared to offer?" Giles asked.

I let my head tip back and focused on the corner where the ceiling met the wall. Was I really thinking about doing this? "Maybe I could ask my assistant? I pay her well but not that well."

"Your assistant is married, if you remember."

"Oh shit, yes." I'd deliberately recruited someone married so I wouldn't end up fucking them and she'd end up hating me and leaving.

The list of potential wives wasn't particularly long— Aurora, blonde cabin crewmember with the long legs, girl with the brown curly hair and great ass who worked at the gym.

No one from work. That would be too messy. I didn't believe in shitting on my own doorstep.

There was the girl who worked behind the counter at the coffee place on the corner. She was pretty and could clearly use the money. But she couldn't be more than twenty. What happened if she turned out to be a monster?

I didn't really know any women socially, other than my friends' wives, or my sister's friends. "I can ask Darcy," I said.

"Well, consider if one of Darcy's very English friends is

the right way to go. Wouldn't someone in New York be better for you?"

I stood up and wandered toward the window and looked out over the city. There must be a woman in this town who needed a big wedge of cash.

"Let me think about it." When I had big decisions to make, I usually knew the right answer in my gut. Yet despite getting married seeming like the only option, it still didn't feel right.

"Just don't take too long. I know your grandfather just had a fall this time, but I'm sorry to say that you don't know whether it could be more serious next time. And you might not get any warning. If you want to keep control of Westbury Group, you need to get married fast."

I nodded. "Thanks, Giles." I couldn't think about my grandfather's death being imminent. I wasn't sure I would ever be ready for such a huge change to all our lives.

I cancelled the call and slung my phone across my desk. What a mess.

John interrupted my reflection as he swept into my office. "So, you didn't close it?" he asked. "This could be a really good investment for us. What's getting in the way?"

Cecily Fragrance was the last thing I wanted to worry about. None of our investments meant anything if Frederick was running the show.

"They want to retain equity. In fact, I think they just want us to play banker—replace the loans at a better rate and let them run the business." John took a seat in his normal chair opposite my desk.

"That's not what we do. We add value by taking management decisions."

"Err, yes. Thank you for reminding me," I said.

"But did you remind them?"

"No, I forgot." The sarcasm was running thick through my veins today. Did he think I was an idiot? "Jesus, what's the matter with you?"

"Calm down, Captain Temper. What the fuck has put you in such a shitty mood? Did your doctor just call to say you have herpes?"

"Fuck off. I'm really not in the mood for your bullshit today."

John and I didn't argue. We joked around a lot but there was rarely an edge. Apparently, today was different. "Sorry. I've just got some family shit going on." I wasn't about to tell him he might be soon out of a job. And frankly, so might I. I would tell him when I had a solution. For once, this was a problem he wasn't going to be able to help me solve.

"Hey, man. Are you okay?"

"I'm fine. I don't want to get out my knitting and talk about my feelings." I needed to forget about Cecily Fragrance and concentrate on Frederick inheriting the estate. "I need to work some shit out."

I'd go to the gym. Clear my head. Sex hadn't worked, maybe exercise would.

"Okay, let me know what I can do. We could always up our offer on Cecily Fragrance. You know we've been holding back a little."

I shook my head. "Money isn't going to do it for them." They knew we'd offered a fair price. John might take longer to realize. But it was clear to me that we weren't going to be investors in Cecily Fragrance. It was as simple as that.

"There must be something we can do," John said. "The figures look great on this business."

I had to talk to him about the issues I was having in relation to Frederick and the Westbury Group. Perhaps he knew of a woman who might want to do a deal of a different kind with me. I needed someone who needed the money but not *too* much. Who didn't mind being married but didn't *want* to be married to me. Someone who looked like I might want to marry her if I was so inclined.

"You're obviously trying to figure it out," John said, getting to his feet when I didn't reply. He couldn't know that I was thinking about how to save my company, not how to take over Cecily Fragrance.

The two issues merged into one in my head like tea and hot water. In fact, perhaps that was a solution—combine both problems and find a solution for both Scarlett and the Westbury Group.

CHAPTER SEVEN
RYDER

I paced up in front of my desk, trying to work out a way of telling Scarlett my plan without scaring her off. I'd called her as soon as John had left my office yesterday. I'd told her nothing of my dilemma but the hope I heard in her voice relaxed me and gave me reason to think I could convince her to do something that would work for us both.

My desk phone buzzed.

"I have Scarlett King in reception for you," my assistant said as I answered.

About time.

"Show her in," I replied.

I slipped my jacket on just before Scarlett entered my office.

"Scarlett, how nice to see you again."

She frowned and I indicated the two gray couches opposite each other. She was clearly suspicious about this meeting. She'd tried to get me to reveal more on the phone but I'd refused. I'd never had a conversation about marriage but I was pretty sure they were best done face-to-face.

She was dressed in black—her hair disappearing into the fabric of her dress. She wore a large silver cuff on her left hand and hadn't brought any kind of bag or notebook in with her.

She took a seat and I sat opposite her, clearing the latest copies of *Forbes*, the *Economist* and *Rolling Stone* from the coffee table that separated us. My assistant would be in with tea in a matter of seconds.

"Thank you for seeing me. I know you must be busy," I said, and she pulled the fabric of her skirt down and tucked it under her legs.

"You said you had a possible solution to our impasse," she said. I'd forgotten how sexy she was. How she carried herself in such a confident way. It had been a complete thrill when she'd undressed and opened her legs when I'd instructed her to. I hadn't expected her compliance, but I'd hoped. I found the most challenging, clever women—the women who ate men alive in the boardroom—were the most pliant in the bedroom. As if they were desperate to give up some of the power they wielded during the day, wanted to take the pressure off and have someone else to decide how they would get their pleasure at night. Scarlett had been no different—she'd just been better than all the rest.

I needed to control the blood flow to my dick.

"Thank you," I said to my assistant, grateful she'd arrived with tea.

She nodded and left the two of us together.

I reached for the teapot. Put the strainer over the cup farthest away from me and poured a cup for Scarlett.

"I don't drink tea," she said.

"You'll like this. It's good for the mornings." In the morning I always had fresh lemongrass. Lapsang Souchong I saved for the afternoons and never served to guests. It was too much for most people to handle.

"I don't drink tea," she repeated.

78

I moved the strainer to my cup and poured. I glanced up to find her watching me.

I set down the teapot, took my saucer and sat back.

She stared back, waiting for me to speak. Her lips were slightly parted and her eyes flickered from my mouth to my eyes.

"Drink the tea, Scarlett. You'll enjoy it."

She shook her head as if she was coming out of a daze. "I don't want the tea."

She was so determined not to follow my wishes it made the thought of her naked, her knees forced apart with the palms of her hands all the more entrancing. She was so different here in my office. "Fine. I want to hear more about what Cecily Fragrance means to you." I needed her to be in the right headspace when she heard my offer. If she had at the front of her mind how important her business was, I hoped that would make her more likely to accept.

She leaned forward, the fingers of one hand curling over the other and resting on her knees, just a few inches from where she'd pulled her legs apart. I took a sip of my tea, in an effort to distract myself from the images flashing in front of me.

"Because you're thinking of changing your mind?"

I placed my cup back in its saucer. "Please, Scarlett. Do as I ask."

She gathered her hair up and then released it. "This is personal. For us both. You don't get it because you're just like every other suit in this city. It's all about profits and margins for you. But for Cecily and me—we like to know that Brenda from marketing's son is just off to college and she's worried sick for him." She flung her arms out wide. "We gave Sean in finance a month off last quarter to go be with his dad while he was dying. This is more than a business for me."

"More?" She'd spoken with passion and I enjoyed listening to her.

Her voice was quieter when she spoke this time. "It's different to what I've had before. I'm more invested. More fulfilled. And I like it. I want to stay. It's my adventure and I'm not ready to give it up."

She was always leaving me with more questions than answers. What did she mean, different to what she'd had before? Her adventure? What was the story with her? I liked her passion. I liked that she'd come here and thrown any kind of game-play or negotiation tactic out of the window.

I wasn't sure I would be able to resist giving her what she wanted, even if she said no to my proposal.

"Why is this your adventure? Why is this business so important?"

She groaned and tipped her head back against the couch so she was staring at the ceiling. "We've been through all of this. You've heard it."

That wasn't my intention at all. I just wanted to know a little more about her.

"I told you I was married, right?" she said. It was the first acknowledgment of the night we'd spent together.

"Go on," I said.

"Well, if you must know—he left me to go have a more interesting life. Told me that life mapped out with me was boring."

I couldn't imagine a single moment with the woman opposite me could ever be boring, but what the fuck did I know about marriage?

She picked at her nail as her hands rested in her lap. "And I guess this job, creating Cecily Fragrance, was me proving him wrong. Showing him that life wasn't so certain. But it turned into something I didn't know a job could be." She shrugged as she exhaled. "I mean, I love it. I worked at an investment bank before and this is so much more fun—I have to decide on our notepaper as well as our accounting software. Everything from ensuring the P&L is correct to looking at our production process. Every day is different." She glanced up at me. "I don't want my ex to be right. That the adventure never works out for me. That I'm destined to be tied to my desk at a financial institution. And I don't want that old life for me either."

She looked surprised as she said it. "It's not just about him. I want this for myself, too." She laughed and put her hands in front of her face. "I feel like I've had a breakthrough in therapy."

I wasn't quite following her, and she must have seen the confusion in my expression, because she said, "It's for me, too. I love where I work. I love that it feels like we're creating a sliver of happiness in someone's life, creating a memory in the perfume."

I liked her passion, her honesty, the way she was fighting for what she wanted. It was rare that I saw that in the people I worked with. Or the women I fucked. I set down my cup and saucer.

"You want me to drink the damn tea?" she asked, picking up the untouched cup in front of her. "If that's what it takes, I'll do it. I'll do anything. I just don't want to give up this company."

"Put the cup down, Scarlett," I said as she began to drink.

She was asking for a lot and that required something in return. And what I wanted most at that moment—more than I wanted full ownership of Cecily Fragrance—was a wife.

"I mean it," she said. "If you want to have veto over a list of things as long as the Nile, it's no problem. I'll drink that weird tea every day. Isn't there some way where we can come to an agreement?"

"I think maybe there might be," I replied.

CHAPTER EIGHT
SCARLETT

The fact that I was in the office of the hottest guy I'd ever laid eyes on and he was a mere foot and a half away had me hearing things. The fact that he'd seen me naked? That we'd had the best sex of my life? It was all combining to make me delusional. I couldn't have heard him right. *Maybe*? I needed to shut up and stop rambling.

But I was sure I'd heard him say *maybe*.

I studied his face, waiting for the next words to leave his lips.

I fisted my hands, trying to keep from launching myself at him. I'd forgotten how completely attractive he was. It wasn't just that his body was something right out of a modeling shoot, or his miles and miles of smooth golden skin, or the deep brown eyes that made me freeze whenever they were on me. It was the way he'd ordered me to put down my cup, and how I was helpless to do anything but obey. The way he'd commanded me to strip naked and spread my legs, and how I'd simply complied. It was the way all his movements were so concise, as if he didn't waste any time or energy on anything.

No doubt he stored it all up to seduce a thousand women.

I squeezed my thighs together and his eyes fell to my groin before jerking back up.

"You say you're looking for an adventure, that you want me to become Cecily Fragrance's financier." He stared past me as if speaking to himself in an empty room. "Maybe we can help each other."

"In what way?"

He caught my eye and grinned. "You're divorced, right?" he asked.

Oh my God. I wasn't about to have sex with the man to keep Cecily Fragrance afloat. That was a step too far. Who did he think I was? "I'm not sure what that's got to do with anything." I pulled my shoulders back. This was a business meeting.

"Legally divorced, not just separated," he clarified.

"I'm not sure what that has to do with you or Cecily Fragrance."

"I have a proposal for you." He chuckled, amused at himself for some reason I didn't understand. "Literally." His tone grew serious and he leaned forward, his fingers loosely threaded through one another, his arms resting on his knees.

"You need me to keep your business, and I need you to help me save mine. Simple, really."

Well, at least it didn't sound like he wanted me to suck him off.

"Divorced, not separated, right?" he asked again.

"Yes," I said, drawing out my response. "Though, I'm not sure what that has to do with anything."

"Everything. I need a wife—and I think you might be the woman for the job."

I was pretty sure I had a halo of cartoon stars above my

head and Daffy Duck was somewhere around holding a frying pan. I had to be concussed. There was no other explanation.

Had Ryder seriously just suggested we get married?

Before I had a chance to respond, Ryder was on his feet.

"What do you think?" he asked, staring at me.

I needed to get out of there. I had no idea what was happening. He seemed normal enough but he clearly had issues. "What do I . . .?" I got up from the couch, Ryder's gaze fixed on me from across the coffee table. "I *think* I'm going to leave."

"I know it's sudden," Ryder said, sweeping his hand through his hair. "I've not really thought it all through, but it *could* work."

"You're not making any sense," I replied, studying his face to see if I could spot any visible signs of a psychotic break or a stroke or something.

Frowning, he pulled his head back.

"Maybe it's an aneurysm," I muttered to myself.

He sat on the couch. "Please, Scarlett, take a seat. The more I think about this, the more I believe this might be an option."

I blew out a breath. Perhaps I'd heard him incorrectly? I perched on the edge of the couch, ready to make a quick getaway if necessary.

"What if I said I'd pay off Cecily Fragrance's loans as you suggested." That was what I'd come here for—I just hadn't hoped to actually walk away with such an offer.

"And in return?"

"In return, you help me inherit my family's estate."

"By marrying you?" I asked.

"Yes."

I waited for him to elaborate but he didn't. Was this about sex? He was a rich, handsome—okay, *gorgeous*—guy with a body Ryan Reynolds would envy.

Was I just super good in bed? Did he just want a little more Scarlett?

"Let's get this straight. You're offering me money for . . . sex."

"What?" His whole body recoiled.

Okay, maybe I wasn't so good in bed.

"Of course not. Jesus, after the other night, you think I have to pay for it?"

"Quite frankly I haven't got the slightest clue what's going on. I think maybe . . ." I looked down at my skirt, embarrassed at his mention of our night together.

"I'm talking about marriage. Not sex."

Was he listening to himself? Nothing he was saying was making sense.

My skepticism must have shown. He raised his palm. "Let me explain."

"This better be good."

"Please, just listen and let me give you the whole story."

I sighed but tilted my head, ready to hear whatever it was that he had to say.

His body mirrored mine and if anyone had walked in it would have looked as though two sane people were having an innocent business meeting. There were no obvious signs of the total lunacy rippling below the surface.

"My family's estate—it's wealth, land and property—has been handed down through the generations via the family trust."

Oh God, I hope this doesn't take long.

"In each generation," he went on, "the oldest male inherits the entire estate. Well, not exactly, which is the point," he said, almost as if he were explaining things to himself. "The oldest *married* male inherits." He shook his head. "The whole thing is ludicrous. My older sister *should* inherit, but the terms of the trust are outdated and old-fashioned."

Okay. Had we just rewound to a Jane Austen novel?

"I've never been bothered about the money or title."

What did he mean, "Title?" Like royalty or something? I stopped myself from asking. I wanted to get out of here.

"The Westbury Group has done well—certainly well enough that I can provide for my mother and sister." He snorted and ran his finger around his collar as if trying to loosen it. "Unfortunately, because the initial investment into Westbury came from the family trust, my cousin Frederick could wrest control of my business when *he* inherits."

God, that sounded serious. Surely, legally that could be stopped?

"So, everything I've worked for—my wealth, independence, my own identity—would be taken from me."

This all seemed a bit farfetched.

"Just because he's married, my cousin inherits." He shook his head. "I can't believe after all this time and effort, everything I worked for my entire life is about to be handed over to someone who hasn't worked a single day since birth."

He pushed his hand through his hair.

"I need a way out—"

"Surely a good lawyer—"

He shook his head. "I've spoken to lawyers, they all say the same thing—get married."

Married?

He let out a long puff of breath. "Ridiculous, right?"

I gave him a small smile. I wasn't sure if I should feel sorry for him or not. "Pretty much, but I'm sure there are plenty of women out there who would line up around the block to marry you."

"And that's the problem." He leaned forward.

This was possibly the most ludicrous conversation I'd ever had in my life. It ranked right up there with my ex-husband telling me he wanted a divorce because I was too boring.

"I don't want a wife like that," he said.

"Someone willing?"

"I get how that sounds." He chuckled. "And no, that's not what I mean. I don't want someone who *wants* to be married to me."

"You're a sadistic weirdo. You know that, right?"

"Only on Tuesdays."

I had to try not to laugh. "Well, it's Thursday so . . ."

"I don't want a wife who has wifely expectations. I don't want to be married. I just want my company. I want someone who wants something from me in the same way that I want something from them. I don't want someone going into this saying they just want the money, when actually, they want more and I'm not prepared to give more. Your motivation to do this would fit perfectly. And me writing off the loan, or transferring it to my wife, is much less suspicious than just a cash payment."

"You want a business transaction." He wanted a fake marriage. "And a divorce afterward?"

"Yes. I want it to be exactly like a business arrangement. Which is why you are the perfect candidate."

Wonderful. The first thing a man who'd dissolved me into a

thousand pieces in bed saw in me the next time we met was a *business arrangement*. It was better than him not recognizing me at all.

Barely.

"But I'm sure you could find plenty of women who would be prepared to marry you for money. I mean, you're easy on the eyes." The corners of his mouth twitched. I shook my head. "You're offering to pay off the loans in full—"

"Cecily Fragrance will be yours, free and clear."

I'd married a man I thought I'd spend the rest of my life with. The divorce had been devastating. It had created an unhealable scar right through my middle that I knew I would wear my whole life.

I'd got it wrong with my ex, and I'd promised myself the next time I'd get it right. That the next time would be forever. I didn't want some guy who saw marriage as a business deal. I wanted someone who wanted me, just *me*, for the rest of his life.

"I can't," I replied, my stomach dropping. This was probably the best chance I had at saving Cecily Fragrance, and I was saying no. "It's just not who I am."

"It's not like I'd expect you to sleep with me or anything," he said.

"That sums up everything wrong with your offer. A husband and wife should want to sleep together."

"Well, I mean, that's totally negotiable. I'm not going to say no, our night together was—"

Was he fucking serious? I stood up abruptly. "Jesus. I'm certainly not going to sleep with you for money; who do you think—"

"Sorry, I was trying to be funny. Wrong time, wrong place." His jaw clicked. "Look, I know I've kind of sprung this on you. But please, at least think about it."

I glanced around, making sure I hadn't forgotten anything, and headed toward the door.

"Weigh up the pros and cons. Think about it like a business deal," he said, standing and pushing his hands into his pockets. "You'd be getting what you want—a debt-free Cecily Fragrance. Surely that's worth considering?"

He made it sound so simple. But I couldn't sell myself just to save a company.

Could I?

CHAPTER NINE
SCARLETT

I stared into my glass of rosé like it was a crystal ball.

"You're quiet. It's freaking me out," Violet said. "Was the sex bad?"

Violet had been messaging me, wanting to know how my night with Ryder had been. I'd managed to put her off last night—I'd needed an early night. I hadn't been so lucky today. She'd insisted we go for a drink when I'd finished work. I just wanted to go home and process everything. "It was . . . complicated," I said.

"What was complicated?" A woman with a familiar voice said.

I looked up to find my sister-in-law, Harper, standing above us.

"I invited Harper," Violet said.

"So I see." I really wasn't up for a big, boozy night out where the main topic of conversation was whether I'd had an orgasm. I put on my best fake smile and shuffled across the padded bench to make room for Harper.

"Can we get a bottle of champagne, please?" Harper hollered across the bar at a waiter three tables over. "We're celebrating," she said, lowering her head to us so she wasn't addressing the whole bar. "I'm so excited! You popped your post-divorce cherry. And with a British guy! Tell me all about it."

Violet tried to avoid the death stare I shot her across the table. I couldn't believe she'd told Harper I hadn't slept with anyone since my divorce.

"Oh, you want the *details*," I said. Well, they wouldn't be expecting to hear this particular story. "He asked me to marry him today." I shrugged.

Violet twisted her mouth to one side as if she were trying to figure out whether or not I was joking.

"He what?" Harper asked.

"He suggested we get married."

Harper smiled politely, glancing across my half-empty wine glass, probably wondering whether or not more alcohol was a good idea.

"Like, as a joke?" Violet asked. "Is that British slang or something?"

I chuckled. "No actually, he seriously wants to marry me."

Harper widened her eyes. "Well, you can't get it right every time. There are a lot of crazies out there. Maybe stick to an American next time."

Crazy was right. Living in Manhattan, I thought I'd seen it all, but getting married in order to inherit? Ryder might be British, but we weren't in the seventeenth century, for Christ's sake.

"Okay, spill, how did that happen?" Violet asked as a waitress came over with our champagne on ice. "Is he crazy in love with you? Do you have a magic vagina?"

As she opened the bottle and poured three glasses, I explained how Ryder turned out to be the man behind the company trying to buy Cecily Fragrance, and how he'd offered to pay off the loans in return for my hand in marriage.

"How long would you have to stay married?" Violet asked.

I shrugged. "I have no idea. I didn't ask him."

"Why? You don't think that's important?" she asked.

Didn't she understand that I'd said no? "Five minutes or five years—it didn't matter. I wasn't going to marry him. For money."

"Not even to save your business? Then you're crazy," Violet said. "There's not much I wouldn't do for that kind of cash."

"I'd definitely do it for five minutes," Harper said with a shrug. "Sign the paperwork and then get it annulled."

"She probably wouldn't be able to get it annulled," Violet said to Harper as if I wasn't even there. "Wouldn't work for his trust thingy."

"Divorced then. Who cares?" Harper said.

"I care," I said. "Divorce is a big deal. Marriage is a big deal. You can't enter into a relationship as a business transaction."

"Of course you can. People have been doing it for centuries," Violet said before draining her champagne. "You over-romanticize things. Marriage is *always* a deal. He has something you want, you have something he wants. Every relationship is like that if you think about it."

"You really do take the fun out of everything," Harper said, shaking her head.

"I'm just practical. Years ago men took pretty wives who had a big dowry if they could offer a title and respectability. Cavemen mated with the most fertile women in the village. It's always a transaction. This one is just more . . . obvious."

"So you think my marriage was a deal?" I asked her.

"I think *every* marriage is. You wanted Marcus because he promised to keep you safe, got along with our parents and has a nice ass."

"Violet, you can't boil down the reasons I wanted to marry my ex-husband to safety and a great ass. I loved him. Marriage is supposed to be about loving each other."

"That was just part of the deal, for you—love I mean. It isn't for everyone."

Harper laughed. "You're so cynical, Violet. But Max's ass was definitely part of the deal for me."

"I am not," Violet replied, shaking her head. "What I will be is a lot richer if you give me his number."

"You're saying you'd marry Ryder—even though you don't know him—just for the money?" I asked, looking at my sister, trying to figure out if she was playing with me.

"For serious money? Of course. I'd be crazy not to." She grabbed the bottle of champagne from the ice bucket and topped up our glasses.

My sister was the most practical, unromantic person on the planet. She also thought like a guy.

"And anyway, weren't you looking for an adventure?" she asked. "Marrying some stranger, it's all about the adventure, isn't it? And even if it's the most boring thing you've ever done, at least you'll be left with Cecily Fragrance, which you love."

According to my ex, I approached life with caution. I thought about all the reasons we shouldn't do something. I didn't like to take risks.

"I agree," Harper said. "I think you should think about it.

It's not like he's paying you for sex."

"How would I explain that to mom and dad?" I asked. "They'd hardly say, 'Go ahead sweetheart, whatever makes you happy.' They've lived in the same house in Connecticut their whole lives, for Christ's sake. They are not exactly all about the adventure."

"Well, first off," Violet said, "I'm not sure what living in Connecticut has got to do with anything. And second, when have they ever told you to do anything other than what makes you happy? They've never pressured us, never told us our decisions were terrible, or our choices wrong. They've only ever supported and loved us. Don't make them the scapegoat just because you're scared."

I twirled the stem of the champagne glass between my fingers. Was I scared? When Ryder talked about marriage in his office earlier, I'd thought he was a lunatic, yet here I was, listening to my sister and Harper tell me how it was no big deal.

"Weigh the pros and cons," Violet said.

That's what Ryder had invited me to do—consider the advantages and disadvantages.

"You'd save your business," Harper said.

"You'd be doing something crazy for the first time in your life," Violet said. "Take a risk. Have a real adventure."

"But I'd be on my third marriage when I find the right guy," I said. "That's a big fucking deal."

"The right guy?" Harper asked. "Your ex was the 'right guy.' You thought you were happy with him, right?"

My insides shifted. "Very."

"I know." Harper squeezed my hand across the table. "What I'm saying is—just because it didn't last forever, doesn't mean it was a failure. It was right for the time. No one said the right guy is the man you spend your whole life with. There could be plenty of right guys."

"Plenty of *right* guys? Is that the deal you have with our brother?" Violet asked Harper.

"Maybe," she replied, sticking out her tongue.

It made sense. There were so many good times and incredible memories between me and my husband that it was hard to coat it all in failure.

But perhaps he was just *part* of my story. One right guy.

"I suppose I could ask him for some more information. I mean, presumably we wouldn't have to live together. And it's probably only for like three months or something."

"Exactly," Violet said. "And if you decide to say no, tell him your sister's interested."

Maybe I would. But perhaps I *was* interested.

CHAPTER TEN
RYDER

There weren't many times in my life that I'd felt nervous, but tonight was one of them. My whole life could be turned on its head this evening. Instead of sitting at the bar, I'd chosen a secluded booth in the corner where it was as private as you could get in the middle of Manhattan. I could still see the door from where I was. There was no way I was going to miss Scarlett if she turned up. I could have called her, to try to state my case again, but I wasn't about to force a woman up the aisle.

The more I thought about it, the more marrying Scarlett made sense. I didn't know her well, but she seemed normal —she held down a job, she was attractive, clever and we shared a similar lifestyle based around work and family. People would buy us as a couple. But most of all, I liked that she'd been so adamantly against the thought of marrying me. I'd had the same reaction when Darcy and my lawyer had urged me to find a wife.

It all seemed so ridiculous.

I'd changed my mind out of necessity. I'd pushed the lawyers as hard as I could, sought second and third opinions. They all agreed—marriage was the only way.

I hoped Scarlett showed tonight.

I swiped my phone open. She was ten minutes late—she'd left me a message earlier asking me to meet her here. I was going to give her an hour. Maybe more. I didn't have anything else to do but wait, and hope. If she didn't show or said no, I didn't know what was next. Scarlett seemed like the only option.

The night with Scarlett had been . . . more than I'd expected. I rarely had a bad night with a woman, but the sex with Scarlett had been a little different. The memory of her face, her hair, her body—it had all stayed with me in a way that I wasn't used to. It was almost as if we'd known each other longer than just a few hours. She'd touched me like she *knew* me. The way she peed with the door open—it was weird but weirdly endearing. The way she liked to kiss. A lot. I couldn't remember a time I'd kissed a woman so much during sex. It had been nice.

Intimate.

Intense

I tipped back my Negroni. Perhaps I'd call her if she didn't show. Try to convince her to take the deal. Or at least maybe kiss me again.

"Ryder?"

I shot out of my seat, cracking my leg on the table. Scarlett. *Shit*, I was normally cooler than this, but I was so damn relieved to see her.

"Hi," I said, bending to kiss her on the cheek. "Let me get you a drink."

She didn't meet my eye as she sat. Fuck, I hoped she hadn't just come to turn me down face-to-face.

As I stood at the bar, I glanced back to our table. Her long dark hair was pulled back, giving me a perfect view of her slender neck. I'd never seen a woman with hair that black. Those full, almost pouting lips I'd kissed so much just two nights ago, those eyes that watered a little as she came. She was just as beautiful as I remembered. I smiled when she glanced at me.

She looked away.

"Thanks for coming," I said as I returned to the table and slid into the booth.

She pulled her shoulders back and looked straight at me. "I'm hoping you'll give me a little more information about this"—she fluttered her fingers through the air —"arrangement you're proposing."

I was in with a shot. Thank God. "Ask anything you like."

She glanced toward the bar as if checking for a waitress. Was she needing a little liquid courage before we got down to business?

A waitress approached and set our drinks down.

Scarlett tipped back her glass, emptying it. Maybe I should have asked for shots instead of cocktails.

Fair enough. This was likely to be one of the most bizarre conversations I'd ever have. I could only assume Scarlett felt the same.

"Let's start with the sex," she said.

"What, now?" She came here to get fucked? I was definitely okay with that, but that's not what this was about for me. "I'd really like you to agree to marry me first." And weren't those words I'd never thought to hear come from my mouth?

"What? No. If we get married, do you expect me to have sex with you?"

Jesus, would that be such a hardship? "There is no expectation from my perspective. And I think it would be good to keep things simple."

"Would I be able to date other men? I assume we'd have to live together?"

I'd been through all this with the lawyers on the phone over the last couple of days. As ever, I was prepared.

"Why don't I give you a little more background?"

She nodded, so I continued. "When my grandfather passes, I must be married—and the marriage has to appear genuine. Should our arrangement ever be challenged, the courts would look at things like living arrangements, trips together and any gifts exchanged. So yes, we have to live in the same place, but that doesn't mean our lives have to change." I took a long sip of my drink. "My lawyer says that the more questions we can head off at the beginning the better. He's suggested a public wedding in England—no elopement. We don't have to make a huge affair of it, but friends and family should go. If we fly over a week ahead of time, that will give people enough time to get to know you—and buy into us."

"You've thought about this," she said, nodding slowly.

"My grandfather's health is deteriorating, when he dies —" I swallowed hard against the thought of a world without my grandfather in it. "I could lose everything I've worked for."

"So could I," she said.

"Exactly why this works for both of us." This was business, not a favor. We would both be saving our business by doing this.

"I'm not sure a week with your family, faking our

relationship, would be so easy," she said, her finger tapping against her cocktail glass. "I'm a terrible liar—people are bound to see right through me."

"You're American." I shook my head with a laugh. "We can blame a lot on that." I grinned and she rolled her eyes.

"Oh my God. Are we really thinking about doing this?" she asked, her eyes betraying her nerves.

"I really hope so."

She ran her finger down her glass, collecting the condensation on her fingertip. "How long? I don't think you said."

"Three months—"

"Okay." She nodded her head.

"Three months minimum *after* my grandfather dies."

She narrowed her eyes. "Is that likely to happen . . . How soon—God, I'm sorry, I don't know how to ask."

I swallowed, while trying to build an imaginary wall in front of thoughts of my grandfather's death. But she was right to ask. "Well, he's eighty-two. Divorce proceedings can't be finalized for three months after . . ."

"He could live another twenty years! There's no way I'm staying married to you for decades—it's just not worth it."

"Gee, thanks," I replied.

She closed her purse as if she were preparing to leave. "You can't seriously expect me just to go along with that."

Shit, I could see how a decade of an arranged marriage might be unpalatable. I'd not thought much beyond actually finding a wife. No one would accept an open-ended offer. No one except Aurora.

"Five years," I blurted as she pulled her purse onto the table and stared at me. "Five years and if he hasn't—if the estate hasn't passed to me by then, we can either renegotiate, or I'll find someone else."

"Five years is a long time, Ryder. Too long."

This was awful, negotiating over the date of someone's death. "Three years. That's my final offer." She'd thought more carefully about the implications of this deal, which was good, as long as she said yes. "We move in together here in New York and you travel with me when I go to England."

"I *have* always wanted to go to England," she said, sliding her purse back beside her. My breathing slowed. "What did you say about dating?" she asked.

"I can't take any risks that my cousin could then use against me," I said, hoping it wouldn't be a deal breaker.

"So no dating." She nodded slowly as if she were trying to picture her future. "Okay, maybe that wouldn't be such a bad thing. I'm terrible at it anyway."

That couldn't possibly be true, but I wasn't going to argue.

"But if I'm going to be celibate, so are you," she said. "I don't want to find out you've got sexist double standards."

Wait . . . No fucking. For three years?

But what choice did I have?

That sounded like a yes to me. "Okay," I replied before I could overthink it. I could go without for a few years if it saved my company. "I'll write it into the contract." And get to know my right hand, hell, maybe even my left, really, really well.

"Okay. When do you want to do this?"

I clenched my fists, trying not to give a high five. I cleared my throat and focused. "You mean when do we sign the contract? Or when do we get married?"

"All of it. But I want my lawyers to look things over. I want you to replace the loans by the end of next week and have it written in that your loans transfer to me automatically at the end of three years or on our divorce, whichever is the earlier." She was leaning forward, her hands placed flat on the table. She meant business. But nothing she was suggesting was unreasonable. "And, I get to pick the ring, right?" She paused before she added, with a huge grin, "I'm a sucker for jewelry."

"Sure." Like I gave a shit about the ring.

"If I have to wear it, I don't want it to be ugly. And of course, we can sell it at the end."

"You can keep the ring, Scarlett." I'd be a complete dick if I made her give me back the ring after what she would be giving up and giving me.

CHAPTER ELEVEN
RYDER

The sun glinted off the aircraft's fuselage as we got to the top of the steps. I hoped the weather would be as nice when we arrived in London.

"But you don't own it?" Scarlett asked as she glanced around the plane.

"No, it's too much responsibility—and a little too flash."

She laughed. "So it's too flashy to own a private plane, but not too flashy to ride in one every time you fly?"

"It's all relative," I replied.

She slid into a cream-leather seat I usually preferred, so I sat across the table from her.

"You don't have to entertain me," she said. "It's a long flight."

"I know. This is where I normally sit. Well actually, I mostly sit there," I said, nodding at her chair. "But I'm just as good with this seat. And anyway, we need to talk."

She opened her purse and began to pull out all sorts of things—her phone, a tablet, a cosmetics bag, tissue and headphones. Jesus, who was she? Mary Poppins? "You want one?" she asked, catching me staring at the tin of mints she'd just set down.

I shook my head.

"Okay. What do you want to talk about?" she asked, looking past me toward the flight deck.

"Nothing specific. But as you're going to be meeting all my friends and family in the days ahead of the wedding, we need to get to know each other. Get our story straight."

She groaned and my cock twitched. "I told you, I'm a terrible liar."

"Then we'll stick as close to the truth as we can. What we don't want is Frederick challenging the legitimacy of our relationship in the courts."

"Okay, well, you tell me what to say and I'll say it."

The plane began to taxi and we fastened our seatbelts, ready for takeoff.

"I want to make sure you're comfortable. *We* need to decide how we met and how long we've known each other. That kind of thing."

She gripped the arms of the chair as we picked up speed, closing her eyes as we took off. "Okay," she said, her voice tight.

So she was a nervous flyer—that was a new detail.

"You're going to be okay," I said. I wanted to comfort her, but I didn't want things to be awkward between us.

"I'll be fine once we're up and I'm drunk."

I chuckled.

We levelled out and she finally opened her eyes.

"You're back," I said.

She released the arms of her chair. "We can say we met because you were interested in buying Cecily Fragrance," she said, picking up where we left off. "That's kind of true."

I grinned. By the time I'd realized she was connected to Cecily Fragrance, I'd made her come three explosive times.

"You know what I mean," she said, narrowing her eyes at me.

"Okay, but we can't say we met a few weeks ago. No one is going to buy a relationship that new."

"I've only owned Cecily Fragrance for two years, so we can't have known each other longer than that."

As I thought about a solution, I took off my cufflinks and placed them on the table and began to roll up my shirt sleeves.

"Do you always wear formal shirts and suits?" she asked.

I glanced down at myself. "I came straight from the office," I said.

"I've never seen you in anything else."

"Now that's not true." I grinned. "You've seen me in nothing."

A hint of pink colored her cheeks. "You know what I mean."

"What about if I met you years ago at a party?" I asked.

"What kind of party?" she asked as she tilted her head.

I paused. "A Christmas party. In Manhattan. I saw you and came over to talk to you. I asked you out and you told me you were married."

"You didn't see the ring?" She fiddled with the engagement ring on her left hand that we'd picked out yesterday.

"I was too dazzled by your beautiful smile," I replied, watching as the corners of her mouth turned up.

"There's no missing that ring," I said, nodding at her new engagement ring.

"You think it's too big?" she asked. "It's a lot bigger than my last one."

I'd hoped it was. Maybe it was the competitor in me, but

even if this marriage was one of convenience, I wanted it to be better than her last one. "The British don't do big engagement rings. That's large enough to look authentically American, but small enough people won't think we're flash."

She tilted her head as she held her hand out to admire her ring. "I like it—it's Harry Winston for crying out loud! But it's also art deco, a classic and very New York."

"You better *love* it. I dropped six figures on it."

She pulled her hand away and rolled her eyes. I hadn't meant to sound like an asshole who only cared about money. "So you met me at a party, you crashed and burned. Then what?"

"Then nothing. I met you again a year ago when I wanted to invest in Cecily Fragrance. Brutal negotiator, you turned down my offer—"

"But accepted the date." She grinned. "I like it. It sounds romantic. Did I remember you? From the party?"

"Of course you remembered me. I was the guy you couldn't forget." I liked this game. We could decide who we wanted to be. That's what I'd been trying to do when I established the Westbury Group. It's what I'd been trying to do all my adult life.

She shook her head. "No. No one I know would go for that. I loved my husband."

She sounded sad. Was she still in love with him? Fuck, I hoped he wasn't going to be a problem. The last thing I needed was for him to want her back, or for her to want out of our arrangement. "Okay, so I remembered you, but you forgot all about me."

Her smile was back. "Sounds good. And why did you want to marry me?"

"You told me we wouldn't have sex before marriage."

She laughed and then stopped herself as the cabin crew came over. "Can I get you drinks? Champagne to celebrate?"

I'd made it pretty clear to people I was flying back to England to get married. I had to act as if I had nothing to hide. As if I'd finally fallen in love.

"Yes, that would be great." Scarlett beamed up at the flight attendant—a woman I'd never fucked, thank God. I didn't want any unnecessary complications on this trip.

"The start of the celebrations," Scarlett whispered. "So, really, why are we getting married?"

"You're the right girl," I said, shrugging.

She nodded and then stopped. "Is it really that simple?"

"You tell me. You're the one who's been married before. Why did you marry your first husband?"

She picked up her glass, pausing before pressing it to her lips and taking a sip. "I don't see how that's relevant. So, I guess, we're just in love. Never felt like this before blah, blah, blah."

I chuckled. "Well, if you left out the *blah, blah, blah,* I think it might be more convincing."

She shrugged and looked out the window.

"I didn't want to lose you a second time," I said.

She turned back to me, her eyebrows drawn together in confusion. "What?"

"That's why I asked you to marry me. I knew when I met you at that party years ago that you were special, and I always regretted that I'd met you too late. I wasn't about to let you slip away again."

"You're quite the storyteller."

"You think it's too much?"

108

"I think it sounds like a fairytale." She glanced back at the window, absently twirling the stem of her glass against the table. "A beautiful story," she whispered. "So yes, let's say that."

I wanted to ask what she was thinking. Why she sounded like she didn't believe in fairytales. But we were strangers. We might have been physically intimate before we'd known anything about each other but, engaged or not, it didn't seem right to ask such personal questions.

She sat back into her chair. "Where did you go to college?"

"Yale. You?"

"Princeton," she replied.

"Did you like it?"

"It was close to home and by then I was already dating my ex—we went to high school together."

"Right." Again, I had more questions for her that I had to push down.

"But yeah, college was good. All those hormones and lack of boundaries. You know?"

I chuckled.

"But I went home most weekends. He was at a local school."

Sounded like he might be a bit of a fuckup compared to Scarlett. She'd probably never realized she was too good for him.

"What about you? Your family's from England, yet you went to college here? Did your parents move?"

"No. I wanted to go to school here. I boarded from twelve."

"Wow, you were a long way away from home. It didn't bother you?"

"I didn't like being away from my sister, but she was older and was away boarding in England anyway."

"You didn't miss your parents?"

"Nope." I took a sip of my drink. "My mother was less of a parent and more of a dependent. My father was never around—he disappeared when we were quite young."

Scarlett flinched but didn't comment.

"School was good, and during the holidays Darcy and I had my grandparents. He was more a parent to us than our mother and father ever were."

She paused as if she were trying to find the right words. "And you're close with Darcy? Even now?"

"Yeah. She's crazy, but sweet and protective and everything I could ever want in a big sister." Thank God for Darcy.

"I'm close with my brother and sister as well. We have that in common." I hadn't noticed the small freckle on her collarbone before.

"What are their names again?"

"Violet, who you met at the bar that night. She's the more bohemian of the three of us. Always has a different job, always willing to try new things. She's a free spirit. My brother Max is older. *Super* protective. He became a father when he was in college, had to grow up fast."

"Are they married?"

"Violet, no. I'm not sure she'll ever get married." She drew an invisible square on the table with her index finger. "But Max married Harper a few years back—and they all know the truth about this." She swept the hand holding her champagne flute between us. "Violet and Harper actually talked me into it. Max wasn't so supportive. He tried to give me the money to pay off the Cecily Fragrance loans, but there was no way I was going to accept that. In the end he gave in and accepted my choice—because he's a marshmallow." She grinned as she spoke about her family. "Gruff on the outside only. He'll do anything for the three of us so long as we're happy."

Scarlett talking about her family made our arrangement seem all the stranger. It wasn't exactly that I hadn't thought of her as a person—I wasn't that callous. It was just I hadn't understood how many people our lie would involve. It made me uneasy—it was much more likely we'd be caught the more people who knew—but I also felt a little shitty that I was asking so much from Scarlett. She was trying to save her business, and I could have just loaned her the money.

"Thanks for doing this," I said.

She smiled. "Thanks for helping me save Cecily Fragrance."

We were bonded together in desperation. Soon to be wedded in matrimony.

Quid pro quo.

Chapter Twelve
Scarlett

Maybe it was the champagne. Maybe it had been getting to know Ryder over the past few weeks while we made arrangements to spend our lives together. Either way, after takeoff, I'd lost my nervousness and settled into something that'd seemed so natural.

Until now.

As the car turned off the road and up a tree-lined private drive, shit got real. Our lies were about to get oxygen.

"So your sister lives with your grandfather?" I asked. "Isn't that kind of weird?" We were sitting side by side in the back of the Range Rover, closer than we had been on the plane. Closer than we had been since our night together.

"It's my family's country home, so it's not like we're sharing bathrooms. You can go days without seeing anyone, though we do normally have dinner together."

His demeanor seemed to have changed a little since we'd landed. Perhaps I was imagining it but he seemed a little taller, his shoulders a little broader. He'd told me during negotiations that he had no sexpectations when it came to our arrangement. Which on the one hand was good because hooker wasn't on my list of life goals. But looking at him, his long legs stretching out in front of him, his large hand resting on his strong thigh, I was beginning to think that negotiating *no sex* into our arrangement would be my loss.

He caught me looking at him and I pretended to be staring at the view.

How big is this place? I didn't have to wait long to get my answer. The leaves of the trees thinned out to reveal a huge . . . house wasn't the word. Building, maybe. "It's like Downton Abbey," I said, trying hard not to press my nose up against the window of the Range Rover to take it all in.

There was a lake directly to my left and beyond that, Ryder's family home. As far as the eye could see were miles of neatly cut grass, scattered with different types of trees. There was a formal flat lawn right in front of the house but the land seemed to dip and rise as it stretched to the horizon. It seemed more like a public park than a private garden.

"Capability Brown designed the gardens," Ryder explained, though I had no idea what that meant. It didn't matter, whoever they were had done a beautiful job.

Jesus. I'd thought Max and Harper's place in Connecticut was big now that they'd added the pool house. But this was on another level. "It's huge," I said. "And old."

"It takes a lot of upkeep."

"I guess you have staff to help."

He nodded. "We have it down to just five full time, some part-time people as well."

"Right," I said.

Ryder chuckled next to me as I looked out of the window. Was he laughing at me? This was a different world. I'd had no idea what I'd be walking into when I agreed to this. I wished Ryder had warned me or I'd used Google for more than my regular search of *Ryan Gosling naked* or *how many calories in . . . whatever I just ate.*

"Lane here looks after us all very well," he said, nodding to our driver. "He runs the place, along with the housekeeper. We also have a cook, a gamekeeper and a gardener. We have to bring in extra hands from time to time. The wedding will mean there are lots of additional people milling about."

"I thought we agreed on low-key."

"Oh, well, yes, of course," he said, dipping his head as if to get a better view of the house in front of us. "We won't go off the estate for anything. We can do the service in the chapel and use the ballroom for the reception."

Was he kidding? "You own a chapel?"

"On the grounds. It doesn't really get used since my grandmother died."

"And a ballroom?" Was he fucking kidding me? I was out of my depth here. Ryder hadn't mentioned anything like this.

"That's standard in a house like this. It's no big deal."

It felt like a big deal. My brother had a lot of money, so it wasn't the wealth that scared me. It was the grandeur of everything. The scale. If a ballroom was no big deal to him, it felt as if there may be other ways he looked at the world that were so completely different to me.

Before I had a chance to wrestle the steering wheel from our driver and race back to Heathrow, we'd pulled up on the gravel drive, in front of the yellow stone steps that led up to the entrance to Ryder's childhood home.

A woman in a smart navy suit stood at the top of the stairs, her hands clasped in front of her, a stern look on her face and a hairstyle that looked like it would withstand a tornado.

Was that Ryder's mother? She was hardly what I'd imagined, but then he hadn't said much.

Ryder stepped out of the car, then turned, took my hand and helped me out. As he closed the door, he waved. "Hi, Mrs. MacBee," Ryder said, grinning like he was seeing a long-lost friend.

I smiled at her but she just nodded. "Is that your mother?"

"No," he said with a laugh. "That's Mrs. MacBee, our housekeeper. Don't worry, her bark is worse than her bite."

Our driver opened the trunk and he and Ryder emptied our bags from the back. "I'll do these," Ryder said.

"No, sir. It's my job."

Ryder sighed but picked up the largest bag in one hand, took mine in the other and we climbed the twelve steps toward Mrs. MacBee.

"You didn't let me have your dietary requirements," she said to Ryder as we reached the top.

"Good to see you too, Mrs. MacBee," he replied with a nod. "Let me introduce you to Miss Scarlett King." He headed down the stairs to help Lane with the rest of the bags, oblivious to Lane's obvious annoyance.

"How do you do, Miss King?" Mrs. MacBee addressed me.

My smile felt tight as it stretched across my face and I took her outstretched hand and shook it. "Oh, please call me Scarlett." No one I dealt with ever called me by my last name.

"Welcome, Miss King," she said and she turned and walked inside.

Had it been inappropriate to ask her to call me Scarlett?

Ryder put his arm around my shoulders as he reached the top of the stairs again. "It's good to be home," he said, turning us both so we faced away from the house, out across the lake. There was nothing but trees and grass as far as the eye could see. Did his family own all this land?

"This is my favorite view in the world," Ryder said.

"It's beautiful."

"Come and I'll show you around," Ryder said, tugging me toward him.

We turned and passed through the huge oak double doors.

"Grandfather," Ryder said as we got inside, the heavy thud of the doors behind making me jump.

An elderly man with a walking stick, dressed in what looked like a robe, came toward us. He held up his hands, his stick swinging like a pendulum. "Ryder, my dear boy, it's so good to see you." He gave me a wink as Ryder put his arm around him in a half-hug. "Even better that you brought your bride." After such a formal introduction to Mrs. MacBee, it wouldn't have surprised me if Ryder had shaken his grandfather's hand.

"Should you be out of bed?" Ryder asked, trying to take his arm.

His grandfather batted him away. "Don't you start. I'm here to meet my soon-to-be granddaughter-in-law." He held out his hands and I glanced at Ryder for guidance. It didn't seem like his grandfather intended to hug me, but . . . I reached out and he took both of my hands in his and squeezed. It was more than a handshake, but less than a hug. I exhaled. "You have no idea how grateful I am to have you here," he said. "You're a very good girl helping my grandson like this." Ryder hadn't warned me that his grandfather knew. Did that mean he wanted Ryder to inherit over Frederick?

"It's so good to meet you, sir."

His grandfather chuckled and I wasn't sure why. Perhaps I should have said *how do you do*. I wish I'd spent more time on the plane quizzing Ryder rather than reading or napping.

"His Grace needs to rest," Mrs. MacBee said from behind us.

His Grace? Shit, what was that about? Was that how I should have greeted him?

"I'll show you to your rooms," Mrs. MacBee said. "I've put Scarlett in the East Wing, and you have your old room."

"Nonsense! This is a new millennium," Ryder's grandfather said. "Ryder and Scarlett will share his room."

I was more than fine to have separate rooms. It would allow me some privacy, somewhere I could escape to. Ryder and I were still getting to know each other—trapping us in the confines of one room didn't seem like the ideal scenario.

Mrs. MacBee scowled. "Before the wedding, I—"

"I may be old and tired, but I'm still the duke around here," Ryder's grandfather snapped.

What did he say?

"Very good, Your Grace," she replied.

I turned to Ryder, wanting to ask him about the odd exchange between Mrs. MacBee and Ryder's grandfather, but he took my hand and squeezed. "They've been bickering like this my whole life." Ryder's grandfather grabbed onto the wooden balustrade with his free hand. "Can I help you upstairs, Grandfather?" Ryder asked.

"No, no, no. I'm just leaning and then I can manage to get to the library. You two get settled in and I shall see you for dinner. Seven sharp. Some of the family insisted on inviting themselves so it will be in the dining room."

Ryder groaned. "Some of the family?"

"It couldn't be helped. Frederick and Victoria want to meet the lovely Scarlett." Ryder's grandfather fixed Ryder with a serious look. "You knew that they'd doubt you. This is the gauntlet you have to run." He released his hand, turned and began to make his way left through a doorway. He held up his stick. "But run it you will. And you'll come out stronger in the end."

I almost jumped out of my skin when Mrs. MacBee said, "Mr. Merriman has been shooting. So it will be pheasant for dinner." I'd forgotten she was still there. "Let me know if I can get you anything to make you more comfortable." She turned on her heel and clipped off down the hall, leaving Ryder and me standing in the oak-paneled hallway.

"This place, Ryder. You should have told me." Portraits of very stern-looking men and women lined the walls.

He shrugged. "It's just home to me. Come," he said, holding out his hand for me. "Let me show you where we'll be sleeping." I slid my palm against his and we started to climb the oak stairs. Brass stair rods held in place worn, moss-green carpet. It looked older than me. Why hadn't they replaced it?

I ran my hand over the oak of the banister. It was so wide I could splay my hand and neither finger found the edge. "How old is this place?" I asked.

"Mainly late seventeenth century. Different parts were built at different times. This entrance hall is gothic, and one of my favorite parts of the house. Do you like this period of architecture?"

I shrugged. "I guess." I had no idea about English architecture—or anything else about who Ryder was, it seemed. We were relative strangers, but over the last few weeks, it had felt as if we'd gotten to know each other. Being here with him, I realized I didn't know him at all. It was like there was a Manhattan version of him and an English version of him.

Midway up the staircase, we came to a split, and Ryder guided us left. "Mrs. MacBee called your grandfather 'Your Grace.' What was that about?"

"Oh, she's just formal like that."

I glanced over at him.

"You know, because technically, that's how you should address a duke."

I stopped and pulled my hand from Ryder's. "A duke? Your grandfather's a duke?"

"I didn't mention it?" he said as if it were no big deal, taking my hand and pulling me up the stairs with him.

"No, you didn't." I would have remembered that for sure. "I should have called him Your Grace?" I asked. "And now I look like the stupid American?"

"It's no big deal. Grandfather doesn't stand on ceremony."

I wanted to punch him in the head. We were meant to be a team. Me being unprepared wasn't good teamwork. "Ryder, it is a big deal to me—you have to tell me these things. I don't want to offend or disrespect your family."

"Okay, I'm sorry. I didn't think about that. We're very relaxed around here. Technically, even I should call him Your Grace."

Wonderful. If his grandson should have called him by this title, I was certain a total stranger should have.

"Seriously. Relax."

We stopped outside a huge wooden door that looked like

something out of a movie set for *Robin Hood* or *Game of Thrones*. It had a cast iron handle and hinges. "This is us." Ryder opened the door and it let out a comical squeaking noise that sounded straight out of an episode of *Scooby-Doo*. He held it open, allowing me to go through into a large seating area with two couches and various cabinets and tables. Beyond an archway, there was a four-poster bed. "This is ridiculous," I said.

"What is?" Ryder asked.

Tears gathered at the back of my throat. It was all too much. All so different from what I was used to, what I'd expected. "What are we thinking?" I wondered aloud. I really knew nothing about this man. When I'd married Marcus, I knew everything about him. That his hair turned almost blond every summer until he was nineteen. I knew that his dislike of carrots was equal to my hatred of beetroot. I knew he was seven before he could ride his bike without training wheels and his brother teased him mercilessly about it.

I hadn't even known Ryder's grandfather was a duke.

Ryder guided me to one of the couches, then turned and rummaged around in one of the cabinets.

"Here," he said, holding out a glass in each hand. "Water in this glass. Gin and tonic in this one."

"Alcohol? That's your solution?" I asked. "Isn't it a bit early?"

"British aristocracy are fond of their booze—you'll hardly be judged for day-drinking—and you need to calm down."

I grabbed the glass from his hand.

"You didn't think to tell me you lived in a place like

this, or that your grandfather is a duke. Isn't that royalty, or something?" I asked.

"No, Fairfax isn't a royal dukedom," he said, as if I'd asked him if it was raining. Didn't he get how ludicrous this was?

"Oh, well that's okay then." I folded my arms. "I'm not sure why I'm making a fuss."

Ryder chuckled. "I like sarcastic Scarlett. But seriously, this isn't that big of a deal, just a little different to what you're used to. I grew up in it, so I just don't notice anymore."

Ryder might be relaxed. But I wasn't. I didn't feel prepared at all. And there was one way to fix that. "We have work to do. I need some paper and pens and you have to take me through what I should be calling everyone." He paused before he nodded. "I don't want to look like some crazy American who doesn't understand the world I'm in."

"Being American is the perfect excuse—people will forgive you anything." He took a seat opposite me. "You shouldn't care what people think. My grandfather and my sister don't care about that stuff and they're the only people who matter."

It was a nice thing for him to say but it wasn't enough. "Thank you. I would just feel better if I knew what was expected. I don't want to embarrass you or your family, Ryder. And I don't want to embarrass myself."

"You would never . . ." He stopped before he finished his sentence. "I'm sorry about dinner. I know you weren't expecting Frederick on our first night home, but as my grandfather said, it was going to have to happen eventually."

"I'm *so* glad you're optimistic." I drained my glass and

set it down. "One of us should be."

"Hand me that." I nodded at the pad on the small table at Ryder's elbow. "You have to brief me. We only have a few hours."

"Whatever you need," he said, completely unfazed by my meltdown or demands.

Ryder's grandfather sounded forgiving, and maybe if we went through things now I could absorb all the information I needed before dinner.

"So, just to be clear, your grandfather, the duke, knows that we're—"

"Yes, he and Darcy know everything. I've never lied to either of them." His expression was serious and businesslike. "My grandfather has always seen me as the rightful heir. It's not that he doesn't like Frederick—just that he was never meant to inherit."

"Okay, and I call him Your Grace?"

Ryder grimaced. "Technically. But, that's not what—"

"How would Aurora address him?" Ryder's childhood friend wasn't a member of the family but knew them well. Perhaps I could follow her lead.

"She would probably just call him sir," he replied.

"Okay, well I'll try to avoid saying anything but I'll call him sir if the occasion arises. How does that sound?"

He held my gaze for a second and then nodded. "You have totally got this."

His confidence in me felt good and my anxiety levels dropped from boiling over to a simmer.

"I'll have to decide what to wear. Will you wear a suit?" I imagined Ryder was hardly going to eat in jeans. I'd never seen him out of a suit.

"My tux," he said.

Of course, because why wouldn't you wear your tux for a casual dinner with family. "Your tux? You're kidding?"

He shrugged. "It's no big deal. Don't worry about it."

Easy for him to say.

I had brought cocktail dresses. One of them would have to do. One of the good things about flying private was that it allowed for more luggage.

"Are you okay with sharing a room?" he asked. "I do think it looks better. My family knows I'm not a saint."

I took a deep breath. Everything had happened so quickly since we'd struck our deal that only now was I realizing it was so much more complicated than I'd ever thought. I hadn't considered sharing beds, bathrooms. Holding hands in front of strangers. Violet had said it was an adventure, but I hadn't prepared myself properly. I felt as if I were standing at the edge of quicksand and only just realized I'd promised to jump right in.

"I suppose since we're about to married, and moving in together anyway . . ." I replied, the reality of the words feeling heavier now than they had when they were discussed in the abstract over the last few weeks.

I had been so reluctant to become single again after my first marriage, but now I was about to be married again, singledom didn't seem quite so bad after all.

CHAPTER THIRTEEN
SCARLETT

"You look beautiful," Ryder said as I came out of the dressing room. His room was really a suite of rooms that had two bathrooms, two dressing rooms, a bedroom and a sitting room. There was even a study. I'd not seen him since I'd told him I was going to get ready.

"Thanks. You don't look so bad yourself." I reached up and tugged at his bowtie and then released it, reminding myself we weren't a real couple.

"That blue looks fantastic with your hair," he said, his gaze skirting over my body.

I nudged him. "Save your compliments for when we're in public."

"I meant it, but okay. Are you ready?"

I guess charm like his was difficult to turn off. "Sure. As ready as I'll ever be."

He took my hand as we walked along the corridor toward the staircase. "How far away is the dining room?" I whispered. "These shoes aren't meant for walking."

Ryder chuckled. "Piggyback?" he asked.

I grinned. "Be careful, I might say yes."

Ryder patiently held my hand as I descended the stairs in my overly high strappy heels. When we were just a few steps from the bottom, the door opened and a petite girl in rain boots came through the door. "It's vile out there," she said to Lane, who took her coat.

"Darce," Ryder called.

His sister looked up and almost leapt toward us, hopping out of her boots and bounding toward us in a cocktail dress and stocking feet. "It's so good to see you." She took her brother's face in her hands and rubbed as if she was petting a dog.

"Get off," he said, knocking Darcy's hands out of the way. "Let me introduce you to Scarlett," Ryder said, not letting go of my hand. "Scarlett, this is my pain-in-my-backside sister."

It was a little awkward as we were on the stairs but she kissed me on one cheek and then the other, all the while beaming at me.

"It's beyond brilliant to have you here, Scarlett. Ryder's told me so much about you. Can you believe Frederick and Victoria insisted on coming over this evening? Apologies in advance for the grilling you're going to get." She waved her hand in the air as she padded down the stairs. "Well, we'll make sure you're okay. Just don't get left alone with Victoria. She might stab you with a fork or something." She laughed and continued to chatter as we got to the bottom of the stairs and headed right in the same direction Ryder's grandfather had taken earlier, down a dim corridor lined with oil paintings that I barely got a look at as we strode through.

"Darcy, where are your shoes?" Ryder's grandfather asked as we entered an oak-paneled dining room with a stone fireplace at one end and a long table in the center. The lighting was low and what glow there was seemed to be sucked into the dark floors and walls.

"I went to check on the horses and lost them. So you'll have to deal with my stockinged feet." She went up on tiptoes as if to emphasize her lack of footwear.

I turned at the sound of someone clearing their throat and found a couple standing close together on the other side of the door.

"Scarlett," Ryder said. "Let me introduce you to my cousin Frederick, and his wife, Victoria."

"How do you do?" I asked, using the formal greeting Ryder had suggested.

"How do you do?" Frederick shook my hand, then Victoria coldly kissed the air by my cheek with a tight smile. There was none of the easy familiarity that Darcy had displayed.

But then, I was probably the last person either Victoria or her husband wanted to see.

A bell tinkled and everyone started moving toward the table.

"Sit next to me, Scarlett," Darcy said, patting the chair beside her. I glanced up at Ryder, who nodded.

The table was covered in a starched, white tablecloth and there was enough silverware surrounding my plate I was pretty sure if I stuffed it all in my suitcase, I could pay off Cecily Fragrance's loans and be done with this charade.

Ryder sat the other side of me, and to the right of his grandfather, who sat at the top of the table. Frederick and Victoria sat opposite us. There was an additional, empty place setting, but before I could wonder who it was for, the dining room door opened.

"So sorry I'm late."

This must be Aurora—Ryder's other option for a wife.

I smiled in her direction as she took a seat but her eyes were firmly on Ryder.

"So, Scarlett, tell me how you and Ryder met," Victoria said. "It sounds like it's been a whirlwind romance."

Ryder draped his arm around the back of my chair and leaned into me. "Not for me. Scarlett doesn't remember, but we met at a party a couple of years ago. Her laugh caught my attention from across the room. And then I saw her." He gazed at me in a performance worthy of an Oscar. "Of course I asked her out then, but alas she turned me down flat."

Darcy giggled, though I wasn't sure if it was as a result of our lie or the thought of her brother being turned down by a woman that amused her.

"It appears you won her over eventually," Frederick said.

"We met at work," I blurted, wanting to add something to the conversation so I didn't appear mute, but apparently my brain and my mouth weren't communicating well.

"You *work* for Ryder?" she asked, scowling as a bowl of soup was put in front of her by Lane, who was serving along with a younger girl I'd not seen before.

"I wish," Ryder said. "Scarlett is a talented entrepreneur —I wanted to buy her business."

"Oh?" Frederick said. "What business is that?"

"It's a fragrance company based in New York. I set it up with a friend of mine," I said.

"A fragrance company? That doesn't sound like the type of investment you normally make, dear cousin," Frederick said to Ryder, glancing down at his soup.

"I like to invest in businesses that make money. Cecily Fragrance has great margins and a strong future ahead of it." I glanced sideways at him and smiled, hoping that wasn't part of the lie we were spinning. The Westbury Group had been very successful and the fact that the company made a real effort to buy us out was flattering.

"Are you investing?" Darcy asked.

"Well, I'm not buying them out but the Westbury Group might provide them with some financing. Scarlett turned me down again."

His grandfather chuckled. "Good decision, my dear."

"I wish I were joking, Grandfather, but Scarlett didn't like my offer at all."

"Well, it seems you found an offer she liked well enough," Victoria said under her breath, her attention returning to her soup.

"I managed to convince her to join me for a drink," Ryder said.

"I'm surprised your ego let you ask her out again," Darcy said.

"He's not used to women saying no to him," Aurora said. "You were a challenge, I suppose."

I wasn't sure if she meant it as a compliment, but it sure didn't sound like one. The way Ryder had described their relationship was that she and her family had been keen for Aurora and Ryder to marry but there hadn't been any affection between them. That might be true for Ryder, but it was clear from the adoration in Aurora's eyes that what she felt was real.

After the soup was the pheasant, which was a just like chicken. I wasn't sure what to expect so was grateful for it to taste so familiar. Each course was served on beautiful china, beautifully presented, and tasted delicious. It was just like a restaurant meal. Did they ever just order Chinese food?

"You okay?" Ryder asked quietly as the rest of the table talked. He shifted his seat slightly toward me and put his hand on my leg. "You're fitting right in. You had nothing to be concerned about. You see?"

"A little," I said, patting his hand. He laced our fingers together.

"You *do* look really beautiful tonight, Scarlett."

"We didn't get a chance to see your ring," Victoria said, interrupting Ryder's easy charm.

I pulled my hand from Ryder and held it up, flat against my chest, not wanting to hold my hand out.

"Oh, it's new, is it?" she asked, reaching for her wine glass and flashing her own antique wedding ring. "I thought Ryder may have given you his grandmother's. She left it to him, you know."

"Victoria," Ryder growled.

"What? It's a simple observation."

Victoria was clearly trying to make a point, but she didn't realize that far from causing trouble for Ryder and me, our arrangement made comments like that simply amusing.

"I'm sure such a young, pretty thing like Scarlett doesn't want an old-fashioned ring like the duchesses' canary diamond ring. Fashions change, isn't that right, young lady?" the duke asked, his eyes twinkling mischievously.

I didn't know how to react. Would I be insulting his dead wife's taste if I agreed with him?

"I didn't want her to feel obligated to accept an heirloom simply because she loves me," Ryder said as he stretched out his arm along the top of the chair behind me.

Victoria rolled her eyes, but didn't say anything.

"Are you planning to move back and live here?" Aurora asked, clearly trying to change the subject. "You know, after the wedding."

"We'll spend time here, but our lives are in Manhattan," Ryder replied. I took another gulp of wine and almost instantly Lane refilled my glass.

"But you won't come back to run the estate?" Victoria asked as if the mere idea was ludicrous.

Ryder fisted his hands. "Things remain as they are— grandfather runs the estate and Darcy assists him."

Victoria was speaking as if the duke was already dead. It was my turn to reach across to Ryder's lap. He brought his hand down to meet mine and we linked fingers, acting like the newly engaged couple we were pretending to be. Except, I wasn't acting. I genuinely wanted to soothe him. Whether or not she knew it, Victoria was being insensitive.

"Are you going to Scotland for your honeymoon?" Frederick asked, as if his wife hadn't just speculated about the consequences of the duke's death.

Honeymoon? We hadn't even discussed it.

I took the opportunity to speak so Ryder didn't snap at Victoria. "We're spending a week here and then flying back to Manhattan. There will be plenty of trips during the course of our marriage, but being here with the duke after his fall is what we both want to do now."

I'd thought we'd prepared well but I couldn't wait to escape back to our bedroom, for it just to be the two of us again. At least there I could relax and just be me for a few hours.

"Are we shooting tomorrow?" Frederick asked Ryder.

Shooting? Was I being left on my own tomorrow?

"Let's see what the weather does—Merriman may need us," Ryder replied.

"He won't let us take the deer anymore, which is a shame," Frederick said as he placed his napkin alongside his empty plate and sat back in his chair.

"That's because you're a terrible shot," Ryder replied.

"Now, now, boys," the duke said. "There's always plenty of pheasant. What will the girls do if the boys are shooting?"

"Maybe we'll go shooting, too," Darcy replied.

The duke chuckled. "Oh yes, well, you are just as good a shot as anyone, Darcy. But Scarlett might not want to join in."

"I don't mind," I said. As much as I didn't want to be murdering deer or anything else, I wanted to be away from Ryder even less. "I'll probably have horrible jet lag anyway. I can catch up on my sleep."

"Did you bring your dress?" Darcy asked.

I nodded. "Yes, I need to make sure it survived the journey." I'd bought the dress with Harper two days before I'd left New York. It was off the rack, which had felt appropriate for our business arrangement, but fit as if it had been made for me.

"I can't wait to see," she said. "Maybe you can show me and then we can go get pampered. Do pre-wedding body prep. There's a hotel with a great spa about ten miles from here."

"I love it there," Aurora said.

"We should all go. We can get to know you better," Victoria said.

"Let's just see, shall we?" Ryder said. "Scarlett and I both have jobs to check in on."

Thank God. Today had been overwhelming enough without the thought that I'd have to spend tomorrow with Victoria without him.

We were a team and I didn't want us split up. I hadn't known him long, but so far he'd kept his word on absolutely everything he'd promised. And his sister and grandfather clearly adored him.

When it came to husbands, I'd chosen worse.

———————

I came out of the bathroom to find Ryder lying on the bed, his jacket off, his bowtie undone and his shoes kicked off to the floor, but otherwise still fully clothed.

An uncomfortable dinner, jet lag and the stress of being on display all evening had taken their toll. I was exhausted.

"You did really well tonight," he said, propping his head up on his hand as I walked to the other side of the bed.

I shook my head. "It was a lot to take in. Thank God for you," I said, climbing up onto the mattress that came up to my hip. "I think Victoria was out for blood." I lay back on the pillows and sank into the bed.

"Yeah, she's clearly not happy."

I chuckled. "I can't believe she said that thing about who was going to run the estate. It was so disrespectful."

"That's what she's like. Her eye has always been on the prize—Woolton—then you waltz in ready to take that away from her, and looking like you do."

What was he saying?

"You're very beautiful, Scarlett," he said, his finger trickling down the side of my arm.

It was nice to feel as if I had someone on my side. I'd missed the feeling of having a teammate, someone in my corner, since my divorce. "I'm glad I passed their inspection. So far, at least."

His hand settled at my waist and goosebumps pulsed out from under his hand and across my body. It was as if we were a normal couple, discussing the day, casually intimate with each other. It reminded me of life with Marcus—a time when I thought I'd found the love of my life. I ignored the sting in my chest and turned to face Ryder so I was mirroring him.

"I don't have to go shooting tomorrow. God knows, I could do without a day with Frederick. I don't see why you should be subjected to Victoria."

"It's fine." It wasn't, but I could handle Victoria. Despite a lukewarm response from Ryder and me, Darcy had seemed excited about the spa and so I'd agreed to go. Which meant Ryder had no excuse not to go shooting with Frederick.

He circled his thumb over the silk of my nightgown. "This is nice. Being here, with you," he said, as if he hadn't been expecting to enjoy my company.

I smoothed my hand up his arm. It seemed like a natural thing to do, though I knew it wasn't. This man wasn't my husband-to-be. I might be marrying him. But it wasn't meant to be a physical relationship.

He pulled me closer. "I know we said no sex . . ."

I ran my palm up his chest. "We really shouldn't." This needed to be about business. I wanted Cecily Fragrance. He wanted a wife. That was all we were doing here.

"It's just you're so beautiful."

I sighed, my nipples tightening against the silk of my nightdress. I'd gotten used to not having sex since Marcus and I split. Ryder had awoken something in me, and I missed how easy it was to fuck and be fucked when I was married.

"And it was *so* good," he said, as if the admission were being squeezed out of him. "Wasn't it?" he asked, shifting his hips closer. "So, so good."

If I could stop the voices chattering in my head for just a second, I could sink into the warmth of him, into being part of a couple again, into the hardness of his body.

I missed all that. I missed having someone who was *mine*.

I reached for his jaw and he bent to kiss me, his lips soft but, like all of him, in control. He led everything—me out of the car, the conversation at dinner, plans for tomorrow . . . my body.

He rolled me to my back as he pushed his tongue into my mouth and sought mine as if he were taking all my worries from me with every touch. Slowly, he created a blurred screen between me and my concerns about the next day, my embarrassment at saying the wrong thing, my pain of losing my husband.

He pulled back. "God, I like kissing you."

I rolled my lips between my teeth, dampening down a smile. I nodded. "I like kissing you too."

"And this?" he said, his hand sweeping down my body. "I like all this, too."

It had been a long time since I'd felt attractive—even longer since I'd believed someone was attracted to me. I'd forgotten how much I liked that feeling.

I reached for my thighs and gathered my nightdress, collected the silk to reveal my legs. I pulled it up and off my body, arching my back, to remove it entirely.

Ryder's eyebrows pulsed up. "Now, I like that even more."

He kissed me again. The scrape of his shirt against my skin made me shudder.

He made his way down my body with his mouth, slow and deliberate, his hands following as though he was trying to commit every part of me to memory. He took his time to explore every angle, every ledge and dip. I held off a groan until he reached my lower belly.

"You're going to have to be quiet," he said, shifting farther down the bed. "These walls are thick, but they're not going to withstand a scream."

He dug his tongue into my slit as I grabbed the back of my legs, pulling them open wide. Why had we not done this since the last time? It felt so good, so right.

His thumb pushed into me like a plug, circling as he licked, dragging his tongue up and around and back. My body seemed to float off the bed, buoyed up by the pleasure. In seconds I was climbing toward my orgasm.

"You promise you'll be quiet?" he asked, breaking his rhythm as he looked up to track my reaction.

"Yes." I reached my hand to the back of his head, urging him to finish what he'd started. "Don't stop."

"Relax and trust me," he said, before diving down to ease my throb.

I didn't *need* to trust him. I knew only too well that he could make me come.

His thumb slipped in and out, my wetness dribbling out between the cheeks of my butt. He slid his index finger against my crack, pressing hard as if he wanted to ensure I knew it was intentional. He found a smooth, rocking rhythm, in and out with his fingers, up and down with this tongue. I floated on the steady pleasure until he slid a finger over my asshole, pressing in just the slightest bit and making me groan. My whole world was awash with sensation—his mouth, his tongue, the slight graze of his teeth every now and then. The press of his hand under my hip bone, holding me still. His thumb sliding in and out, his finger mirroring the rocking motion.

It was all too much. And he knew.

He released my hip and pressed his hand to my mouth, clamping down so I could release the cries that I'd been trying to hold inside. I gave in, pleas and curses and moans vibrating against his palm as I came, writhing against him, into him, my only thought how much I wanted to be with him. Right here. Right now.

Nothing else mattered.

Not Cecily Fragrance, not Marcus.

Not my future or my past.

CHAPTER FOURTEEN
RYDER

I was so hard I could hardly breathe. I slid my zipper down carefully, not wanting to scrape it across my erection and blow my load.

Scarlett hadn't been quiet. Even knowing that people might hear, she hadn't been able to hold back and I totally fucking loved it. She'd barely said a word at dinner, no doubt intimidated by the alien chatter and the jostling for dominance that had taken place. But here? In this bedroom, just her and me? She wasn't intimidated and she certainly wasn't quiet.

I carefully maneuvered myself to lie beside her. Her belly rose and fell in the most delicious way. I couldn't look. Jesus. I tried to think about hunting with Frederick.

"You look angry," she said. "What's on your mind?" She rolled toward me and I kept my eyes on the ceiling, trying to ignore how her breasts sat high on her chest, her nipples pointing at me, daring me to squeeze them.

"You want to ask me what I'm not thinking."

"What?" She slid her hand over my stomach and I grabbed her wrist.

"No," I barked.

She pulled her arm back as if I'd bitten her.

"Sorry, I'm going to come if you touch me." I squeezed my eyes shut as I felt the mattress dip beside me. What was she doing? I couldn't help but think about the way she moved so unselfconsciously when she was naked.

"You are?" she asked, her voice sounding farther away. I opened my eyes a fraction. She sat cross-legged, her elbows on her knees, looking at me from the middle of the bed.

I groaned. She was going to be the death of me. Her still-wet pussy faced me, her dusky pink nipples jutting out as if desperate for touch.

I fiddled with the fastening of my pants. I needed to get naked. Now.

"You want me to help you with that?" she asked, as if I were unloading the trunk of a car.

I glanced at her. The glint in her eye told me she was clearly teasing me.

"If you don't behave, I'll bend you over my knee." I couldn't look at her, but managed to slide off my trousers despite the mental image of her ass in the air, red from my palm. Removing my clothes had calmed my cock. Slightly. For now.

I stripped off my shirt and boxers, sighing as I stuck my hands behind my head. I was ready for round two.

I caught her staring at my dick. "Like what you see?" I asked.

She tilted her head toward my face, her eyes following as if she couldn't bear to turn away from my erection. I almost grabbed her right then and pulled her onto me, but I wanted to make this last.

"Well, I know what it can do, so yeah, I like what I see." And there it was—that complete honesty. It wasn't something she said because she thought it was the right thing to say. It was what she believed, what she felt.

I chuckled. "Come show me how much," I said. "Straddle me." I wanted an uninterrupted view of those tits as I fucked her.

She crawled slowly toward me, her breasts swaying as she moved. Christ she was beautiful—like a more intense and perfect version of every woman I'd ever fucked. Was it because I knew her a little now? Was it because I liked the open, fresh woman she was?

"You're bossy," she said as her palms flattened against my abdomen and she settled atop me.

"You like it," I replied.

Her shiver in response was all the confirmation I needed. She liked to be told what to do. Maybe not outside of the bedroom, maybe not even outside of the two of us. But she liked *me* telling her what to do in bed.

And *I* liked that.

I grabbed her hips and pulled her toward me until she slid over my cock, her wetness coating me. She tilted forward and pushed her hips back, her clit connecting with my root.

Her head fell forward, her long hair skirting my body. She moaned and swiveled her hips. Pressing her clit to my cock. I let her rub herself against me, let her think she was in charge for a few moments before I tightened my grip. "I want inside you," I whispered.

She paused and then nodded. Did she have to think about it? I reached for my wallet on the bed stand and pulled out a condom. She watched as I slid it onto my cock, which jerked under her greedy gaze.

"Be gentle," she whispered. "I want it to last."

"You do it," I replied, happy for her to take charge for a bit.

I wanted to shove my way inside her tight, wet heat and fuck her without mercy. I didn't want to hurt her, and I definitely wanted her to enjoy it. But more than anything I wanted her to come. Hard.

I released her hips and fisted my hands at my side as she took a hold of my dick, her small fingers wrapping around it tightly, like she might drop it. She placed the tip at her entrance and sighed. It was as if it was what she'd been waiting for, and now she'd got it, she could relax. I liked the idea that she'd been waiting for my cock.

She squeezed my tip with her muscles and I had to stop myself from thrusting off the bed, slamming into her. She panted as she lowered herself a little, squeezing her eyes shut. "So big," she muttered.

She let out a half breath and then began to move in small, sharp shifts.

The sight of her parted mouth, her bouncing breasts, her flexing thighs—heaven.

She sank lower and the pressure of her muscles surrounding me was just perfect. I almost blacked out— overdosing on pleasure. If drugs felt this good, I'd be an addict.

"Ryder," she said, panting.

I'd been lost in her until then, watching every part of her except her eyes. She looked panicked. Why?

"It's too much." She placed my hands on her hips and it took a second or two for me to connect the dots. She wanted me to fuck her, didn't want to be the one in control.

I clenched my fingers into her flesh and brought her down fully onto me. She whimpered. "Yes," she whispered. "More."

Jesus, it took everything I had not to explode.

I sat up and flipped her over. "I'll give you more," I said. At that moment I didn't care if she screamed the house to the ground. I was about to overflow at the feel of her, at the sight, sound, touch of her. And I wanted her to be where I was. "I'm going to give you everything."

I thrust up and she squealed and bent her legs, taking me deeper until I couldn't get any further inside her. I pulled out and pushed again in long, slow strokes, dipping my head to her shoulder and sucking up a mark on her neck that tasted of tangerine and heat.

My glutes spasmed as I pushed into her, forcing her legs wide. She slid up the bed and I hooked my hand over her shoulders to keep her in place.

"Like that? Like it when I fuck you good and hard?" The words came out sharp as she moaned in response. She loved it.

It was as if she hadn't had this before—like it was all new and fascinating to her—what I could do, how her body responded.

She grabbed my neck, her fingers curling around the nape. "I like how *you* like it," she choked out. "How you like fucking me."

She'd summed up exactly what made it so good. We were two opposite sides of the same coin, enjoying how we made each other feel—each relishing the pleasure of the other—it heightened every move we made.

"I do, I rejoice in fucking you, in making you come."

She stiffened and gasped then scrambled for a pillow, brought it over her face and screamed into it as she climaxed.

I didn't care about the noise. Not anymore. My grandfather was on the other side of the house, my sister had heard worse, and I didn't give a shit about the staff. I was fucking my fiancée. So what? I pulled the pillow from her face and sped up my rhythm. Pushing against her pulsating muscles, chasing my release.

My orgasm was seconds away, carried from her to me. I came in sharp, desperate strokes, groaning out loud.

I collapsed on top of her, every last bit of energy drained from me.

Absentmindedly, she wound the hair at the back of my neck around her index finger. It was such a small thing, but so intimate I almost couldn't bear it.

I pressed my lips to just behind her ear to interrupt her touch. I couldn't move to do more even if I wanted to.

"I think we were loud," she said once my breathing had slowed. I rolled off her to my back, laying one of my legs over hers, somehow wanting to keep touching her but having had no practice in postcoital cuddling.

"I don't give a shit," I replied, turning my head as she put her hands over her face.

"I hope no one heard. I tried, Ryder. I really tried."

I grabbed her wrist, pulling her arm over my belly. "Hey, don't worry about it. I don't think I exactly held back either."

"But your grandfather," she said. "It's so disrespectful."

"Don't sweat it." I threaded my fingers through hers. "He's on the other side of the house. He definitely won't have heard."

"You think?"

"Absolutely." I glanced at her tight nipples, flat belly

and glossy hair that spanned across my bed in a fan of black. "You wanna test my theory and go again?"

If I was going to fake-marry someone, I could have done a lot worse. Scarlett King was clever, beautiful and fucking fantastic in bed.

CHAPTER FIFTEEN
RYDER

Even nice days in October began with bleak, cold mornings. That I'd been pulled out of bed and away from Scarlett's warm body to go hunting with Frederick, of all people, only added to the misery.

Still, I knew I was going to have to have a conversation with Frederick on my own at some point. I just had hoped it wouldn't be while we both were carrying guns.

Merriman, the gamekeeper, pulled up and put the hand break of the Land Rover on. "Let's go from here," he said.

I opened the door and headed to the trunk, Bracknell, Merriman's golden retriever, following me.

I hated shooting. Some people enjoyed it because of the land, the fresh air or being with their dogs. But for Frederick I knew it was the sense of power he had from killing things. He made me sick. For Merriman, it was all about estate management. That was the only way I could justify it. I knew Frederick went on organized hunts, where they were shooting pheasant especially bred to be shot. That was just fucked up as far as I was concerned—creating something to kill it.

"I doubt you do much shooting in New York," Frederick said. "You a little worried about being rusty?" he asked, handing me a shotgun.

I'd always been a better shot, even though Frederick did it so often. "Not that worried, no. No doubt Merriman will be better than both of us as usual."

Merriman pretended he couldn't hear us bickering as he always did. Everyone at Woolton had gotten used to our fighting. Even as children, there'd never been a time when we were friends, despite us being just a year apart in age. Frederick had always been so resentful. So keen to find fault in everything and everyone. Being near him had been exhausting, even as a kid.

Merriman led the way with Bracknell and the cartridges, luckily, and Frederick and I followed over the uneven, dew-covered ground.

"You should have worn walking shoes," I said as Frederick stumbled. Why had he worn wellies? And why the fuck was he wearing tweed? Merriman and I were happy in our wax jackets and jeans. This wasn't a formal day shooting with all the pomp and ceremony. It was two cousins out with the gamekeeper.

"Rubbish. Just because you live in America doesn't mean *I* have to let my standards slip."

I sighed but didn't reply. There was no point. He was always so keen to look like he fit in, rather than just relaxing and letting it happen.

I glanced up at the sun, pushing through the mist of the morning. I hoped Scarlett would be okay at the spa. I knew Darcy would look after her, but Victoria? There was no telling how she'd treat my fiancée. I was even worried that Aurora would be less than friendly when I wasn't around. She was a sweet girl, but I had a sneaking suspicion that she wasn't married by now because she'd thought I'd eventually come to my senses. She'd been close to my mother, sister and grandfather as a child, but why she still spent so much time here as an adult? It didn't make sense to me.

Merriman stopped and took off his bag, setting it on the ground. Without glancing behind him, he tossed a small bottle of water toward us. It was unexpected and I didn't quite catch it, and it bounced at my feet.

Frederick chortled as he caught the second one. "You still think you're going to beat me?"

"What can I say? If it happens, it's because my beautiful fiancée kept me awake and, rest assured, it will not bother me in the least." I grinned, happy to fuck with Frederick and tell the truth at the same time.

"Yeah, right. What an excuse. As if you two are actually sleeping together," he said. Interesting. He clearly suspected my relationship with Scarlett.

I chuckled, trying not to show any weakness. "You think we're saving it until our wedding night?"

"I doubt she'll go through with it. If she's got any sense, she'll take the money you've obviously paid her and walk away. Unless, of course, you're paying extra for the sex."

If I hadn't been holding a shotgun, I was pretty sure I'd have taken a swing at him. Scarlett wasn't marrying me for money—not really. She was only trying to save the company she'd put everything into. Just like me. And she wasn't sleeping with me for money, that was for sure.

"Or maybe she just wants to be a duchess."

"She didn't know about the title when I proposed." That was true too. I hadn't deliberately left that part out but I'd not really considered the fact that while she was married to me, she'd be my duchess.

"Yes, all very convenient. She's the perfect woman, who suddenly has you popping the question, and just in the nick of time, too."

"What exactly are you implying?"

"I'm not implying anything. I think I'm saying it quite openly. There's no way your romance, or whatever you want to call it, with that woman is real. You just want to inherit."

"You're a dick, Frederick. If what you were saying is true, why on earth wouldn't I have married before now? Why didn't I simply marry when Grandfather had his stroke?" Lying didn't sit easily, but what choice did I have? "Or at any time in the last decade?"

He didn't know anything had changed. There was no way he could know how the Westbury Group was linked with the estate.

"I'm not quite sure yet." He shrugged. Confidence and swagger weren't attributes that fitted him and he looked stiff instead of relaxed. "But these things tend to have a habit of revealing themselves as I'm sure that woman will."

That was a threat if ever I heard one, but I was too incensed to worry about what plans he had to try to reveal the true nature of our relationship.

"*That* woman? My *fiancée's* name is Scarlett. You might not like it, Frederick, but Scarlett is going to be my wife."

"Your whole relationship is a fake, and we both know it."

"Because it's not convenient to you? You should have been a fly on the wall in our bedroom last night—no one was faking anything. You might have a sexless marriage, but I certainly won't. Hell, take one look at Scarlett." I scoffed. "As if I can keep my hands off her." I didn't have to lie to him. Everything I was saying was true.

Frederick sniffed and wiped the end of his nose with the back of his hand. "Victoria is a very attractive woman."

"Yeah? I reckon you haven't had head since you married her." My jaw tightened. I was pissed at Frederick and irritated at myself for letting him affect me.

Merriman cleared his throat as Frederick grimaced.

"Gentleman," Merriman said. "Can we concentrate on the matter at hand?"

I turned back to Merriman. "Sorry." What I wanted to do was punch Frederick out and go back to the house. I'd expected Frederick to bait me, been waiting for it. But why had I let him get under my skin? I didn't usually. I just didn't like the way he was talking about Scarlett. She was an innocent party in all this. How dare he talk about her like that? "You have my full attention," I said, nodding at Merriman, not able to hear a word he was saying. Frederick had barely spoken to Scarlett. Who was he to judge her so quickly? If he'd bothered to get to know her, he'd realize that she was a sweet, feisty, sexy, funny woman who any man would be lucky to marry.

Chapter Sixteen
Scarlett

I glanced around the dimly lit circular relaxation room with the gold, domed ceiling. In different circumstances, this place would probably be a great getaway. But right now I'd rather be almost anywhere than at a spa with Victoria and Aurora. I'd thought that Ryder had said they weren't particularly friendly with each other, but watching them chat at the juice bar, completely ignoring Darcy and me, they looked thick as thieves.

"Don't worry about them," Darcy said from next to me. We were on day beds, waiting for the next treatment. The spa was quiet and I hadn't seen any other guests. After the full body massage I'd just had, and the countless orgasms last night, I should be more relaxed than I was.

I smiled and turned toward her. She put her magazine down and looked at me. "I'm not. I'm just relaxing." I settled my mango and ginseng smoothie onto the floor and started to look through the magazines littering the small side table.

"I bet Ryder told you the story regarding Aurora, but probably left out all the details that matter. She's been after him since she got her braces taken out. She's been a total mess since he announced your engagement."

I glanced over at the two of them again. "Ryder said they were never together."

Darcy swung her legs off the bed and leaned in close to me. "No, they never dated. I think when he was about fifteen they kissed, but that was it."

I found that really hard to believe. Who could be hung up on a guy for so long if he'd never given her any reason to hope?

"Ryder has always been very clear that he'd never marry. He used to joke that George Clooney stole his idea," Darcy said.

"But she thought he'd change his mind?"

"I guess. But Ryder never even had girlfriends. There was nothing to suggest he was going to settle down."

"Unless she thought he was playing the field and one day he'd come back, make a life and children with her."

"If that's what she thought then she's delusional. Ryder is as ruthless with his women as he is in business dealings," Darcy said, then paused, her expression turning guilty. "Though I've never known him to deliberately upset someone." She tossed her magazine onto the bed and picked up her sludgy green drink. "I told him to marry Aurora. I knew she'd be willing." Darcy shrugged. "But Ryder wouldn't agree to it, said it would hurt Aurora that he could never be a real husband. So I don't think he led her on."

"Did she know he'd only inherit if he married?"

Darcy glanced over at the juice bar. "Everyone knows that, though I don't think it was the money she was after." She paused, frowning. "Well not entirely, anyway. I think she liked the idea of the whole package—the title, the social status. But mostly I think she loves him."

"And you two are friends?" If Darcy knew about our arrangement, would she have told Aurora? And if she knew, would Victoria find out?

"Yes, we've always been friends. Though my feelings are not so warm where Victoria is concerned. The woman doesn't have friends." She laughed. "That sounds bitchy, but I'm being factual."

"But Aurora and Victoria look close," I said with a nod toward the bar.

"They're not close. Victoria's probably pumping her for information about you. But Aurora doesn't know anything. She might suspect ulterior motives—she knows how Ryder is, after all—but you and he were so cute at dinner last night. More than anything else, I imagine she's jealous."

"What are you two talking about?" Victoria asked as she sat on the bed next to me.

"My brother," Darcy said. "I was just telling Scarlett how cute they look together."

Victoria rolled her eyes but at least she didn't say anything.

"How did you say you met again?" Aurora asked.

More questions. It seemed like I was being thrown a rope so I could hang myself. "As I said last night, I don't remember the first time we met. It was at a party a couple of years ago apparently." Aurora took a seat at the end of my bed and I had to shift my legs up to make room for her.

"You have amnesia or something?" Victoria snapped.

"No. He asked me out and I said no."

"I thought you didn't remember," she said.

I shook my head. "I don't, but Ryder's told me the story more than once. Of course, he could be totally making it up.

But then, I was married. I wouldn't have been paying attention to other men."

"Married?" Aurora asked. "And you're divorced now?"

"Well she's not about to commit bigamy, is she?" Darcy laughed. "The wedding is the day after tomorrow, for goodness' sake."

I smiled. "Yes, we're divorced now." It was the first time that the mention of my divorce hadn't caused a physical pain. Perhaps my heart was healing as everyone had promised it would. "My ex and I grew up together, were childhood sweethearts." I cringed as I realized I was describing a situation close to Aurora and Ryder's. "We started dating at fifteen. Got married at twenty-one. We were too young."

Except, *I* hadn't been too young. Violet had told me more than once that people came in and out of our lives, travelling with us through different parts of our journey, and that my ex-husband had been my companion through my teens and early twenties. For him, I'd been a temporary part of his life, but I'd been happy to spend the rest of my life on the same road together. And now instead of sharing the minutiae of lives, I had no idea where he was even living. And he would have no clue that I would be in England and about to be married. Things change so quickly.

"And it's amicable?" Victoria asked. "Or was it a bad breakup?"

"Victoria," Darcy said, shooting her a dirty look.

"It's as amicable as these things can be. Definitely better now that some time has passed." And that bit was true.

"And you looked Ryder up when you got divorced?" Victoria asked.

I curled my toes, gripping the cotton cover of the day bed. "Nope." Now it clearly felt like Victoria was trying to catch me out. "I couldn't, as I said last night. I didn't even remember meeting him. We ran into each other at work. Well, he wanted to purchase the business I co-founded."

"Oh right, so it's buy the business, get the girl for free?"

"Victoria," Darcy and Aurora said in unison.

"My business partner and I refused his offer, but I agreed to a date."

"That's so cute," Aurora said. "I have to say it was a bit of a shock. Ryder's always liked women, so I was surprised to hear he'd decided to settle down."

"Just say what you mean—Ryder's a slut," Victoria said. "He's fucked most of New York from what I understand. I hope you know what you're doing."

"That's my brother you're speaking of, Victoria. If you say another—"

"Well, I have to say, he's certainly honed his craft," I interrupted.

For once Victoria didn't have a response.

Darcy laughed. "Yes, you sounded like you were having fun last night," she said.

Oh my God, how humiliating. I covered my face with my hands. "I'm so sorry," I said. Ryder had warned me to be quiet. It was just so difficult when I was with him. I took a deep breath. "I just mean I have no reason to doubt his loyalty." I took another sip of my juice.

Darcy chuckled and thankfully we were interrupted by two members of staff calling Victoria and Aurora back for their next treatment.

I watched both disappear behind a heavy curtain.

"Oh my God," Darcy whispered. "That was perfect. You even managed to blush when I pretended I'd overheard the two of you."

"You made that up?" Thank God. We had to be more careful next time. I didn't want Ryder's grandfather and sister overhearing us. And anyway, there probably wouldn't even be a next time. Last night had just been . . . I couldn't call it a mistake—it had been too good for that—but it wasn't the deal that we had struck.

"Well, I thought I'd made it up . . ." She narrowed her eyes at me. "Were you and Ryder . . . together?"

I held my breath, unsure what I was supposed to say. "He must have told you how we met," I said.

"Remind me."

Ryder and Darcy were close, and I wanted to keep the lies to a minimum. Ryder wouldn't mind if I filled her in, would he?

I quickly explained how I'd had my first ever one-night stand, then run into Ryder at work the next day. "So it's not as if we first slept together after . . . you know."

"He proposed." Darcy finished my sentence for me.

"Exactly."

"But you're *still* sleeping together?" she asked.

"Just last night." It wasn't like it was a regular thing. And I had no idea if it would happen again, despite the day after tomorrow being our wedding day.

"Twice is double the number of times he normally sleeps with a woman," she replied and swung her legs back onto the day bed and opened a magazine.

I lay my head back and stared at the glimmering ceiling. He probably wasn't around the same woman more than once. Sleeping together again had been a matter of circumstance.

Would it happen again tonight? I enjoyed his company. And his cock—that was for sure. And it wasn't as if dating had worked out that well. Maybe having a career and a lover would be my path for the next part of my life.

"Scarlett!" Ryder called from the bedroom.

"I'm in here," I replied. After my massage I was covered in oil and had decided to take a bath when I returned to Woolton.

The bathroom door swung open and Ryder and his tousled hair filled up the frame. "Shit," he said, finding me in the tub. He turned to leave. "Sorry."

"Don't be. Come in." I wanted to catch him up on my conversation with Victoria. And I kinda liked that he'd come looking for me—all rumpled and handsome.

He paused and turned back to face me. "Are you sure? I —"

"Come in and shut the door—you're letting the cold in." My husband and I had always caught up on our days while I took a bath. Sometimes he'd join me. It had been sacred time as a couple.

He chuckled and clicked the bathroom door closed, wandering over and sitting on the tiled ledge surrounding the bath. "You don't mind me being in here?" he asked. But he didn't insist on leaving.

"Should I?" He'd seen me naked in far more compromising positions. And the thick bubbles covered the surface of the bathwater in any event.

He shrugged. "I don't know. I thought you might want

155

your privacy." I knew a man who looked like he wanted to talk.

"I'm fine and you're a sight for sore eyes. I want to hear about your day. So why not now?" I smiled. "How many birds did you kill?"

"A sight for sore eyes? Does that mean the spa day was difficult?"

"Tell me about the birds," I said. I wanted to hear about his day.

"I'll tell you about the birds and Fred-a-dick when you tell me about Victoria."

I laughed. "You know you sound like a fifteen-year-old boy when you call him that," I said.

"What can I say? He brings out the worst in me." He reached down and swept his fingers into the water. "Nice," he said.

"You can join me if you want. Plenty of room for two." I drew my knees up to show him how much room I had left in the tub.

He looked at me and narrowed his eyes. "And then you'll tell me about Victoria?"

"I'm not suggesting Chinese water torture. It's a bath, not blackmail." I rolled my eyes. "And anyway, Victoria wasn't anything I couldn't handle."

He stood and stripped off his shirt. "A bath actually does sound great."

I watched his pecs curve and pulse as he flung his shirt to the floor and started on the fly of his jeans. I caught sight of the row of three freckles on his hip bone that I'd found last night and smiled. I was ridiculous. Every inch of this man's body was delectable, but I focused on three tiny freckles. As he pushed down his jeans he turned his perfectly biteable ass toward me and I was easily distracted. "You have a great ass," I said.

He chuckled. "Back at you."

He stepped into the water.

"Sit between my legs and I'll give your back a rub."

"My favorite place to be, Miss King," he replied as he steadied himself, grasping either side of the tub and took a seat in *my* favorite place for him to be.

The muscles under his skin were tight and I snapped open some bath cream.

"It's cold," he said as I squirted it onto his shoulder.

I laughed. "Don't be a baby. I'm going to make you feel great." His hands gripped my calves and pulled my legs tight around him.

I began to pinch and knead the muscles at the base of his neck, working my way down his shoulder, first one side and then the other. His body slowly relaxed with every touch. "It feels good," he mumbled.

"I told you it would." He sank back onto my chest, and I slipped my arms under his. "Fred-a-dick got you tense," I said.

"Apparently, you're the cure for that," he said.

"Wanna talk about it?" I asked.

He turned his head to look at me. "Nope. I can't even remember why he pissed me off now."

"Families are complicated," I said.

"Yeah, you can say that again. I'm lucky really. I have my grandfather and Darcy—a lot of people don't even have that. They've never let me down. I can count on them for anything. And I would walk through fire for them."

I squeezed him tighter. "You don't wish you had more of a relationship with your parents?" I asked.

He skidded his hand over the surface of the water. "My grandparents were my parents really." That wasn't an answer but I couldn't tell whether he was being deliberately evasive.

"You don't miss your mom?"

He sighed, his body pressing against mine. "An idea of her perhaps. But I can't miss someone who I never knew, who was never around."

"I suppose." I let a beat of silence extend between us.

"I wouldn't wish the parents I had on anyone and I wouldn't want to be the people they are. But at the same time, I can't complain about the privileged life I have."

"I'm not sure any privilege makes up for not having a mom."

He didn't respond and then scooped up some water and splashed his face.

"Will I meet her?" I asked.

Ryder shook his head. "I have no idea where she is at the moment." He cleared his throat. "Haven't seen her for a couple of years."

I couldn't imagine what it must be like not to have parents—to not have seen my mother in years. "I'm sorry," I said.

"Don't be. Not now. When we were kids it was . . . more difficult. But now? Like I said, I have my grandfather and Darcy. That's all I need." He spoke with conviction as if he, his grandfather and his sister were in a fortified castle, with high walls and a deep moat. No one was allowed in or out. But I got the feeling he'd just let me peek over the edge, just for a few minutes.

I swept my hand down his chest and he turned to look at me. As he did, I bent and kissed him on the nose before I had a chance to think that maybe I shouldn't. I was used to doing what came naturally with the man I was with. I'd never had to check myself or wonder if it was too much.

Ryder grinned up at me. He didn't seem to mind. "You have suds on your head," he said.

"I do?" I asked as he dusted them off.

"They suited you. But you could wear naked with anything and you'd make it look great." He chuckled. "God, am I being a cheeseball again?" He turned back around and we both faced forward.

"Again?" I asked.

"You called me a cheeseball the first night we met," he said, his exhale pressing against my belly.

"I did?" There was nothing cheesy about Ryder.

"Yeah, it threw me off my game a little. You don't remember?"

I remembered him being charming. And gorgeous. And I remembered wanting to see him naked but not being cheesy.

"Nope." I stroked my finger down from his hairline at the top his neck to the top of his spine. Even the most innocuous part of the man's body was a turn on. "I don't remember you being a cheeseball. Are you giving me fake compliments?"

Was his flattery just a knee-jerk reaction to being with a woman? A line he used often? Victoria had certainly painted him as a man who'd do whatever it took to get a woman into bed. "Or did you mean it?"

He paused before saying, "Yeah, I meant it. You're beautiful. Unselfconscious and open, which is really attractive." He took a breath, my hands rising and falling with his chest. "I find it *very* sexy."

I pressed my mouth against his shoulder to stop myself from grinning so wide my face split in two. He *did* mean it. I could feel it, and it could never be cheesy if he meant it.

He squeezed my legs and then trailed his thumb down to my ankle before he stood. He was getting out? I wasn't ready.

"Your turn for a foot rub," he said as he sat back down opposite me, took my ankle and began to work his thumbs into the sole of my foot in firm, determined strokes.

"This is nice," he said. "I've never . . ."

Shared a bath?

Talked about his family?

Slept with a woman more than once?

All of the above?

His thumb hit a particularly tender spot and I groaned, closing my eyes. When he stopped, I opened them to find him looking at me.

"The sounds that you make . . ."

I tilted my head, inviting him to finish his sentence.

"I like them."

I grinned.

"They make me . . ."

His eyes grew darker and he didn't need to say anything for me to know what he meant. I slid my foot from his hand, and found his erection below the water.

"Giving me a foot rub gets you hard?"

"The noises that come out of your mouth do," he replied, capturing my foot with both hands.

"I don't mean to be so loud." Had I been loud with

Marcus? Since we'd moved in together, we'd never had a reason to hold back but at the same time, I couldn't ever remember trying to. With Ryder I was only too aware of how much the sound was bursting out of me.

"I like every noise you make." He smoothed his hand up the inside of my leg. The water chased upward, lapping over my pussy. I wasn't sure if it was the water, his words or his stare that heated my body.

I wanted his fingers, higher, sweeping over my clit but instead his hand went back to my foot, his thumb circling over my heel.

His cock jerked against his belly and when I looked up his eyes met mine—hungry.

"Clean enough?" I slid my foot from his hand, braced my hands on the side of the bath and stood. "Because I want to get a little dirty." The suds still clung to parts of my body as Ryder swept his eyes over the length of me. I held out my hand and he grinned.

CHAPTER SEVENTEEN
RYDER

"Fucking croquet? Really?" I muttered under my breath as we started to descend the stairs. I really would have preferred to spend the day in bed with Scarlett. Last night in the bath, the bed, the floor and against the wall had been a much more preferable way to pass time than with a bunch of people I didn't know or didn't care for.

She squeezed my hand and whispered, "Don't be so miserable. It's a beautiful day and I've never played."

"I'd prefer to play with you."

Frederick and Victoria were coming over as well as my aunt and uncle and Scarlett's sister, brother and best friend, who'd arrived yesterday and were staying at the nearby hotel. No doubt Darcy would have invited about fifty more people as well because she knew everyone within a fifty-mile radius. The wedding was tomorrow and we'd see all the same people again.

"You *are* going to play with me," Scarlett said.

I growled. "Not like that. I mean naked. I want to play with you *naked*." Fucking Scarlett King was my new favorite thing to do. The more sex we had, the better it got—and it had been pretty damn good to start off with. The fucking last night should have been recorded for a *How to*

Have the Sex of Your Life training guide or something. We'd had sex after the bath and before dinner. And then after dinner. And then this morning I went down on her because she looked so sexy as she slept, I hadn't been able to help myself.

She knew what I liked now. The drag of her nails on my back, over my cock. I knew how she enjoyed my tongue pressing on her clit and my thumb in her ass. And she enjoyed me talking a little bit dirty to her. I'd never considered that sex with someone I knew could be better *because* I'd bothered to get to know her. I'd always assumed that any positives of having been around a person longer would be outweighed by the negatives. But now that I thought about it, I couldn't think of too many negatives of being around Scarlett.

"You've played with me naked enough. We have to go out into the world and interact with people with clothes on," she said.

Okay, maybe her lack of willingness to have sex twenty-four hours a day was a negative.

"You're such a spoilsport," I replied, but couldn't help but grin as she laughed at me.

As we got to the bottom of the stairs, the door opened and people flooded through. I'd have been happy to spend the day with just Scarlett, Darcy and Grandfather, but Scarlett was right, we needed to mingle. Much as I'd have preferred a simple wedding, something restricted to immediate family only would raise suspicion.

Scarlett withdrew her hand and ran toward the three people in the hall. I recognized one of the girls she greeted with a hug from the bar when I'd first met Scarlett. It was clear the sisters were close. Scarlett had spoken to her several times since we'd arrived in the UK.

This morning, my blow job got interrupted when Violet called to say they'd landed. I wasn't sure I was going to like the girl.

"Ryder," Scarlett called, beckoning me over as Frederick and Victoria arrived. As I'd rather speak to anyone but them, I took Scarlett's outstretched hand. "You've met Violet."

"Thank you so much for coming all this way," I replied, kissing her on both cheeks.

"As if I was going to turn down a chance to come to England," Violet said. She glanced at Scarlett, who was clearly giving her some kind of pointed look. "And my sister's wedding, of course."

"And this is my brother, Max, and Harper, his wife."

After introductions were made, we all headed outside to the croquet lawn. I wrapped my arm around Scarlett's waist as we walked. The leaves were still mainly green on the trees and the sky was a bright robin's egg blue, unusual for this time of year. As we turned the corner, more people gathered by the lawn came into view. It looked like Darcy had invited everyone I'd ever known growing up. My sister should have talked to me first. No doubt, people wanted a look at the next Duchess of Fairfax. Except, Scarlett wouldn't be, not really. And certainly not for long.

A line of buffet tables set with white tablecloths and silver bowls of covered food flanked the croquet lawn. Darcy had gone to a lot of effort. People milled about, clutching drinks and glancing over as our party walked toward them. Darcy hovered near Grandfather, who sat in a chair facing the lawn, chatting to my aunt and uncle while

Darcy fussed over the buffet tables.

Lane stood behind one of the tables, pouring out Pimms into tall glasses.

"Are we pretending it's summer?" I asked, tipping my head toward the drinks.

"I thought it would be a taste of England for our American friends," he replied.

"The way you make it, Lane, we'll all be passed out by tea time," I said, scooping up two glasses, handing one to Scarlett.

He nodded. "Exactly my plan, sir."

I guided Scarlett away from the table.

"What is this?" Scarlett held her glass up and inspected it. "And why is it garnished with salad?"

"Pimms, and it's not like it comes with a salad bowl. It's just cucumber. And some fruit." I picked a slice of cucumber out of my drink and held it to her lips. "Try it."

She took a bite and grinned as I popped the other half in my mouth.

"Look at you, so cute together," a woman said from behind us. Scarlett and I turned as one. "It's as if you're made for each other." Victoria grinned at us from beside Frederick. Victoria only smiled when she was being vicious. I wasn't sure whether or not Scarlett had picked up on the jibe or whether or not she took Victoria at face value.

"Awww, thank you, Victoria. That's what Ryder keeps saying—that we're made for each other. I keep asking him where he left his stiff upper lip, but of course I love it when he says it." She glanced up at me, grinning. "That dress is fabulous on you," she said, turning her attention back to Victoria. "It really shows off your body fantastically."

Victoria twitched, her smile slipping, just a fraction, as she tried to work out whether or not Scarlett was being sarcastic or genuine. "Thank you," she muttered.

"You are so welcome. I'm sure you get a million compliments a day about your figure," Scarlett said, glancing at Frederick.

Scarlett was a thousand times better than Victoria at pretending to be charming. Perhaps because she simply *was* charming. Still, Scarlett had clearly decided to kill Victoria with kindness.

My fiancée fucking rocked.

"I have the teams," Darcy announced, waving some cards in the air. "Gather 'round."

"You're going to teach me?" Scarlett said as I handed her a mallet.

"Sure," I said, bending to kiss her smiling mouth. I wasn't sure I'd ever absentmindedly kissed a woman before. Certainly not just to have that additional connection, to feel closer to her. Kissing had always been a part of sex. But now we were pretending to be a couple, it seemed to be the natural thing to do.

"Your usual colors?" Darcy asked and I nodded.

"You want red or yellow?" I asked Scarlett, walking toward the starting point.

"You mean you can't guess?" she replied. "I would have thought my name would give it away."

I chuckled. "Of course, Miss King. I'll take yellow. You toss." Rummaging in my pocket, I pulled out a fifty pence piece.

"Who are we playing against?" Scarlett asked as we scanned the crowd from the center peg.

"Hopefully not Frederick and Victoria," I replied, turning the silver coin between my fingers.

"Oh, I don't know, that could be fun."

"You're crazy." I pulled her close, circling my arms around her waist. "Victoria doesn't know what to make of you at all."

"Oh, don't tell me you don't enjoy my teasing." She pushed my hair from my face. "I know you better than that."

There wasn't much I didn't enjoy about her. "You certainly seem to know what you're doing." She raised her eyebrows. "With Victoria, I mean," I said.

"And I'm great in bed," she said and winked at me.

I couldn't argue with her there.

"Looks like it's cousin against cousin," Frederick called as he strode toward us carrying a mallet.

Scarlett turned in my embrace so we could face him as a team. I'd never in my life, other than with Darcy and Grandfather, been so certain someone was unquestionably on my side. I'd never thought it was even possible outside the three of us.

CHAPTER EIGHTEEN
SCARLETT

"Grip the shaft at the top with both hands, your right below your left," Ryder instructed from his crouched position in front of me. "Make sure you're clenched tight."

His grin told me he was trying to provoke a reaction with his dirty croquet talk. I wasn't sure if it was for my benefit or for Frederick and Victoria, who were looking on. "Like this?" I tilted my head. "Or tighter?"

Ryder stalked toward me as I stood over the croquet mallet and came behind me, smoothing his hand over my ass.

"Your arse looks fantastic," he whispered into my ear.

Wasn't that kind of comment wasted if no one could hear it? Or did he just like my ass? He crouched beside me, facing the little white hoop sticking out of the ground. "How many times are you going to say the word shaft to me during this match?" Ryder chuckled. I glanced up at the crowd at the side of the grass. Most of the guests were looking in our direction— as if the four of us were actors on a stage. As if they were waiting for the first punch to be thrown, blood to be spilled.

"That's right. Now, take the shot."

I swung the mallet and it cracked as it hit the ball.

"That's my girl," he said as my ball ended up exactly where he'd told me to put it. He wrapped his arm around my neck. Pulling me toward him, he placed a kiss on my head.

We watched as Victoria took her turn. I had no idea why Ryder spent any time with his cousin and his wife. There was clearly no love or affection shared.

I kept my eyes firmly on Ryder's butt as he played. God, he had a great ass. Great legs. A great, great dick. I'd wanted to save my company so badly that I would have married him if he were the least attractive man on the East Coast. But I might not have been sleeping with him if he wasn't so sexy it made my knees weak just being within a mile of him. And I definitely wouldn't have been having so much fun if he wasn't so easy to like. Easy to be with.

"Good shot, sexy," I said as his ball went through the hoop. I still had little clue about what was going on in terms of the rules of the game. But it didn't matter—Ryder was guiding me through it. He seemed to like teaching me step by step, and I liked him taking so much time doing it.

He winked at me as he came back to join me.

"Was it a good shot?" I asked under my breath. I was pretty sure the ball was meant to go through the hoop.

"Of course it was. I made it."

I rolled my eyes. "Modesty isn't your strong suit, is it?"

"Not false modesty. I'm very un-British like that." He clamped a hand over my hip.

"Tell me one thing you don't think you're good at?" Surely he wasn't 100 percent confident about everything.

He shrugged and I slid my arm around his waist. "Plenty."

"Tell me," I said. I wanted to find a chink in his armor, know more about this man I was sharing a bed with.

"I can make you a list of all my faults, if you like."

"Ahhh, I see. You can't admit when you're wrong."

"Maybe I don't want to admit that I have faults *to you*."

His words brought me back to reality. We weren't a real couple. We didn't share intimate stuff like this. This was a show. The touching. The whispering into each other's ears. It was an act designed to convince our audience that we were in love.

I dropped my hand from his waist and tried to move away. I'd been so caught up in the sex, the fun. So happy to stop grieving the end of my marriage. I'd let my guard drop, forgotten that it was all a lie.

It was my turn, but Ryder wouldn't let go of my waist when I tried to move forward to take it. "I'm bad with women," he said.

It was such a ridiculous thing to say—such an obvious lie —that I yanked his hand from my waist without responding and took my shot. It went straight through the hoop and I couldn't help but be proud of myself. Ryder hollered from behind me and I turned to find his smile as wide as Africa. Bad with women, my ass.

I narrowed my eyes as I approached him. "No lying," I said.

"Lying?"

"Don't give me some bullshit that you're bad with women. I shouldn't have asked. I was having fun and . . ." And what? Got carried away? Was trying to build intimacy? "Just forget I asked."

As we watched Victoria take her shot, Ryder leaned down to whisper in my ear. "I have no idea what's happening. Why are you angry?"

"It's your turn," I said. He looked at me as if I weren't finished talking about this. "Your shot," I said.

"Oh, right, yes."

He went over, barely stopping to hit the ball and making what I was pretty sure was a shitty play before stalking right back to me.

"You didn't answer my question. Why are you angry?"

I kept my forced smile in place feeling like a crazy person, trying not to let on what I was feeling to our audience. "I'm not mad." I wasn't angry at Ryder. I was irritated at myself. "I just don't appreciate you lying to me."

"I wasn't lying. I *am* bad with women."

"Right," I said. What did it matter if he was lying? He was just a business deal; what did I care?

"I'm not talking about sex. Obviously, I can seduce a woman." He swept his hand through his hair while his cousin took a ridiculously long time over his shot. I wanted him to get on with it so I could step away from this more than awkward conversation.

"I mean relationships. I've never spent time with a woman who wasn't Darcy or . . . I don't know what I'm saying, really. I just don't have a track record for hanging out with women. But with you—"

Frederick finished his shot and before Ryder had a chance to finish his sentence, I walked back over to my red ball. Ryder thought I was fishing for compliments. But I didn't want his platitudes. I needed to remember what this was . . . and what it wasn't.

His hands were at my waist before I realized he was behind me. "Relax and hit a long, smooth stroke."

"Ryder," I said with a sigh. Couldn't he tell I had to have just a few seconds to get myself together—switch my gears back to our deal?

"I'm not letting go. Take the shot."

"If you don't move, I'm not going to be able to make this shot."

"I don't give a shit. Take the shot. I'm not letting go."

Jesus, what had crawled up his ass? I swung my mallet and my shot was no better than his last one had been. Frederick and Victoria were through the next hoop already. We were getting our asses kicked.

He took my hand and we walked a little farther away from Frederick and Victoria than we had been between the other shots. "Look. I'm having a lot of fun hanging out with you. Just being with you, and it's made me realize that I've never had that before." He scrubbed his hands over his face. "I've never spent time with a woman just because I liked her company."

Sure he had.

He clearly knew what I was thinking. "Of course I've spent time with women; it's a prerequisite to getting laid. I've just never done so fully clothed, or just because I enjoy their company. All I'm trying to say is that I like sleeping with you, but I like just hanging out, too." He shrugged. "Maybe if I'd realized it could be this good, I would have given it a shot sooner."

I paused before I said anything, trying to process what he was saying.

"Have I pissed you off?" he asked.

"Your shot," Frederick called from the other side of the lawn.

"Christ, the guy's a prick. Can't he see that we're having a conversation?"

The crinkle in his forehead and his annoyance at

Frederick interrupting us was irresistibly cute.

"Kiss me," I said.

"Kiss you?"

I grabbed his collar and pulled him toward me. "I have to ask twice?" It was the only answer I had to his confession. I didn't want him to realize how good it felt for him to tell me he liked my company. Because the way he'd said it sounded genuine. Unguarded. And after dating a million men since my divorce, it was a relief. Because I felt the same. I liked his company, too.

He grinned and bent to kiss me. But I didn't let him pull away after a quick press of his lips. I wrapped my hands around the back of his neck and slid my lips against his. He groaned and pulled me closer as his tongue met mine, urgent and needy.

Just before my knees started to buckle, wolf whistles and cheering came from behind us and I released my hands. I'd forgotten we were on stage.

But then, I wasn't performing when I kissed him. And something told me he wasn't that good an actor either.

"Go and get this old duke something to wet my palate," Ryder's grandfather said to Ryder as the three of us sat opposite the croquet lawn, watching Darcy and Violet play against Max and Harper.

Ryder stood and patted his grandfather on the shoulder. "Of course. Scarlett—"

"You can be without her for just a few minutes, Ryder. I'll take care of her," the duke said.

The sun was starting to go down and the air had a cold edge to it that hadn't been there earlier but the light was beautiful, the sort I imagined painters always tried to recreate.

"This has been a lovely afternoon," I said as I watched Ryder walk toward the drinks table.

"Made all the better for your presence. I've never seen Ryder quite so at ease with himself."

"I guess our arrangement takes the pressure off."

"How so?"

"You know, because it doesn't matter if his friends or family like me. Or if I do or say the wrong thing. It matters to me, of course. But Ryder doesn't have to worry."

"I'm not sure that would ever be a concern for Ryder. That young man has got a mighty will. No one can make him do anything he doesn't want to do. Or force him to have an opinion that isn't his own."

I smiled. That was true. "I guess." I shrugged.

We clapped as Harper's ball went straight through the hoop. She hadn't been playing very well up until then, and I could tell from her determined face that she wasn't about to let the game, or the other team, beat her.

"Did I ever tell you how I met my wife?" the duke asked as the clapping died down.

"I don't think you did," I replied.

"I was twenty-five. And the last thing I wanted to do was settle down. It was the sixties and I took full advantage of the free love, though in the end, I still had my responsibilities to the estate and my father."

Looking out over the lawn, he continued. "My mother picked my wife for me. She was very suitable. Came from a good family. Bred to understand her duties and responsibilities to the estate very well."

I wasn't quite sure what he meant. "Duties?" I asked.

"The Woolton Estate, being Duchess of Fairfax—it's all a big responsibility. It takes a lot of work. And my mother understood that. Of course, I tried to resist the union for as long as possible. I refused to meet my wife for months. But eventually, my parents invited her to our annual summer garden party." His face broke out into a huge smile and he began to shake his head. "I didn't think she was suited to me in the slightest and I hated my parents for forcing this stranger onto me. I thought she was meek, and far too serious."

"I had no idea. I'm sorry that you were forced to marry someone you didn't love." I might be marrying Ryder, but I was doing it out of choice and it was going to last a maximum of three years. The duke had married for life.

He patted me on the hand. "Don't be. Marrying the duchess was the best thing I ever did." He was giving me whiplash. "Sometimes, the most unusual circumstances can throw two people together—that doesn't mean they're not perfect for each other." He sighed. "It took me a while to realize what I had, to understand her strength and vulnerability, her character and her beauty. And when I realized who she was and recognized I'd fallen in love, I kicked myself for not valuing her more highly, more quickly. From that moment on, she was a treasure to me."

"Here you are, Grandfather," Ryder said, interrupting our conversation and handing the duke a glass. "What are you two talking about?" he asked, taking a seat and turning toward the game. I'd lost interest in who was winning. I was more intrigued about what the duke had been saying. His message was clearly meant for me to take as a lesson, but I wasn't sure what it was he saw in Ryder and me that made him think that his experience could be applied in our circumstances.

"I'm just telling Scarlett here about your grandmother, and how much I adored her."

"You treated her like a queen," Ryder said.

"Because that's what she deserved. And she treated me like a king in return." The duke chuckled.

"You were made for each other. Two sides of the same coin," Ryder said.

"You're right," the duke replied. "We grew to be."

"You used to tell Darcy and me about how you met at the summer ball and how you swept her off her feet."

He nodded. "She liked me to tell that story. Said she loved the romance of it, even if most of it was exaggerated."

Ryder chuckled. "She was a very special woman."

The duke turned to me and winked. "We Westbury men have a habit of finding the right woman—even if we don't realize it at the time."

Chapter Nineteen
Ryder

"You look . . ." Darcy pursed her lips as she straightened my lapel and stared into the full-length, free-standing mirror I was facing.

"Handsome?" I suggested.

She shook her head. "Like the groom."

"Thanks, Darce." I rolled my eyes. My sister never threw around compliments and apparently she wasn't about to make an exception just because it was my wedding day. "It's a good bloody job since I *am* the groom. Is Scarlett ready?" I checked my watch. Music from downstairs filtered into the room.

"Last time I saw her she, Violet and Harper were trying to figure out how drunk was too drunk for a bride."

"Jesus." She needed to be drunk to go through this? Way to make a guy feel good. "You think she's having second thoughts?" I asked.

Darcy frowned as if she was thinking about her answer. "I think she's messing about with her girlfriends."

It sounded like she was trying to get loaded, as if she needed the liquid courage just to marry me. "Do you think I should be forcing her to go through with this wedding?"

"Forcing her?" Darcy said, picking up the red rose and

lily of the valley that was to be fixed to my lapel. "You're not forcing her to do anything. You're paying her, remember?"

Of course, I hadn't forgotten I was paying her. It had started off as the perfect solution but the more time went on and I got to know her, the more time we spent together in and out of the bedroom, the more it was clear that getting married was bigger than I'd let myself imagine.

"You're both getting what you need out of this," Darcy said.

I wasn't sure it was an equal trade. "I feel like I'm taking more than I'm giving. I'm a selfish fuck." I stared at the flowers in her hand as Darcy began to fiddle with the pin at the back.

"You're so dramatic. She's getting what she wants. You're getting what you want. What's the big deal?"

An awkwardness lodged in my stomach. I wasn't sure Scarlett was getting what she wanted. She'd been married before. She knew what a normal wedding day would feel like—a day when the bride and groom were in love. Wouldn't this be more difficult for her? Knowing how it should be? "Isn't your wedding day a big day for a woman? Isn't it meant to be about love and the start of a life together?"

"Have you developed a Disney addiction I'm not aware of?" Darcy asked, straightening her skirt. "Scarlett's not some naïve eighteen-year-old girl you've tricked into marrying you. She knows what she's doing. And anyway, she likes you."

The corners of my mouth twitched at the thought that Scarlett liked me. "Maybe." The feeling was mutual. She was cool and sexy. Funny and charming. She'd handled Frederick and Victoria like a pro, and Grandfather had clearly taken to her. If I could have designed a fake wife from a blank sheet of paper, I couldn't have imagined better than Scarlett.

Fuck, I'd seen the woman naked. No question. I'd won the fake-wife lottery.

Darcy's gaze flickered between my lapel and the reflection of the flowers in the mirror, then she straightened out my jacket one last time. "I don't see how the deal you struck with Scarlett is all that different to all those women you shag on a regular basis. In fact, that's much worse, them you use and just don't give a shit. So why have you suddenly grown a conscience when it comes to Scarlett?"

"It's not the same." But she was right. I used all the women I slept with but it was mutual. "I don't pretend anything else is on offer when I sleep with a woman."

Darcy frowned. "You said you'd been completely upfront with Scarlett."

"I have." I wasn't quite clear why this felt so different. But it was. The women who came before her, rightly or wrongly, hadn't mattered to me. Because I didn't know them, and I didn't want to. But I did know Scarlett. Liked her. More than that, I respected her.

"You might be feeling like you got the better end of the deal, but as long as you are both happy, then surely that's all that matters?"

"It's not too late to call this off." I let out a long exhale.

"How does that help anyone, you idiot? Scarlett ends up losing her business. You end up losing yours. You upset Grandfather, me—"

"I don't know, okay?" I pushed my hands through my hair.

"Maybe I can just loan Scarlett the money and talk to Frederick."

Darcy folded her arms and cocked her hip. Damn, I was in trouble. She'd been doing the same pre-fight dance since we were kids. "Don't be stupid. Frederick doesn't give two shits about you. He'd relish the opportunity to hurt you, to ruin you. And anyway, it's far too late to try for a deal. If you were to offer him the title and the estate right now in exchange for signing over your business, he'd laugh in your face. And then what? If you try to marry Scarlett anyway, he'd know it was all for show."

Of course, she was right. I knew that. I'd known it since I first heard Frederick could get control over the Westbury Group upon my grandfather's passing. It was why I'd proposed this deal with Scarlett in the first place. If there'd been another viable solution, I'd have thought of it by now. It was just that now I knew Scarlett, it was more difficult to have her lie for me. It was bad enough that my grandfather and sister were embroiled in this deceit. I was asking a lot of Scarlett. And although she seemed to be taking it in her stride, I couldn't help but think I'd underestimated her role in my scheme.

"You could always buy Scarlett a wedding gift as an additional thank you," Darcy said.

I nodded slowly. I could but I was sure Scarlett wouldn't be interested in further financial rewards. "You know, she's not that girl." Satisfied with my reflection, I turned away from the mirror and glanced around for the rings. We'd agreed on a simple service. No bridesmaids, no best man. It seemed the right thing to do. If this was a real wedding, I think I'd prefer simple in any event.

"You don't think she's interested in the title, do you?" Darcy asked.

I laughed. "No. Not at all. I just mean that it's her business that she's trying to save. She's very passionate about it. The money is just what she needs to do that."

"Sounds like someone else I know."

Scarlett and I were similar in lots of ways. I'd long since stopped caring about the money I made. I was one of those people who genuinely enjoyed their job—the deal, the sense of responsibility I felt for my employees, the feeling of building something of my own. It was a satisfaction unlike any other. Scarlett had that, too.

"Then what are you worried about?" Darcy asked.

I was saving something important to Scarlett and vice versa. It was a good match from both sides. But that knot in my stomach just wouldn't go away. "If I wasn't paying her, you think a woman like that would marry me?" I asked. I wasn't sure what had made me ask the question but as I did, I realized I'd been thinking the same thing for a couple of days now. Would a woman as sophisticated and beautiful as Scarlett ever want to settle down with a selfish, confirmed bachelor like me? I'd always assumed I could get married if I wanted. But perhaps the right woman wouldn't be interested.

Darcy didn't answer and when I glanced up to stare at her in the mirror, I found her looking at me. "If you didn't need to marry her, would you?" she asked.

I chuckled, but it was forced. "You know I'm not the marrying kind. Too many women to limit myself to just one."

Normally, Darcy punched me in the arm when I said

something like that, but this time she acted as if she hadn't heard me. "I think she'd be lucky to marry you even if you weren't paying her. And something tells me she knows that."

"What do you mean?" Had she spoken to Scarlett about me?

"Just that I like the two of you together. I've seen you in uncomfortable situations, making decisions about things that don't sit well with you, but when you're with Scarlett, I don't see any of that. I see you being yourself, the way you really only are with me and Grandfather. Something tells me that if you weren't such a confirmed bachelor, Scarlett might just be woman enough for you."

CHAPTER TWENTY

RYDER

Scarlett King was my wife and I was her husband. And it didn't feel as strange as I'd expected it to.

We'd left most people downstairs, drinking and enjoying the music. When my wife had said she was tired and her feet hurt, I'd brought her upstairs.

"The sun will rise before they all get to bed," Scarlett said, smiling over her shoulder at me as she entered our bedroom.

I didn't respond. I was too taken with the skin exposed by her backless dress.

"They seemed to have had a good time." She kicked off her shoes as we got inside and she reached around her back for the buttons of her dress toward the bottom of her back.

"Hey, let me," I said, gently knocking her hands away.

"Thank you."

I hooked my fingers under the fabric, stroking her smooth, soft skin. I wasn't sure any woman I'd ever known had had skin as perfect as Scarlett's. I popped the first satin button free of the loop of satin that held it in place, revealing a tiny amount of extra flesh.

"You think everyone enjoyed themselves?" she asked.

I couldn't care less. "Did you?"

She tilted her head, creating a beautiful porcelain curve.

"Yes. It was so much fun. You're a good dancer."

I popped open another button. And another.

"You said that already." I'd had fun twirling her around the dance floor, but it was an excuse to hold her close and to keep her away from people who wanted our attention. I was happy just to be with her. We'd held the reception in the ballroom and because there hadn't been many people for the wedding breakfast, it had left a lot of room to dance.

"We've only been married a few hours and I'm repeating myself. I'm boring you already."

I wasn't sure Scarlett was capable of boring anyone. "Never."

Pop. Pop. Pop. Her dress undone, I watched as she took half a step forward and peeled the satin off her shoulders, stepping out of her gown revealing her pale-cream lace underwear. She turned and I had to reluctantly drag my eyes up her body to meet her satisfied smile.

"It's La Perla. You like it?"

My gaze swept down to take her in again. Her dress had been seemingly simple and demure. But underneath it, she'd been hiding an outfit that would make a priest hard. Her breasts spilled out of the cups of her bra. A corset pulled her waist into a sleek hourglass, the white fabric almost see-through. A tempting tease. The tops of her thighs were circled in lace and, framing her pussy, hung the straps of her garters.

"Yeah, I like it," I said, my voice croaky and coated in lust. I cleared my throat but let my eyes continue to wander up and down her body. At every point the lace gave way to flesh—the top of her thigh, either side of her garter, her breasts—there was a promise of something that I wanted to savor. Memorize. "You're so fucking beautiful."

184

She lifted her arms, stretching her body, her hips gently swaying as she fiddled with her hair, pulling out a pin.

"Let me," I said, desperate to undress, untie, undo her.

I stepped forward, careful not to brush my body against hers. I wanted to take this slowly. Savor her. If I felt too much of her heat too soon, I'd be lost. Her hair had been fixed up, but I preferred it down. I liked the way the silky strands felt against my skin, between my fingers, over my cock.

She pulled a pin free and her hair tumbled down her shoulders. She shivered, though I was pretty sure it was more than her hair giving her goosebumps. She wanted me just like I wanted her. We were equal in our lust for each other, and in so many other ways. I knew I could make her laugh and she had me chuckling more often than I could remember. She was as passionate about what she did as I was. She had a real sense of family—I was just as lucky.

I wanted her and she wanted me.

And now, we were married.

I pulled out the final pin and slid my fingers through her hair and over her scalp. "There. I like it better like this."

She closed her eyes in a long blink. "Then I'll only wear it down from now on."

I groaned at the thought that she'd change the way she wore her hair for me. To have a smart, independent woman want to please me above herself? It felt more powerful than anything I'd ever experienced. I couldn't resist her any longer, and I slid my hands around her back and pulled her against me.

"It's our wedding night," she whispered.

"Yes," I said. Perhaps those words should have made me pull away—after all, I'd been running from commitment my entire life. But nothing about being bound to the woman in my arms frightened me. "I'm going to make sure you remember it."

"I know you will," she said.

As I lifted her, she wrapped her legs around my waist and twined her arms around my neck, pressing her mouth to my jaw as I walked us over to the bed. It seemed fitting that I'd fuck my wife in a bed—traditional. At least for the first time tonight. Back in New York, I'd have her in every room in my apartment. I'd enjoy hearing her screams echo out across Manhattan.

As I set her down on the mattress, she dragged her hands down my chest. "You're still dressed."

"Yes, too busy looking at you."

She began fumbling with my buttons but I stepped away. Not because I didn't want to be naked. Not because I didn't want her touching me, but because I knew I'd be faster. I stripped off my shirt and pants and was undressed in just a few seconds.

Scarlett stared at me from where she lay propped up on her elbows.

"Just a few more hours and I'm going to make you scream so loud Manhattan will have a run on ear plugs."

"Hours? How—"

"It's thirty-six hours until we fly to New York." I stalked back to the bed and gripped her ankle, pulling her to the edge of the mattress. "Forty-two hours until we land. Then after customs and the journey into town, I figure it's forty-four hours max until I make you come in my apartment where you can be as loud as you like."

Her breath hitched as I fisted my cock on an upward stroke. "Are you wet, my bride?" I asked, using my free hand to push between her legs. Her panties darkened with her juices. God, I loved how her pussy smelled.

"Always," she replied.

"I'm going to fuck you while you're wearing that until it's worn and ragged and soaked in our come." I quickly unwrapped a condom, covered my dick and slid her underwear to one side. I pushed my tip over her clit, trailing down to her entrance and back up. She was more than ready and I was done holding back. I pushed in, just a fraction of the way home, and exhaled. God, it felt good. Right.

Slowly, I pushed deeper.

"Oh God," she cried.

"No, baby, you need to be quiet for just a few more hours."

"I can't. It feels so good and it's been too long."

It had only been a day, but I understood how she felt. I couldn't get enough of this woman. Of the way she held my dick inside her, squeezing tight. Or the way her breath felt against my skin. Or how she tried to choke back her groans. I learned more about her with each fuck. And every time, I felt myself falling a little further under her spell.

I pulled back the crotch of her panties, the elastic adding to the friction on my dick. I lost my focus in the acute pleasure of her and I fell forward, my hands bracing against the mattress. "Christ, you feel good."

I needed her closer and like an awkward teenager, I maneuvered us both up the bed. I liked her body heating mine and mine responding in kind. I liked being able to whisper in her ear about how good, tight, smooth she felt.

I slid my hand down the lace of her corset, then sank into her on a curse. "Christ, just as I think it can't get better with you," I choked out.

I kept my pace slow and steady but every atom of my body tightened with the pleasure of fucking her. It was as if I was only a breath away from an orgasm every time I touched her.

"My husband," she whispered, gripping my shoulders.

Her words lit a fire within me.

I was her husband.

It might be in name only, but while we were married, I'd work hard to deserve that title—I wanted her to be happy. Wanted to *make* her happy.

Her hips twisted, her fingernails digging deliciously into my skin. Jesus, it was too much. Being over her like this, her beneath me, taking my dick like it was the best thing I could give her. It was more than I deserved.

"Ryder!" she called. I knew what she needed and I was going to give it to her. Lifting myself without breaking my rhythm, I placed my palm over her mouth. Her body relaxed as if she was finally able to let go, and as she did, her muscles began to pulse around me.

"Oh, so soon," I said. I savored her growing tightness around me and it was as if her orgasm lit mine. Her eyes fluttered as her scream vibrated across my palm. Fuck. I was gone. I clenched my jaw as I pushed into her in jagged, uncontrollable thrusts.

Totally focused on finding the edge, I couldn't control the groan that ripped through my body as I poured into her, desperate to let her have every last drop of my come.

I slumped over her, needing her close, wanting to prolong the togetherness.

"Ryder," she whispered, trailing her fingers down my back.

"Christ, did I pass out?"

Her body moved below mine as she laughed. "No. I can vouch for the fact you did not pass out. You did, however, make a lot of noise."

I'd always liked a little dirty talk during sex, but I'd never been loud in bed. It seemed I couldn't help myself when Scarlett and I fucked. It was different—more intimate.

I rolled over and discarded the condom. Then settled in and pulled Scarlett close so she rested against my side, our legs twining. "Fuck it. I was fucking my wife. What do they expect when you're just so goddamn sexy?"

She leaned across my body and dropped a kiss on my nipple at the same time as she slid her hand over my cock.

"You're insatiable," I said.

"With you, apparently I am."

My chest expanded at the thought that I was the best she'd ever had. But it still wasn't as much as she deserved.

"I'm going to do as much as I can to quench your thirst tonight, Mrs. Westbury."

"Big promises." She pushed up on an elbow, her hair falling over her shoulders providing an ineffective curtain across nipples just peeking out of her corset. I pulled one between my forefinger and my thumb.

"Yes, I think I can keep up."

She straddled me, her hands flat on my chest, her ass in the air. She was perfect—unselfconscious, sexy. Mine. And I was hard. Again.

"Let's see, shall we?" she said.

Tonight was going to be a long, glorious night.

Chapter Twenty-One
Scarlett

I squeezed my legs together beneath my desk, my nipples grazing against the lace of the bra with the movement. I hoped no one in the office saw me wince as I shifted in my chair. I could still feel the press of Ryder's palm against my inner thighs, his hand wrapped around my hair, pulling my head back so he could graze his teeth on my neck. I was really sore. All over. I'd have been more than happy to have more of Ryder, despite the aftereffects. We'd barely stopped touching each other since the wedding six weeks ago—it was almost as if someone had set down an hourglass as we took our vows, and from then on it had been a race to fit in as much sex as we could before the last grain of sand fell and the marriage was over.

Not that I was complaining. I wanted Ryder as much as he seemed to want me. But then, maybe he always had a voracious appetite. I knew this wasn't my default setting, that he'd awakened something primal and insatiable in me. But it wasn't *just* physical. There was endless talking in the middle of the night. Even though we were exhausted, I had no desire to sleep and apparently, neither did he. When we weren't making each other come, we were sharing our lives. We talked about his grandfather. His time in boarding school. The fact that his mother hadn't been at the wedding and no one seemed to mention it. We talked about Violet and Max and why I'd spent so long in a job I didn't like. I talked about how much I'd loved my husband and how devastated I'd been when he'd left.

Nothing was off limits.

Except for the feelings I didn't want to acknowledge. I didn't tell Ryder I no longer constantly thought of my ex. I didn't mention that I was beginning to believe that life after the divorce could not just be bearable, but really good. Fun and full of things I'd never dreamed of.

And he never mentioned how we acted like newlyweds in every way despite the fact that our marriage was only true on paper.

"How are those numbers?" Cecily asked as she took a seat on the edge of my desk.

"Good, I'll have November's P&L by the end of the day. And I think it's going to be ahead of budget." I wiggled my mouse on the spreadsheet on my screen.

"Awesome. We should celebrate. Do you and Ryder want to come over to dinner this Saturday?" Of course I'd told Cecily of the arrangement Ryder and I had. She'd tried to talk me out of it at first but I was determined. This was my business as much as hers. And I wasn't giving her anything. I would just replace her half of the loans with a loan of my own, on much more favorable terms than were currently in place. She'd eventually relented, understanding that I either married Ryder or we went bust.

I'd never accepted a social invitation for us both. I'd been to a couple of his work functions but our free time was mainly spent at his apartment, together and alone. "Sounds good." I wasn't sure if Ryder would want to hang out with my friends. I wasn't sure it made sense in the context of our arrangements. Being together at a public business function helped legitimize our marriage and living together was a requirement. But a private dinner with friends was new territory. I wasn't sure. "I'm free but I'm not sure about Ryder. I can ask him."

There was nothing about the way we interacted, either in public or behind closed doors, that suggested we weren't a couple. Ryder touched me constantly. He'd grabbed my ass on the croquet lawn in front of his entire family, for Christ's sake. It would be interesting to see how he reacted—how far our arrangement went.

"Okay, let me know. How is shacking up together going?"

I couldn't help but grin. Living with Ryder Westbury was definitely an adjustment. His apartment, situated in Tribeca, was nothing short of beautiful and big enough to get lost in.

"It's different." Before the wedding, I hadn't realized how much living together was going to be a huge shift in my life—from the commute to having to be considerate of someone else when you left your dishes in the sink. "For both of us I think. We're getting used to sharing space."

It wasn't that his company made me uncomfortable. It was just the opposite. But last night, he'd proudly led me into the guest room that he'd cleared out for me. To give me "*my own space*." The crushing wave of disappointment had threatened to drown me until he'd kissed me. One thing had led to another, and as usual, we'd ended up fucking all night. Still, even the morning after, that damn guest room underlined the fact that we weren't a couple—this wasn't *our* apartment. It was his place and I was a glorified boarder.

We might act like a married couple, but ultimately, I had my own bedroom in his apartment. I had to remember that we weren't really together. Great sex was simply the icing on top of our business arrangement. I was going to have to make an effort not to forget.

"Have you rented out your apartment?" Cecily asked.

I shrugged. "Not yet." I'd had a couple of agents around about renting my apartment, but the more I thought about Ryder giving me that room yesterday, the more I wanted to hold on to it. I needed to retain the independence that it represented. I understood I couldn't stay the night there. If anyone was keeping tabs on us, spending nights in separate apartments would give us away for sure. Having met Frederick, I wouldn't be surprised if he had someone checking up on our situation back home. We'd pulled off the wedding, but Ryder had always been so vocal about not wanting to inherit. Such an abrupt change of heart was bound to cause suspicion in someone like Frederick.

"You don't hate him though? I mean, it's going okay?" Cecily asked.

"I don't hate him at all. He's been a perfect gentleman and his family is lovely."

She crossed her arms. "A perfect gentleman? How disappointing. I'd hoped that maybe there'd be a spark between you. That it might turn into something."

Hopefully the heat in my cheeks didn't give me away. Cecily didn't know we were sleeping together.

"He's totally gorgeous. And as rich as God," Cecily said.

And hung like a horse. And a devil between the sheets.

And attentive and caring and funny. Urgh. I was going to have to work very hard to separate reality from whatever was going on with Ryder and me.

Cecily snapped her head up. "Speaking of . . ."

I followed her line of sight to find Ryder heading across the office, grinning at me. "I brought lunch," he said as he reached my office and held up a brown paper bag.

I rolled my lips together, trying to stop myself from smiling.

"And a parcel." He produced a package, just smaller than his hand.

"I'll leave you two guys to your married bliss," Cecily said, slipping off my desk.

"Hi," I said as she left. "I was just thinking about you." As soon as the words left my mouth, I wanted to suck them back in. I shouldn't be saying shit like that to him. It sounded too intimate.

He handed me the package. "I've been thinking about you all morning, too."

We both had to get better at separating real life from our arrangement. I knew myself well enough to know that I couldn't withstand his compliments and lovely gestures along with the physical intimacy and still remain emotionally closed off.

"Will you shut the door?" I asked.

"Sounds good, does it lock?"

I ignored his comment but as soon as the door shut he came over to me, pulled me from my chair, wrapped his arms around my waist and bent to kiss me. There was no one here. No audience to perform in front of. Just as there hadn't been behind closed doors ever since we'd flown to England.

"You feel good. I've missed you."

"You can't have missed me already. You saw me this morning." He'd fucked me from behind before breakfast as I'd gripped the chest of drawers beside his bed. Sex with Ryder was how I'd always imagined it could be—how I'd always hoped it would be with Marcus. It was spontaneous, passionate and plentiful.

"It's been too long," he said, releasing me to take a seat on the other side of the desk. "Hungry?" he asked, diving into the paper bag he'd brought with him. "You didn't eat much at breakfast so I thought I'd better make sure lunch came to you." He pulled out an avocado and shrimp salad and slid it over to me.

"Thanks." Lunch was a really thoughtful gesture, and I found myself wondering if it was just a coincidence that he'd chosen a salad I'd have chosen for myself.

"You like shellfish, right?"

"Sure," I replied, opening the plastic box and taking a fork from the center of one of the rolled up napkins that he'd picked up. "So what brings you here, husband?"

He shrugged. "I told you. I missed you. And I wanted to give you this." He nodded at the package next to the empty bag on the table.

Maybe he *had* just missed me. There was nothing in our rulebook that said we couldn't be friends, was there? And friends could miss each other, couldn't they? "What is it?" I asked.

He grinned at me. "It's wrapped up. How would I know? I'd forgotten Grandfather gave it to me just before we left for the flight back. I found it when I was rearranging things in your room yesterday." He unwrapped his sandwich and took a bite. "Eat," he said with his mouth full.

I rolled my eyes and dug my fork into the salad he'd brought for me, ignoring the mention of my newly allocated space.

I couldn't remember my first husband ever bringing me lunch while we were married. He'd worked just a couple of buildings down from my office, though I couldn't recall ever meeting during the day. We were both always so busy working toward a future we weren't going to share.

"How was your morning? Make a billion dollars? Two billion dollars?" I asked him.

He narrowed his eyes at me. "My wealth is meant to impress you. Not provide ammunition for your sarcasm."

I laughed. "Oh, thanks for telling me. I'll know for next time."

"Does anything impress you?" he asked, tilting his head to one side as he looked at me and I reached out and swept his hair off his face.

"Plenty of things."

"My penis?" he asked and I laughed again.

I feigned my best thinking face before saying, "Your bed is really comfortable. You have a very impressive mattress. And I sleep like a baby on it."

"Not what I was hoping you'd say and it sounds like a problem rather than something to be impressed by." He frowned. "A new bride shouldn't be getting a good night's sleep."

"Oh I have no complaints about the amount of sex we're having, that's for sure." I popped a cherry tomato in my mouth.

"It's a lot, huh?" he asked.

Christ. It was probably all too normal for him. But not for me. I wanted Ryder. All. The. Time. I'd never wanted sex so much in my life.

"But I think I'd rather risk my dick falling off than stop. I see you, and I want you. Even now, watching you with that plastic fork is turning me on."

I wiggled my eyebrows. "Cutlery does it for you?" I twisted the fork between my fingers. "Where do you want it?"

He smiled and shook his head. "*You* do it for me." His gaze went from me to the view of Manhattan. "I can't keep my hands off you." His tone was thoughtful, as if he couldn't quite understand the pull between us.

I reached across my desk to wipe the tiny bit of mustard from the corner of his lip with my thumb. He grabbed my hand and took my thumb in his mouth.

"Like I said, I can't keep my hands, mouth, dick off you."

I tilted my head. "I'm not complaining." I couldn't imagine a time when I wouldn't want him to touch me.

We stared at each other for a couple of long seconds, smiling.

"Open it," he said, releasing my hands and passing me the package he'd brought with him. I took it and turned it in my hands. It was sealed tightly with a hundred miles of tape. I finally pried off the packaging to reveal a blue-velvet jewelry box with worn edges, as if it had been well loved. I glanced at Ryder, who was staring at the box. As I picked it up a small cream envelope fell away from the bottom.

I pulled out the card.

Dearest Scarlett,

I gave this necklace to the woman I'd grown to love on our first anniversary.

I hope you'll wear it as a reminder that love can flourish in the most unexpected places.

Congratulations on your marriage. I wish you many happy years together.

Yours sincerely,

The Duke of Fairfax (Your grandfather-in-law)

"A wedding gift from Grandfather?" Ryder asked as I put the card back in the envelope.

A gift that came with a huge hint that my marriage might turn into something more than a business arrangement. That it could turn into love.

Life didn't work like that, did it? It may have for the duke, but not for me.

I released my held breath and nodded as I swept my hand over the velvet box. The hinge creaked as I opened it. A delicate, gold chain adorned with large raindrops of amethyst and diamonds sat on a bed of cream satin.

"It's beautiful." I stroked my fingers over one of the tear-shaped stones.

"It was a favorite of my grandmother's."

I glanced up to find Ryder staring openly at the necklace.

"I can't accept this. It's got such sentimental value to your family, Ryder." I pushed the velvet box toward him.

He fiddled with the clasp, then said, "Of course you can accept it. You must. My grandfather likes you a great deal, and he obviously wants you to have it."

I couldn't show him the card. I didn't want to make

things difficult between us or lead him to believe I didn't understand what we were to each other. We were simply making the best out of a situation that had been forced upon us. The sex was convenient. Ryder was thoughtful and polite —just as any decent guy should be given the circumstances.

What we weren't, and never would be, was in love.

That wasn't part of our arrangement. And I had to keep telling myself that.

"Let me put it on you," Ryder said, reaching for the necklace.

I pulled my hair to one side as he moved in behind me. "I feel like I shouldn't. It doesn't belong to me." The cool stones hit just below my collarbone.

"It does belong to you, though. You're the next Duchess of Fairfax."

I giggled. "You can't say that.

"Why not? It will be your title." He pulled out my chair so I faced him. "It suits you, brings out the violet flecks in your eyes."

I tried not to grin. "I have violet flecks?" I took the hand he extended and let him pull me into his arms.

"Only if you look very closely," he said, pressing his body against mine. "And believe me, I do."

I linked my arms around his neck as he stared into my eyes, then collapsed into laughter.

"You can't laugh. I'm being romantic," he said.

"Aww, I'm sorry. It's just you're very sweet. No one you do business with would ever guess. But I'll make it up to you tonight. I'll cook." It would be fun to poke about in his kitchen.

He winced. "I have a dinner."

It shouldn't have bothered me, but for some reason it did. He hadn't mentioned a dinner. I let go of his neck.

"Sorry, it's a meeting with a company John forgot to tell me about."

Relief fluttered in my stomach and I smiled. "No problem. Cecily has asked me to go around to her and her husband's place for dinner on Saturday. Want to come?"

Ryder pushed his hands through his hair as he leaned on the table. "Sorry, I can't. I have an awards thing. It's been in the diary for months."

A public business event I wasn't invited to? I began to gather up our lunch cartons. A last-minute thing that John had forgotten to tell him about was one thing, but a big business event that had been arranged for months? Why hadn't he mentioned it?

"Oh. Okay. I just thought I'd ask," I said, sealing the salad container and putting it into the paper bag it came in.

"It's at their house?" he asked. "The dinner with Cecily?"

"Yes. We just made our numbers this last month so we're celebrating."

He nodded. "Oh, that's good."

"Yes, it's not a formal thing." I wanted him to say he wanted to make it or ask me to rearrange it to a time when he could celebrate with us but he didn't. He didn't say anything at all. I dumped the remains of our lunch in the trash. "I better go. I have a meeting." I started to walk toward the door of the boardroom.

"Don't forget this," he said.

I turned and he handed me the blue velvet jewelry box. "Thanks."

"Hey," he said, backing me against the door, his hands braced on either side of my head. "I'm sorry about dinner, but I won't be late. Wait up for me?"

He had no need to be sorry. It was nice of him to apologize. He didn't owe me anything. But did I want to wait up for him? The sex was amazing, but it was pulling me deeper. I wanted to be with him tonight, and every night. The realization hit me like a punch in the face. What was I playing at?

I smiled and nodded, knowing that I would be tucked up in bed, trying my best to sleep when he returned. I needed to create some distance between us.

Because more than that? I wanted him to change the rules.

I wanted more.

"Good morning," I said as I walked into the kitchen to find Ryder sitting on one of the white stools at the breakfast bar. The *Wall Street Journal* was folded on the counter next to him and a bowl of what looked like fruit and yogurt sat half eaten.

"Good morning. Sleep well?" he asked, his tone neutral and not as if we'd not seen each other for the longest time since we left for England.

I'd heard Ryder call my name through my closed bedroom door when he'd returned the night before, but I hadn't responded.

"Sure," I replied, which was a total lie. I hadn't slept at all. I'd lain awake all night, wondering if I'd made a huge mistake. Not in marrying Ryder and saving Cecily Fragrance from financial ruin, but by not being more cautious in keeping things . . . separate between Ryder and me. Sleeping with him over and over had confused things. Liking it was worse. Wanting anything from him—like for him to want to celebrate my successes with me—was as far as my feelings for Ryder were going to go. The creeping affection I felt for him, the way I wanted to tell him every little thing that happened to me while we were apart, it had to stop. It all had to stop.

At least the night of no sleep and the constant churning of my thoughts had given me a plan.

"You got a busy day?" he asked.

I glanced up as I poured my coffee to find him staring at me through narrowed eyes. Had he always been so devastatingly handsome?

That would be a *yes*.

I nodded. "I really do."

"Okay," he said, drawing out the vowels. "You want to eat out tonight? There's a great Mexican place on the corner that's really—"

"Actually, I'm going to head back to my place. I need to pick up a few things." I needed some space. To regroup. Draw a line in the sand.

"You want me to come? I can help," he said.

I eyed him over my coffee cup. "That's okay. I can manage. And if it gets too late, I might stay over there anyway." I turned and poured the remains of my drink down the sink and put my mug in the dishwasher.

"Scarlett," Ryder said. It wasn't a question, and I didn't know him well enough to know whether it was going to turn into one.

"I have to run. Like I said, busy day." I closed the

dishwasher with a click and headed back to my bedroom. I shouldn't have bothered with coffee.

He grabbed my wrist as I walked by, forcing me to halt and turn to him. "Did I do something?" he asked.

I was being a bitch. He hadn't done anything apart from be gorgeous and generous and kind and funny. But it was just too much. "Of course not." I forced my lips into a smile. "I'm just tired. I'll let you know if I decide to stay at my place."

Slowly, he released my arm. Part of me wished he hadn't. If he'd tried to kiss me, I would have fallen into the pull between us and any hope of keeping my feelings shored up would be gone.

CHAPTER TWENTY-TWO
RYDER

"Can you hold my calls and make sure I'm not disturbed for thirty minutes?" I called to my assistant. I probably should have walked the four paces it would have taken to get to her desk on the other side of my office door, but no doubt after five years working for me, she was used to my impatience. She just got up and closed my door, which was exactly what I'd hoped she'd do.

I exhaled and leaned back in my chair. I needed a break from my day. I'd had meetings one after another. I should be staying later in the office. But I'd been wanting to get my fill of Scarlett. I'd had little chance to think about my wife's mood this morning, but every time someone had left my office or there was a pause in the conversation, that was where my mind wandered. I smiled as her beautiful face drifted into my thoughts, but my good mood didn't last long as I remembered our interaction this morning—it had been short and cold. I'd been disappointed not to have found her in my bed last night when I'd returned from dinner.

Worse, the client I'd taken out had been a waste of time. There to stroke his ego more than to entertain my offer. So all in all, the evening had been dull, but then most things were when compared with a night in bed with my Scarlett. I'd been looking forward to seeing her when I got home. We hadn't spent much time apart other than during working hours, and I felt her absence more than I'd expected to. I wanted to know how her day had been, and I wanted to see what she looked like wearing that purple and gold necklace and nothing else. Except maybe heels. I'd planned to have her pose for me, to snap a picture of the vision she'd make. In the snatches of time I'd had during the course of the day, I'd set up the shots in my imagination. One of her facing away from me, coyly looking over her shoulder. One sitting on the chair in my bedroom, one leg draped over the arm, revealing her mesmerizing pussy.

But I'd raced back from midtown to find the apartment quiet and Scarlett's bedroom door closed. I figured she'd taken the chance to catch up on her sleep; I just didn't get why she'd used the guest room.

It didn't make sense. We'd slept in the same bed for weeks. Why would anything change now? I picked up my cell and dialed her number, smiling as I realized she was at the top of my recently called list.

No answer.

She'd been cold at breakfast. It had been the first time since she and I had flown to England that we hadn't fucked in the morning. I'd half expected to take her on the kitchen counter, but had to settle for jacking off in the shower.

Had she received some bad news I didn't know about?

I tried her number again. Voicemail. I stared at the phone, trying to figure out what to do. If she was really planning on staying over in her apartment, that would be another night I wouldn't see her. Perhaps I should surprise her and turn up with takeout. But when I'd offered to help her with her things, she'd seemed pretty adamant she didn't want me there.

My mobile began to vibrate in my hand and my stomach dropped with relief, but as I looked at the screen, it was the very last person I wanted to hear from.

Frederick.

"Hi, Fred. How are you?" I sounded bored even to myself. Why was he calling me? I'd only seen him a couple of days ago.

"Ryder. I tried your office line but they told me you were in a meeting."

It was as if he were constantly trying to catch me out in a lie. "Just finished. What can I help you with?" For a split second I thought he might be going to tell me he was going to challenge my marriage, but he'd never do that over the phone. He'd dispatch his lawyer for that sort of thing.

"You can buy your cousin a drink. I'm in town and thought we could catch up for dinner."

In town? He hadn't mentioned being in New York when I'd seen him in England. And as far as I knew, he'd only ever come to the US once, back when he was at university.

"You're in Manhattan?" I asked. He was also arrogant enough to assume I'd just drop whatever plans I had for the evening.

"That's right," he replied, as if it wasn't odd at all. "Just in a cab from JFK. Staying at the Mandarin Oriental, but I'm not in the mood for anything too much. I thought maybe Scarlett could whip us up a stew or something."

I laughed out loud. His assumption that Scarlett would cook spoke volumes about what he thought of women. "I'm not sure Scarlett is a stew kind of woman, but I can make a mean grilled cheese sandwich."

His response wasn't immediate. "Well, whatever you

were planning to have for dinner, will it stretch to three?"

"Scarlett and I haven't made any plans."

"No plans for dinner?" he asked. He seemed surprised. Like it was a big deal. Maybe he was here just to see if things between Scarlett and me on home territory seemed suspicious.

"I told her to have a big lunch so we didn't have to waste time eating when we could be in bed." That would shut the little prick up.

"I'll be at yours at eight. Grilled cheese, whatever that is, is fine," he replied and hung up the phone.

Shit. This was the last thing I needed. Uncomfortable, I stood and began to pace as I dialed Scarlett.

Still voicemail. After the beep, I left a message, telling her that Frederick had arrived unexpectedly and asking if she could go to her apartment another night. I had no idea whether she'd call me back, check her messages, or change her plans. I needed a backup plan—a story to tell Frederick in case she just didn't show.

I glanced at my watch. It was five minutes to eight and I'd still not heard a word from Scarlett. Perhaps she'd just been stuck in meetings all day. I tried to remember if she'd said anything about a big project at work that would mean she was out of contact, but she hadn't said anything at lunch yesterday and I'd barely seen her since.

I dialled her phone one last time. Voicemail. Shit. I would just have to tell Frederick she'd been caught up at work and hope he'd buy it.

I glanced around the apartment, trying to see it through my cousin's eyes. Would he see anything out of the ordinary? Could anyone tell that we weren't a real couple from just being in this place?

Right on time, the buzzer went. If I found Scarlett on the other side of that door, I'd happily give up my day job and go volunteer at a homeless shelter. I glanced up at the ceiling in a final plea to whoever was up there as I pressed the intercom.

"Mr. Westbury, your guest Mr. Westbury has arrived."

Looked like I was keeping that day job.

"Send him up," I replied.

I headed to the door, ready to show him in. Fuck. Scarlett's room. What if he went in there and realized she'd slept in there last night? I turned right down the hallway and opened the door to Scarlett's room. The bed was made and there were toiletries on the dressing table. Quickly, I scooped up the jars and bottles and put them into a suitcase that was lying next to the bed. I didn't have time to ask myself what it was doing there. As I zipped it shut, there was a knock at the door. I swung open a closet, slid the case inside and slammed the door shut.

I quickly scanned the room. It was almost as if Scarlett had disappeared. There was nothing of her left in this room. I felt a pinch in my gut. *Where is she?*

As Frederick knocked a third time, I opened the door. "Hey," I said, smiling as if I were pleased to see him.

"I finally made it to the Big Apple. Cabbie was bloody rude, I have to say."

I swept my arm toward the living space. "That's New York for you. You get used to it. Can I get you a drink?"

He took in the apartment as if he were shopping for real estate, scanning every wall and ceiling. "I'll have a gin and tonic. Nice place, Ryder. Where's the lovely Scarlett?"

I headed over to the kitchen and pulled out two tumblers. "She has a big thing on at work. Sorry, if we'd known you were coming we could have rearranged things."

"Oh," he said. "She won't be back at all?"

"Well, I hope at some point." I chuckled. He wasn't about to be recruited by the CIA for his sleuthing skills. "She does live here, after all." I lifted up my cell. "She's going to keep me posted. I know she'd want to see you while you're here. Did you bring Victoria?"

"No, I'm here on business."

Business? Frederick took an income from the estate and lived off Victoria's trust fund. Unless his business was to discredit my marriage, I couldn't imagine what he'd be doing here. I glanced at my phone again. Why wouldn't she just call?

After I poured our drinks I stalked over to the couches where Frederick was making himself at home. "How's the hotel?" I asked.

"Fine. Nice views. So, what's for dinner?" he asked.

"I thought we'd go out. No one cooks in New York City."

"Well, that is a shame. I was looking forward to a cozy evening in. Do you mind if I use your lavatory?"

I cringed. I hadn't checked the bathroom. "Sure, the guest bath is just on your left there," I said, pointing back toward the entrance hall. The guest bath shouldn't have anything incriminating in it, should it?

As Frederick left the room, I began to pace, clutching my phone, waiting for it to vibrate. It wasn't just that Frederick was here, I wanted to know where Scarlett was. I hadn't heard from her and I was beginning to grow concerned. Anything could have happened to her. This was New-York-Fucking-City. She could have been mugged or kidnapped. She could have gotten caught up in the middle of an armed robbery. She could have been pushed onto the tracks of the subway, or run down by a cab.

Where the fuck was she? I wouldn't be half as tense as I was if she was here. I wouldn't be worrying if something had happened to her but also because when she was close, she always gave me something to smile about, whether it was her perspective on a problem at work or the slide of her hand over my chest.

When had I become that guy?

I ran my free hand through my hair as Frederick reappeared.

"You okay, old chap? You look a little on edge."

I shook my head. "I'm fine." But I wasn't fine at all. I wanted to be discussing my day with Scarlett, not Frederick.

A bang on the door interrupted my list of catastrophic things that could have happened to Scarlett. Was that her?

I sprinted to the front door and she almost fell inside as she struggled with the key in the lock. "Goddamn key," she said, muttering into my chest.

I was so stunned and happy to see her, I didn't notice that her hands were full as I pulled her against me.

"Hey," I said, squeezing her tight.

"Errr, hi. Can I just . . ." She wiggled free of my arms and I saw the bags she was carrying.

"Sorry, let me help you with that." I was so relieved at being able to touch her again I nearly forgot Frederick was sitting on my sofa.

She didn't meet my eyes as she handed me a bag that had a bunch of tulips poking out of the top. She'd had time to go shopping, but not call me back?

I wanted us to have a few moments together, maybe share a kiss hello, but she swept past me and into the living room. Frederick had turned to face us and Scarlett beamed when she saw him. "Frederick! How lovely to see you. Welcome to New York." She pulled him in for a hug. "What are you doing here? You should have said you were coming, and I could have rearranged my work schedule."

Frederick smiled, probably relieved Scarlett had released him from her hug. British aristocracy didn't indulge in such things. "Last minute plan. I thought I'd surprise you."

Scarlett turned to me, still not looking me in the eye and pointed at the bags I was carrying for her. "Can you put those on the counter? I've got tarragon chicken if that works for you?" she asked, looking at Frederick.

"Sounds great," Frederick replied. "Can I do anything to help?"

"No, tell us about your trip. I'll put Ryder to work as my assistant." She grinned and turned to look at me for the first time since she arrived. Even though I could tell it wasn't as natural as usual, her gaze was like the sun, warming my body, relaxing and unknotting each tense muscle.

"Can I get a glass of wine please?" she asked as she began to unload the bags she'd brought onto the counter.

I wanted to drag her into the bedroom and have a private conversation. Ask her where the hell she'd been and why she hadn't been answering my calls. Thank her for changing her plans, tell her I missed her.

Instead I opened the wine fridge and took out a bottle of Pouilly-Fume I knew she'd love.

I poured the wine, tuning out of the chat she was having with Frederick.

"Thanks," she said, not looking at me as she arranged what she'd bought in front of her. But I didn't set the drink down. I stepped so close that I could smell that now-familiar scent of warm tangerine. It wasn't perfume. It was just her.

She looked up at me, her eyes slightly narrowed. She was pissed. Perhaps because Frederick's arrival had interrupted her plans, but it felt like more than that. I set the glass down on the marble, the satisfying scrape of two hard surfaces sliding together making me realize I'd not been focused on Frederick since Scarlett had walked in the door.

I circled my arms around her waist and pulled her toward me. She curled around my biceps and dug into my muscles, as she resisted my embrace. I bent my head to her neck, not wanting her to reject my kiss. "I missed you," I whispered against her skin.

She yielded a little, her thighs scraping against mine. "I've been busy—"

I didn't want to hear her excuses. I was just pleased she was back. "I'm glad you're here."

"I'm hungry. Can you let go of your wife for just a few minutes so she can prepare the chicken?" Frederick called from the sitting area.

"Honestly, I'm not sure I can," I replied, lifting my head but not taking my eyes from Scarlett.

She tried to twist away but I held her tight. I didn't know where she'd go if I released her. I bent my head again to her ear. "Whatever I did, I'm sorry."

She nodded against my cheek. "Let's cook dinner."

I stepped back slightly, but kept my hand on her lower back. "What can I do?"

"Get me an ovenproof dish for the chicken and a salad

bowl?"

Christ, she was amazing. She didn't know this kitchen well, yet she was doing a great job covering that up by getting me to assist. "And the colander. You can wash the salad."

I grinned. I didn't think there was a person alive other than my sister who would instruct me to wash salad.

"You don't mind eating at the breakfast bar do you, Frederick?" Scarlett asked as she prepared the chicken while I placed the things she'd asked for on the counter in front of her.

Frederick wandered toward us, his drink in his hand. "Of course not. I'm here for the company."

Sure he was.

"I have to say, this place isn't what I thought. I'd expected it to have more of a woman's touch," Frederick said, glancing around.

Scarlett laughed. "Give me a chance, Frederick. You must know that it was Ryder's place before we got married," she said, chopping the tarragon. "But I've had a few ideas of what I might like to do with the place."

Was she saying that just to placate Frederick, or did she really want to redecorate? Not that I minded.

I'd let my designer pick almost everything for this apartment. If Scarlett wanted to make changes, I'd be happy with that. "What kind of ideas?" I asked.

She shrugged. "Oh, just some things in the bedrooms," she said, sliding the onion from her chopping board into the frying pan. "I was thinking of switching things up a little."

Fuck, I hoped that included her sleeping in my room. I'd missed her warmth next to me this morning when I woke. It'd felt like a piece of me had been missing all day. As I passed behind her, I placed the pepper mill on the counter and took the opportunity to press my body against her and kiss her shoulder.

"You really can't keep your hands off her, can you? I get that you're newlyweds, you know. You don't have anything to prove to me," Frederick said, grinning.

I flexed my hands and resisted the urge to punch him. "I can't help myself." I wrapped my arms around Scarlett's waist as she continued to chop. Not because Frederick was here, but because I wanted to.

Because I could.

Because I'd missed her.

I couldn't remember the last time I'd ever missed anyone. Maybe my sister while I was away at school. But no one as an adult. What was my wife doing to me?

CHAPTER TWENTY-THREE
SCARLETT

"Give us a call if you decide to extend your trip," I called out to Frederick behind the elevator doors as they glided shut. I hadn't missed an opportunity to top up Frederick's wine all night. He left fed, a little drunk and hopefully convinced that Ryder and I were the real deal.

"I really hope he doesn't," Ryder mumbled as the elevator began to whir and I turned to go back into the living area.

"You think that was a test?" I asked.

"Of course it was a test. The man's been to New York once in his life and he's suddenly here on *business*." He emphasized the word like it was the most ridiculous thing he'd ever heard. But it didn't seem so impossible. Surely, Frederick could have just hired a private investigator.

The door clunked behind us. As soon as I walked into the living room and felt Ryder's eyes on me, all my resolve to keep my emotions detached from him began to wobble. Being alone together, it was so easy to slip into married life or into that pretend world where I wasn't pretending.

How had I let things get this far? Why had I allowed myself to want something more from this man? I knew better. I'd missed him last night and I had no right to. And that was the reason I needed to leave.

"I should go," I said, heading toward my bedroom.

"Go?" he asked, his voice following me down the hallway. "Where?"

"I told you I was going to stay at my apartment tonight."

He took hold of my wrist and pulled me back from the entrance to the bedroom. "Scarlett," he said, his brow furrowed.

I glanced down at my feet. The way he looked at me was as if he really wanted me to stay—not because of our arrangement or because Frederick had just left. It was so easy to think that this was real.

"I feel like I've done something wrong, but I don't know what. Please tell me. Let me make it better."

I took a deep breath. It wasn't anything he'd done. Ryder had been nothing but nice to me. Too nice. "No. It's not that."

I tried to free my wrist but he tightened his grip. "Then what?" he asked. "I missed you."

I shook my head. It was him saying things like that which made it so easy for me to trick myself into thinking this was something that it wasn't.

"Scarlett? Did something happen at work? Or with your ex?"

I glanced up to find Ryder scanning my face as if he was looking for clues. "No, it's nothing like that," I replied. "I'm just tired."

"Too tired to talk?"

"Talk?" Presumably it was a euphemism for sex. "Yeah, I've had such a busy day."

"So don't go to your apartment," he said. "I don't want to spend two nights without you in my bed." And there it was again, that pulse in my stomach at his words, dissolving the walls around my heart. Exactly the sensation I shouldn't be feeling. Because I shouldn't *be feeling* anything. But his closeness chased away the fight in me, and Ryder must have sensed it. He released my wrist only to pull me into his arms. "Don't leave me tonight," he whispered.

"But I have to," I said. I needed to rebuild my walls and I couldn't do that pressed against Ryder's body.

"Don't. Sleeping on your own isn't allowed. The guest room is not for you to sleep in. And neither is your apartment. You belong in my room. *Our* room."

Was he just telling me what I wanted to hear? His expression was concerned and genuine. The problem was that I wanted to believe him so badly.

"Scarlett," he whispered for no reason in particular.

I reached up and trailed my finger along his jaw. He felt like mine, but I knew he wasn't. It was just so easy to pretend.

He pressed his lips to the corner of my mouth. "Where have you been all day?"

I was sinking deeper and deeper into him, into a life with him. And as much as I knew it was the last thing I should be doing, I couldn't stop.

I turned my head in answer so my lips aligned with his. I glanced up from under my eyelashes.

"I want to make this right," he said in a half whisper before kissing me properly, prying my mouth open and sliding his tongue against mine. He stepped forward, pressing me against the wall. He ground his hips against me, his erection thrusting against my stomach. Perhaps I'd be better able to resist him if he couldn't do the things he did to my body.

I threaded my hand through his hair as he reached beneath my skirt and yanked my panties down. The lace brushing the back of my thighs was like a match against a striker, everywhere he touched me burned.

If only he'd *stop* touching me.

"This pussy," he said, casually rubbing his fingers along my folds. "I've missed it. You can't torture me by denying me."

As if I had an arsenal able to torture him. As if he didn't have all the power here.

"I've not had you in thirty-nine hours." He ran his teeth along my neck and my hips bucked off the wall. "It's far too long." He pushed two long fingers inside me and I sucked in a breath, my knees buckling. I needed this. His fingers. His cock. His mouth. I wanted everything from him.

Which is why I should resist him.

He slowly started to circle his thumb around my clit, his free hand on the back of my ass, pulling me into his touch. Between dirty words he plundered my mouth.

I sagged, but he held me in place, his fingers circling and pushing, pressing and pulling. My orgasm whispered from a distance.

Just a few hours ago, I'd needed space. Just a few minutes ago, I'd wanted to go home. But I had no control around him. During my first marriage, I'd always known what was coming—what lay around the bend in the road. But with Ryder, I was in new territory.

"Ryder," I managed to say. "We shouldn't." But I knew it was futile to fight my attraction to him. I wasn't sure it was possible to be in a room with him for more than a few seconds without wanting him.

"You want me to stop?" he asked. He released my ass and for a moment I thought he would let go of me entirely and the thought was horrifying.

I shook my head and his fingers delved deeper inside me while he tried to undo his fly with his other hand.

He let out a gasp as his dick sprang out of his pants and he rounded the crown with his hand. "You're so tight. I want inside you."

I was seconds away from coming on his hand; I wanted to be able to milk his cock. I wanted him to feel what he did to me. "Yes, deep inside."

He dropped his lips onto mine, the heat of his tongue pushing deeper. I missed kissing him. As much as I might know it wasn't what I should be doing, everything was okay when I was kissing Ryder, when we were close like this.

I whimpered at the loss of his fingers. He grabbed my ass and lifted me up and against the wall. I squeezed my legs around his waist, desperately wanting him inside me but knowing it would almost hurt until I was used to him again.

His tip brushed my entrance.

"I'll go slow," he whispered. He must have known what I was thinking.

I nodded, gasping as he filled me.

"Fuck," he said, stilling. I pressed my hips down anyway, wanting him too much to wait. "No," he said, sharply. "I'm not wearing a condom."

I wanted to get fucked. Needed him to fuck me.

I didn't care about a condom. I didn't care about getting in too deep. I didn't want anything but the feel of his cock against my walls, driving hard flesh inside me chasing away my doubts. I'd do anything to get it. "Leave the condom," I said.

I wanted him close.

"I'm clean. I got the results just before the wedding." His words were breathless, his pupils dilated, his normally sleek hair a little mussy.

I nodded. "Good, me too," I said, trying to sway my hips to get him deeper.

"Are you on the pill?" he asked.

"Yes." He slipped in just a little farther. Nothing was clear in my mind other than my desire to come, my need for Ryder.

Slowly and with such control, he lowered me onto him until I was oh-so-full, so close to him.

I pressed my palm against his chest, knowing that any movement would set my orgasm off. I wanted to simmer in the *just before* for a few moments longer.

I concentrated on the way my skin looked against his, how his fingers felt digging into my ass, how he smelled of home. Despite every uncertainty—how I knew my heart would be safer—being here with him like this just felt right.

My body dropped in the realization and I clasped him closer, dipping my head to kiss his jaw, his shoulder, his mouth as he pushed into me relentlessly.

I threw my head back as he drove me harder and harder so close to the edge of my climax.

"Oh Jesus, I love your expression right before you . . ." He jabbed his hips up like he couldn't help himself and it set my orgasm free. It rippled across my body in waves, getting stronger and stronger as I dissolved, my heart spinning in my chest.

The understanding that he was fucking me, unable to do anything else until he'd had his own orgasm, prolonged my climax; his desire for me was the ultimate stimulation.

Just as the edges of my orgasm ebbed away, he grunted and dug his fingers deeper into my ass cheeks as he poured into me.

His breaths were hot and fast against my neck, my head lay back against the wall, my legs wrapped around his waist.

He growled, shifting us so he took more of my weight than the wall. I expected him to set me down, but instead he carried me into his bedroom.

"I fuck you here. You sleep here. Not in the spare room. Not in your apartment," he said. "Let me see." He lifted my skirt as if to admire his work. "My come belongs here. In your pussy, dripping down your legs. You understand?"

I shivered.

He raised his eyebrows as if reminding me I hadn't answered. I nodded. "I understand."

"Don't leave again." He tugged off my skirt, discarding it behind him, and undressed quickly, standing over me naked.

I didn't move. I didn't dare.

His eyes darted from my face down my body and back up. "Open your legs, Scarlett." It was the same request he had of me the first time we slept together, but this time felt different. Before I'd been laid bare in front of someone I never had to see again. But now? I was living with this man. Maybe even sharing my life with him. But seeing the burn in his eyes, the need in the rise of his shoulders, I did what he asked willingly.

He groaned. "Yes. Like that. Nice and wide." Gripping his cock in his fist, he took a step closer, standing between my open legs that were dangling off the side of the mattress.

"I need to fuck you all the time," he said, using the tip of his cock to circle my clit. "And you need it, too. I know you do."

He was right. I'd been on edge all day—a symptom of not having him inside me for longer than it should have been. If I couldn't survive a day without him physically, what did that mean for me? And if he felt the same way, did that mean something more? Or was it just physical, just sex?

"I'm going to fuck you again. Nothing between us. Just my skin against yours. And you're going to come again and again because you need to understand what you're missing when you don't sleep in my bed. When you try to avoid me."

A strangled vowel left the back of my throat. I knew exactly what I'd been missing, that was why I'd avoided him. Didn't he get that?

He gripped the top of my thigh, tracing his thumb across the juncture between my legs, rubbing the mixture of my wetness and his come into my skin like he was emphasizing his point. It was as if he was trying to mark my skin with *us*.

Without further warning, he pushed into me and I cried out. I never got used to the size of him, despite it only having been minutes since he was last inside me. "See how I fill you up? Nothing else can do that. No one else. Only me."

He grunted, stroked his hand over my belly and around my waist, pulled out and thrust sharply again. The hint of pain intensified the pleasure and I knew this was unmistakably us. It was how we fit together. No man would ever make me feel like this again. So possessed.

He dug his hand into my waist, the other one curling around my shoulder. I closed my eyes in a long blink. I knew the next thrust from him would be the deepest yet. He pushed sharply into me, and I started to unwind.

Ryder knew my body well enough now to read every sign. I could hide nothing from him when we fucked.

"See how quickly you come? How fast *I make you* come?"

I couldn't react or respond. I had no control over my body or mind. It was all his.

I shuddered as my climax rushed over me; the drumming in my ears reached a crescendo, every part of me dissolving, my whole body trying to float off the bed.

The next thing I was aware of was Ryder chanting "So beautiful. So beautiful" while rocking in and out of me.

I smoothed my hand up his arm and gazed at him—the edges of his hair were damp with sweat and his broad, rounded shoulders glowed as if he had just finished a workout.

"Flip onto your stomach," he said, pulling out of me.

I tensed. What did he have in mind? I'd had his finger and thumb inside my ass. I'd never experimented with any anal play with my ex, but with Ryder there was no saying no and I found I liked it.

He turned me over and dragged me back toward him so my legs hit the floor. "I know you can't stand, baby, but I need to be in that ass of yours."

I gasped. And I flung one hand back, covering my bottom. A finger was one thing. His dick was quite another.

"You're so wet, baby; it's going to feel so good." He delved inside me with his fingers and as if to prove his point, began to lubricate my ass. "So, so wet."

Normally he circled and stroked my ass, relaxing me until I was almost begging for his fingers. But today he was impatient and his thumb pressed through the circle of muscles before I expected them to. I moaned into the mattress. How could I still feel this turned on despite coming twice?

"Oh yes, you're getting good at this, aren't you?" He thrust his cock into my pussy, complementing his thumb above. "You want more." It wasn't a question.

His cock stayed buried inside me but his thumb was quickly replaced by two fingers nudging at the muscles. I gripped the bedding. Could I handle this?

"You're doing good. So good," he said and I took a breath at the same time as the thrusts increased in pace.

He waited just a second before he began to rock his fingers and cock in and out of me. It was too much, too good, too full.

Pinned to the bed by the sensation, I couldn't move. I was exhausted but my orgasm wasn't far away. It was almost as if I were having hundreds of tiny climaxes that were building and building into something—I didn't know what.

Ryder's thrusts jolted into me and I knew he was close. His movements became less controlled, his voice tighter and louder.

"So tight. So smooth. So good," he growled.

My body began to clench as my climax took over and Ryder cried out, folding over my back, his breath hot on my neck as we came together, floating, grasping. Joined. I'd never felt so much like an *us*.

CHAPTER TWENTY-FOUR
SCARLETT

"So dinner on Tuesday?" Violet asked from the other end of the phone. I had her on speaker as I scanned my emails that had built up during my morning full of meetings about Cecily Fragrance's new store opening in Southampton. "I'm not taking no for an answer. I don't see you enough."

I thought back. In the three months since Ryder and I had returned from England, I hadn't really gone out with my friends. And I couldn't remember him ever going out with his friends without me. Ryder and I liked hanging out together.

"Sure. Come over and I'll cook," I replied and she groaned. I stopped what I was doing and stared at the receiver. What was her problem?

"You're so boring. I was going to get Harper to come out and Grace, too. I thought we could have a few shots and a little fun. I've been over to your place every time I've seen you for months."

"Sorry, I've just been so busy at work; it's just nice to be at home in the evenings."

Home. After my night in the guest room, he'd dismantled the bed. He'd never made me feel like I was a guest. When I'd mentioned his couch was too hard, we'd gone shopping for a new one that weekend. I don't think he even noticed when I rearranged his kitchen and he told me how much he liked the flowers I bought each week. There was never a moment I felt awkward or uncomfortable there.

Violet sighed. "Maybe if you weren't up fucking all night, you could manage a night out with your sister. Even Harper was saying she missed you."

Maybe I had been neglecting my family in favor of my husband. "I'm not up all night fucking." Just part of the night. Every night. And mornings, too. When it was as good as it was between Ryder and me, why wouldn't we want to spend our time together? It felt real—a relationship, a friendship, a partnership. And I resolved that while it did, I'd go with it. "There's just a lot going on in the business. But a girls' night sounds good." I could always get home before Ryder went to bed. That way, I'd still see him, even if it was for a short while.

"Great. I'll speak to Harper and Grace. I need a bit of bonding time without men."

"Well, I'm always up for girl time. You know that."

"You could have fooled me," she said. "But I'll set something up. There's a great new hipster place in the East Village we should try."

I groaned. "You know that the three of us are hardly the hipster type."

"And I keep telling you, you need to expand your horizons. You never know, we might find your next husband there."

Next husband? "You make it sound like I'm a praying mantis."

Her tut echoed down the phone. "I just mean that when

your thing with Ryder is over, you might want to change things up a bit. A hipster's an option."

It had been three months, and I'd promised Ryder three years. Violet was jumping the gun, but I wasn't about to rain on her parade. "I'm not sure hipsters will ever be my type, even if I'm on my ninth husband, but it's not me you'll have to convince. I'm pretty sure Harper will want to go to somewhere uber-glam." Frankly, if I was going to spend the evening without Ryder, I wanted to make sure it was somewhere nice, but I'd let Harper take the fall for this one. I knew she'd be happy to.

"Well, it's my party, so I'm picking the place. Does Tuesday work?"

As long as it wasn't Friday. Friday nights in with Ryder were my favorite nights of the week. I couldn't remember how it started but it had become a ritual that we'd start the evening with a bath and a classic movie in bed with popcorn, which inevitably led to sex. Then we often ate grilled cheese in our robes and flipped through the channels while talking about work, family and books and then, eventually, we had more sex. "I think I might be busy on Friday but otherwise . . ."

"Okay, any day other than Friday. I'll arrange. Gotta go."

As soon as Violet hung up, my desk phone buzzed again.

"Your gorgeous husband just arrived. Again," my receptionist said over the speakerphone. I grinned. Ryder made it to lunch at my place a couple of times a week. I wasn't quite sure how he managed it, but there was always a "reason" for his visit. A meeting in the area, or his banker had just canceled on him. I liked that he felt he needed to explain his appearance to me. It was as if he wasn't sure I'd want to see him if he didn't have an excuse.

"Thanks. Send him back." Usually he just wandered through, so I wasn't sure why he'd stopped at reception.

"He's on his way. I just had to call you to tell you how lucky you are." No one but Cecily knew about my arrangement with Ryder, and Gail in particular was taken in by our story of a whirlwind romance. I could see how it would be easy to fall for. I couldn't imagine most husbands were attentive enough to have lunch with their wives a couple of days each week.

He appeared at the door to my office, grinning and holding up a white paper bag, which presumably contained our lunch. "That meeting with Bob got canceled, so I thought I'd grab a bite with you if you're not busy."

I beckoned him forward with the tilt of my head and the curl of my hand. I was never too busy to see him.

"We never lunch in your office," I said, unpacking the containers from the paper bag.

"That's because you never stop by."

True. Since the night of Frederick's visit, things had evened out between us. I'd relaxed. Stopped asking if I'd given too much of myself away. I'd tried to live in the moment and enjoy our time together, however short. Because it was more of a marriage in many ways than I'd ever had the first time around. "You're always welcome."

He grinned and I smiled back. I avoided his office. I was pretty sure there were plenty of women who had seen him naked there. From what he'd told me in the three months since we'd come back from England, he'd been quite the player. I never asked him if he'd been faithful to me since our wedding. If he hadn't, I didn't want to know. But I was pretty sure he'd only been with me. But he didn't get much opportunity to sleep with other women. We spent most of our time outside working hours together.

"John wants me to go to some shitty gala dinner next week," Ryder said as he took a seat on the other side of my desk.

Despite having seen each other this morning. Fucked. Shared our mood. Talked, drunk coffee together. Even though, tonight, we'd fuck, talk, eat dinner together. There was always more to talk about. More to say.

"Like a benefit or something?" I asked. Ryder didn't trust a lot of people but John was an exception.

"An awards ceremony. Waste of bloody time if you ask me, but he's convinced I need to be seen at these things."

I opened up the boxes of food. Thai. Nice. "Well, it's just an evening. What can it hurt? You can always sneak out after the main course."

"You'll come though, right?" He handed me a paper napkin wrapped around a plastic knife and fork. "You'll make it bearable."

My heart squeezed and I glanced at him. He must have felt my eyes on him because he looked up and smiled. What he'd said was not meant to have any particular meaning attached to it, but to me it showed me how much we were a team, a unit—a couple. Did he see it, too? Wasn't this more than just an arrangement? Surely if this was just business, he wouldn't be sitting across from me. But we never talked about us. Never discussed our three-year deal. We were only a few months in but I was at the point where I didn't want to put a time limit on us.

I wanted to know if he felt the same.

"Sure," I said, poking my fork into the box of Thai food I'd opened. I liked the idea that a work event would only be manageable if I was with him. "There's no place I'd rather be."

"There's no place I'd rather have you." His eyebrows darted up. Ryder was able to make anything sound dirty.

"I'm serious," I said. "I like spending time with you."

He paused, his fork hovering over the paper container. "I like spending time with you, too."

"I mean, even without . . ." I circled my hand in the air, not wanting to be too serious but at the same time wanting him to understand what I was trying to say without having to actually say the words. "You know. The deal. I still like it." Christ, I sounded like a thirteen-year-old girl with a crush on her brother's best friend. I rolled my eyes at my pathetic attempt at sharing my feelings and the corner of Ryder's mouth began to twitch. This was his chance to say something.

The beginning of Ryder's smile was interrupted by his phone vibrating on the desk between us. Darcy's name flashed up on the screen. I took a forkful of food.

"Do you mind?" he asked.

I shook my head, my mouth full of Thai noodles.

"Hey, Darce, what's up?"

I couldn't hear her, but I could tell Darcy was speaking really fast. Ryder's face fell and he stood. Under his suit I could see every muscle tense as he closed his eyes.

"Yeah, we'll get there as soon as we can."

I dropped my fork. Something had happened. Something bad.

Ryder took a breath and hung up the phone. "We have to go," he said, glancing around as if looking for something.

"What's the matter?" I asked, my heart pounding.

"Can you come?"

"Yes, anywhere." I didn't need to know what had happened—I would go wherever Ryder asked me.

I gathered up my phone, tablet and bag as Ryder punched numbers into his cell. "I need the plane to go to England as fast as possible." England? Something had happened to Darcy or to the duke.

He hung up and we headed out. I'd message Cecily when we were in the car. I didn't want to waste time. Ryder needed me.

As we stood in the elevator to take us down to Ryder's car, I slid my hand into his and squeezed. "Grandfather's had a stroke," he whispered, his voice so low I almost couldn't hear. "He's at the hospital."

I squeezed his hand again and leaned across and lay a kiss on his shoulder.

CHAPTER TWENTY-FIVE
RYDER

The practicalities of death somehow seemed to help me cope with losing my grandfather. That and having Scarlett by my side. We'd barely spent a moment apart since landing to the news that my grandfather had passed away.

I sat back in the green leather chair at my grandfather's desk. I used to sneak into this office when I was a kid and climb up on this chair, pretending I was just like him. I'd known even then that if I became half the man he was, I'd be okay.

Now the chair was mine. The soft leather under my thumbs provided a kind of comfort as I took another meeting with Giles to begin the process of turning over day-to-day operations to Darcy. I'd had no idea of all the complications my grandfather dealt with on a daily basis.

"Darcy should be here," I said. I had no interest in running things. As far as I was concerned, the estate, the house, everything was Darcy's, regardless of what the official documentation said. I just wanted my business.

"The paperwork today doesn't need Darcy. She knows what she needs to do, and I'll guide her through the rest." My sister had been preparing for this moment for years. She knew the estate better than anyone. She loved her life here.

I'd been selfish all these years thinking that she'd be fine as long as I provided for her financially. I'd thought Frederick having this place would be no big deal but now my grandfather was gone, I was so relieved that Frederick wouldn't have any claim over it. Darcy would be happy. I'd have control over the Westbury Group. Everything was how my grandfather had wanted it.

"Thank you, Giles. We're lucky to have you."

We'd been in England two weeks. The funeral had been yesterday and this morning I woke for the first time thinking of life back in Manhattan. Scarlett hadn't mentioned going back, though she must be wondering how long we'd stay.

"Darcy's incredibly strong, but she can't do this without you," I said. "She will need your wise counsel."

"Oh, I think she'll do just fine, whatever life throws at her. You're both resourceful and independent. The old duke said that was what he admired in you both—the way you dealt with your mother and father. He worried it would damage you, but he said that you both had the ability to turn the most negative situation into a positive one."

My parents had been the last thing I'd been thinking about since my grandfather's death. I'd called my mother to let her know about her father's death the day after it happened. The call had lasted less than a minute. I wasn't sure if she was incredibly upset or just disinterested. She'd thanked me for letting her know and then made her excuses to end the conversation.

I'd not heard from her since, despite sending her funeral details over email.

We all grieved in different ways, but apparently, it hadn't occurred to my mother that Darcy or I might need her here. Because we didn't. We never had.

The thing about death was it turned your attention to the living. In the last two weeks I'd thought a lot about my future. I'd never thought about having children before, but my grandfather's death had made me see it as a possibility—as the next natural step. I could imagine having a daughter with Scarlett's long, dark hair, riding one of the estate's ponies—tiny riding boots on—her face bearing a scrape of mud. My son on Scarlett's lap as she read him a story as my grandmother had done for Darcy and me.

"At some point we should talk about the dissolution of your marriage," Giles said.

His words caught my attention, yanking me out of the vision of my future I'd created. "Pardon?"

"We need to transfer the loans you made to Cecily Fragrance to Scarlett and begin proceedings. We can wait three months to file everything but there's nothing to stop us getting things ready now."

Could Giles hear the pounding in my chest as well as I could? I focused in on my breathing, trying to keep calm. The last few months with Scarlett had changed me. I'd never properly *known* a woman, other than my sister. I may have slept with a lot of women, but I hadn't understood how much the right one could add to my life. I'd fought so hard for so long to be independent, I'd never realized how amazing it was to share my day with someone. Being with Scarlett had been nothing like I expected. I liked her. I trusted her. I wanted to get her naked morning, noon and night. The thought that it was all going to end and she would go back to her corner of Manhattan and I would go back to fucking three different women a week hadn't occurred to me in a while. Somewhere along the line, our situation had morphed into something I wasn't expecting.

"Ryder?" Giles asked, knocking me out of my mental fog.

"Well, of course, the loans should be transferred across to Scarlett as soon as possible." But the divorce? I enjoyed our life together. And I thought Scarlett did, too. Was divorce what she wanted?

I'd not slept with anyone except Scarlett since we met, and instead of it making me feel hemmed in and tied down, I felt freer than I ever had. It felt as if she was on my side, shoulder to shoulder with me. We were a team, a unit . . . a couple. Did divorce mean we'd still date, fuck, live together? If not, I wasn't sure I was okay with that.

"Exactly. So I've left an envelope with Scarlett to take back to the US to have her lawyer review, but everything is in order, just as you agreed."

"Fine." The funeral had only been yesterday. She hadn't left my side all day. We'd been stuck together like glue for the last two weeks. And I'd been so grateful. It was only right that she have that money as soon as possible. If I'd have thought about it, I would have transferred the loans from me to Scarlett months ago.

"You just need to sign here and here," Giles said, pointing at a dotted line on the bottom of a page.

I took the lid off my pen and signed. Then he presented another page. "And here for the divorce application."

I set my pen down. "I think I need to speak to Scarlett about this part." Maybe divorce was inevitable, but that didn't mean I had to accept it without a fight. I stood. "I forgot that I said I'd help Darcy with something." I headed toward the door. I needed air—time to think. I didn't want to discuss my divorce, or the fact I didn't see any need for one. I liked Scarlett and the life we had together. I wasn't ready to give that up.

I had to speak to Scarlett and find out if she felt the same.

"Scarlett," I called as I took the oak stairs up to our bedroom. I'd expected to find her in the library; she seemed to gravitate toward the place on the rare occasions we weren't together, but when I'd checked it had been empty. "Scarlett," I called again. If she was sleeping, I'd wake her. We needed to have this conversation. I didn't want to go back to Manhattan and have her go back to her flat. It didn't seem right. If necessary, I'd convince her to let me redecorate her place before she moved back in. Then she'd be forced to stay a little longer and then by the time that was done, hopefully I'd be able to convince her—maybe even rent her flat out. We didn't have to consider forever, but surely she'd give us a chance. Things had been good between us. There was no reason to walk away now.

I opened the door to our bedroom, expecting to see her napping on the bed, but she wasn't there. I glanced around. "Scarlett," I called out. Was she taking a bath? I charged into the bathroom, hoping to find her covered in bubbles and staring back at me, a wicked grin on her face. But the bathroom was empty as well. Maybe she'd gone over to the stables with Darcy? I took out my phone and dialed her mobile. It rang from the other side of the room and I saw it light up on the nightstand. Shit. She took her phone everywhere with her. Where was she? I stalked over to her phone and found it sitting on a large, brown envelope. Her name had been crossed out in blue pen and in her neat handwriting she'd spelled out "Ryder."

My heart began to thud against my chest.

I grabbed the envelope and turned it over in my hands. The flap opened easily and I pulled out the papers, scattering them onto the bed. The ebony type jumped out at me: *Divorce*, *Loan Settlement*. I rummaged through them and found her signature at the back, just above her name. I turned the document over. It was the loan settlement. I tossed it aside and grabbed the other document. She wouldn't have signed the divorce papers without asking me, would she?

I flicked through the pages of the divorce petition. All signed, as if it were just more loan documentation. As if it meant nothing to her. As if *I* meant nothing to her. The floorboards outside my room creaked. I gathered up the papers and stuffed them back in the envelope. Perhaps she did want to discuss what was going to happen between us. After all, even though the envelope had been addressed to me, it had been left on her nightstand, under her mobile phone.

I quickly replaced the envelope and phone and headed toward the door to meet Scarlett as she came in.

But when I yanked open the door, Scarlett wasn't standing in front of me as I'd hoped. I glanced left and right, but only found Lane coming out of the summer suite.

"Sir, can I help you with anything?" he asked.

I shook my head. "No, sorry. I thought you were Scarlett. You haven't seen her, have you?"

He opened his mouth as if to speak, then stopped, frowned and finally said, "I dropped her off at Heathrow, sir."

Heathrow?

My face caught fire. "Oh, yes. Of course, you did."
Heath-fucking-row?

"Did she leave something behind? I can have it sent over
by courier if needs be."

"No, that's fine. I just wasn't quite sure what time she
was leaving." I nodded and closed the door, clenching and
releasing my fists, hoping the action would take away from
the slice through my chest.

She'd taken her money and left. Like all I'd ever been
for her was a damn job. Had she really been faking our
whole relationship this entire time?

Jesus. I'd been played—and it hurt more than I could
ever have imagined. I'd thought the death of my grandfather
had been bad enough. But this? To find out the last three
months had meant nothing to her. Was I really such a
dreadful judge of character?

I'd spent my life carefully limiting the number of people
I cared about. Because I knew from bitter experience that it
was only the people who were close to you that could hurt
you. My parents had taught me that lesson early and hard.

And Scarlett had just sent me to grad school.

CHAPTER TWENTY-SIX
RYDER

"Come on, Darce! I'm going to be late." I stood at the bottom of the stairs, ready to go into London to meet the shareholders of a potential new investee company. Darcy was meeting old school friends. I really didn't want to spend nearly two hours in a car with her, but I'd not left my room after Scarlett's disappearance, which meant Darcy would have eaten alone. I was a selfish prick, but I just couldn't bring myself to explain Scarlett's absence. It showed an embarrassing lack of judgment on my behalf. I'd always prided myself on being able to pick out people I trusted and people I didn't.

I clearly wasn't as tuned in as I thought I was.

"I'm coming," she shouted back, the slam of her bedroom door echoing over the landing.

She appeared at the top of the stairs with a frown. "Where's Scarlett?" I rolled my eyes. She thought I hadn't gone to dinner because Scarlett and I were too busy fucking. How wrong she was.

"Come on," I said, ignoring her. The gravel crunched beneath my shoes—something I missed when in Manhattan. The feel of the stones under my feet meant I was home.

"You're mighty moody today, Ryder. If Scarlett doesn't want to chaperone you to London, it's not my fault."

I climbed into the back of the Bentley, slamming the door before Lane could do it for me.

I pulled down the armrest between us and opened my laptop. I'd have to spend the journey working or at least pretending to work. The last thing I wanted to do was talk about Scarlett.

Darcy and Lane exchanged words outside the car, then the opposite door opened and Darcy got in without a word. She fastened her seatbelt and began to mess with her phone. Good. Silence was what I needed.

I began to scan through emails that had come in overnight. Despite being across the pond for over two weeks, things seemed to be running smoothly. John was handling anything that required face-to-face meetings. I occasionally joined by video conference but other than that, it was business as usual. I knew my grandfather would hate to think he'd pulled my focus from the Westbury Group, so I'd made sure I'd kept on top of things.

"What did you do?" Darcy asked from next to me.

Assuming she was talking to her phone, I ignored her.

"Ryder. What happened with Scarlett?"

Fuck. I did not want to discuss this.

I glanced up to see that Lane had brought up the privacy screen. Had Darcy asked him to? Was that what they'd been muttering about before Darcy got into the car?

"I'm busy, Darcy."

I knew I wasn't going to be able to shut her down, but it was worth a shot.

"Lane said Scarlett flew back to New York yesterday."

I shrugged. "What's your point?" I asked, keeping my eyes fixed on my laptop screen.

"What did you do to make her run?"

Right. Typical of my sister to assume I'd done something. I wasn't the bad guy in this situation. I was the goddamn victim. I'd opened myself up to a woman and where had it got me? Used and thrown out.

"I don't have time for an argument, Darcy. I didn't do anything. The estate has passed. She got her money. We're done. It's as simple as that."

Christ, everything about her departure had been so calculated. I'd thought that she'd become friends with Darcy but she'd clearly not even said goodbye to her.

"You sent her away?" Darcy asked.

"No. If you must know, she didn't tell me she was leaving. Giles gave her the papers and the next thing I knew, she'd gone."

Silence. Of course, now that I wanted Darcy to say something, to condemn the woman who had abandoned me, my sister had nothing to say.

"She just left? She didn't say anything to you?"

"Not a word. Went upstairs to find her to . . ." Tell her I thought we had something. Ask her if she wanted things between us to continue. God, I'd been such an idiot. "And she'd cleared out. Signed the papers and got the first plane out."

"You sound pissed off." Darcy's tone had mellowed. Surely she and I were on the same side?

"I *am* pissed off. She could have at least said goodbye."

I glanced across and Darcy was staring right ahead of her, her mouth twisted. "I thought . . . I mean, I know it was an arrangement and everything, but you seemed to get on really well."

I let out an incredulous huff.

"And I thought it was, you know, physical between you two."

I scraped my hand through my hair. "It was . . . and maybe more." She'd been my partner, my confidante, my friend as well as my lover. Nothing from my side had been faked. "For me, at least."

"Did she just say she wasn't interested in things going any further after Grandfather's death?"

"We didn't even discuss it. I was going to ask her whether she wanted to keep seeing each other but—"

"You never discussed it?" Darcy asked.

"I didn't have a chance. She just left as soon as she signed the loan documentation, which transferred the loans to her business to her."

"But you said that she signed the papers. Surely you said *something* when you handed those over?"

"Giles gave them to her."

"What?" Darcy shouted.

"He's going through all the paperwork. I went to talk to her about it and she'd gone." Why the fuck was my sister pissed at me?

"Jesus Christ, you're an idiot."

I slammed my laptop lid down. "I know. I shouldn't have trusted her, but she fulfilled her end of the bargain. Those loans had to be transferred."

"Oh my God. I can't believe we're related. Are you really that stupid?" She twisted so she was sitting sideways in her seat, facing me.

"Darcy, if you're just going to insult me, I have no real interest in continuing this conversation."

"For some unknown reason, Scarlett liked you. It was obvious how much she cared about you to anyone who bothered to look."

I'd thought so, too. But Darcy was ignoring the facts. Scarlett had *left*.

"She came with you when Grandfather died. She didn't have to. She had plenty of excuses to stay in America. And given the smile you've worn since you met her, I think you liked her too."

"You're forgetting an important detail," I said.

"Oh? Like how you're forgetting that Scarlett, who's been your wife in every sense of the word for *months*, got served with divorce papers by some stranger without so much as a thank you from her ungrateful shit of a husband?"

"I told you—I didn't know! Giles took care of it."

"How would she know that?"

I paused for a second, trying to work through the implications of what Darcy was saying.

"Have you been hit on the head or something? Scarlett was probably devastated."

Devastated? Darcy shook her head. "She thought she was building this great relationship with a man and then the first chance he gets, he ends it and doesn't even have the decency to do it to her face."

"But I didn't end it. I don't even *want* to end it."

"How would she know that? All she knows was that she was in England, supporting you, and the second Grandfather was buried, got handed her marching papers."

I let Darcy's words sink in. Had Scarlett run away because she hadn't gotten what she wanted, rather than because she had? My sister never had a problem telling me if she thought I'd behaved insensitively or I hadn't taken her feelings into account. "Why wouldn't she say something? Why would she sign them? She just ran off."

"Because she's humiliated." Darcy sounded exasperated.

Perhaps Scarlett had fled because she'd been hurt—abandoned me only because she'd thought I'd given up on her. "You think maybe she didn't want the divorce?" I held my breath; was there still a chance for us?

"If you insist on being so bloody obtuse then I really can't continue this conversation. For the first time in your life, you have a shot at a real relationship. With a woman you like and trust. Frankly, you don't deserve her if you're not going to give her the benefit of the doubt, and realize how much she's hurting."

"Hurting?" All my thoughts were competing in my head. Could Darcy be right?

"Well, aren't you?" Darcy asked.

Every part of me hurt. I didn't work properly without Scarlett. She made me into a better man, into a man who could make connections with people, care about people—love. "I miss her."

Darcy snorted. "Exactly. When have you ever said that about a woman? And you just threw it all away."

"Is it too late?" I asked, my body tensed in panic.

"I have no idea. But if she means something to you, I suggest you leg it back to New York and beg her forgiveness."

Before Darcy had finished her sentence, I'd hit the button to take down the screen between us and Lane. "We need to turn around. I need to get to Manhattan."

"That's some diversion, sir," Lane replied.

Except it wasn't a diversion. I hoped it would be the route to my future.

CHAPTER TWENTY-SEVEN
SCARLETT

"So, just like that, you're divorced?" Violet asked, leaning over the table at the Hotel Gansevoort in the meatpacking district. I counted the black and white tiles over Violet's shoulder, from our table to the door. I didn't want to think about what had happened. In fact, I just wanted to forget the whole thing. The sooner everything became official, the better.

"The paperwork still has to go through." Sadly, I already understood the legal process of divorce. It wouldn't take long, but it didn't happen overnight. My second divorce and I wasn't even thirty. If my first ex-husband hadn't made me feel so worthless and boring, I probably wouldn't even have a second ex-husband. I'd wanted it to be an adventure. Instead it had been a disaster.

"And he didn't mention it?" she asked.

"No, but like I said, our deal was done. The estate passed and I was no longer useful."

Violet shook her head. "That just doesn't seem right. You seemed so happy together in England. The way you looked at each other and touched one another, it was like you were a real couple."

I'd much rather be drunk than having this conversation.

The kinda drunk where I couldn't remember my own name. I picked up my cocktail and took two huge gulps.

"Is it nice to be back in your apartment at least?"

I nodded, avoiding Violet's gaze. "Sure." I hadn't been back to my apartment since I landed yesterday. I couldn't face it—it was the ultimate reminder that Ryder and I weren't together. I couldn't be home alone. If I could have moved out of New York, I would have. This city seemed to be at the core of my unhappiness. I'd relocated here to prove to my ex that I didn't need to have the next forty years of my life planned out. I'd come back here, now things were over with Ryder. This place represented my failures.

"I'm worried about you. I know you liked this guy, so why are you pretending that it's no big deal that you broke up?" Violet asked.

I sighed and sat back on the leather bench. "What's the alternative? I'm sick of being miserable. Crying isn't going to make me happy."

"So, you admit you're upset?"

"Is that what you want to hear? You want me to wallow in how awful my life is?" Was my sister trying to torture me?

"Yeah, that's what I want—for you to be miserable."

I glanced up as she rolled her eyes at me. "I'm trying to help. Just be honest with me and tell me what happened. You know what they say, a problem shared is a problem halved."

"You're ridiculous. No one says that."

"Humor me. I'm your little sister. You know I get my own way eventually, so just give in now. It's easier."

As much as I might complain, I wouldn't have agreed to drinks tonight unless I'd really wanted to see Violet. I covered my face as my eyes began to water. "I've been such an idiot, Violet." I gulped back my tears.

The bench dipped slightly beside me as Violet sat down, wrapping me in a one-armed hug. How had I let myself have feelings for a man who was so clear about what he wanted from me—sex and a wedding ring? How had I misread the signs so badly?

"Can we have another two rounds," she asked a passing server. I wasn't about to complain, alcohol couldn't possibly make things worse.

"I'm going to kick his fucking ass," Violet muttered. Her sympathy burst through my wall of indifference like a wrecking ball. I still couldn't believe after all Ryder and I had shared, he hadn't even had the balls to give me the papers himself.

It shouldn't matter. I always knew divorce was the next step in our relationship. Ryder wasn't the kind of guy to settle down. He'd told me as much over and over again. Still, for a man who'd never had an adult relationship, he was awfully good in one. So attentive and kind and . . . loving.

It had felt so real.

"What a douchebag," Violet said under her breath. "But at least you got your company."

True. And I should be grateful that Cecily Fragrance was free of debt. At least my career wouldn't collapse. There had been one good thing to come out of my divorces. The first divorce had pushed me into business, and the second had saved it. But if I'd known how much it would hurt, how high the cost to my heart would be, I never would have married Ryder.

"I can't believe he was so cold," I said.

"Well, he is British."

So? Ryder had never been cold *with me*. Darcy had been nothing but kind and friendly and their grandfather had a heart as warm as the sun. Just as my tears had slowed, a fresh batch appeared.

"His grandfather gave me a necklace. I think it led me to hope that maybe we could work out." The duke had hinted that even though our relationship hadn't had a conventional start, that there was a chance of it turning into something real, just like his own marriage had. "Ryder's grandfather really grew to love his wife—but only after they got married."

"And you were hoping Ryder would grow to love you, too?" Violet asked.

I nodded. "How could I have been so naïve?"

"Because you'd grown to love him," Violet concluded when I didn't say anything.

She didn't need my confirmation. We both knew she was right. I hugged my arms to my stomach, wanting the sharp pain to subside. When had I started to love him?

"You're such a good judge of character, normally," Violet said, almost to herself.

"How can you say that? I'm about to be divorced for the second time in two years."

"Well, when you put it like that. It's just that the first guy you married was a good guy—"

"Violet," I groaned. "I don't want to hear how my breakups have been all my fault."

"I'm not saying that at all. Hear me out. He *was* a good guy. You were both just too young. And Ryder? I mean I didn't know him that well, but he seemed decent. Seeing you together at the wedding? I just don't get why he'd just serve you with divorce papers when you had such a good thing going."

"He saved his company. And mine. The deal is done."

"Maybe," Violet said.

"There is no maybe. That's how it went down." I blotted my eyes with a cocktail napkin. I had to get it together. "I'll be okay. It was just a shock. I'll go back to my apartment tomorrow." Ryder hadn't misled me, hadn't lied. I needed to put my big girl pants on and get the fuck over him. I picked up my drink and tipped it back.

"I thought you were back at your place? You're not staying at his apartment, are you?" Violet asked.

Shit, I hadn't meant to mention that. "No, I just stayed here in the hotel last night. I didn't want to go home—"

"Scarlett, why didn't you call me?"

"Because I don't want to sleep on your couch."

"I don't want you on my couch either. But I could have come over and had room service on you."

I nudged her in the ribs and she giggled, sipping her cocktail. "I mean it. I love room service. If you're staying here tonight, count me in, sister of mine."

I knew she wanted to stay to keep me company, to hold me if my tears started again. But I appreciated that she covered up her concern with faux selfishness. Violet always knew just what to do. "Shall we go get in our jammies and find a cooking show to watch?" I asked.

"Sounds like a great idea. And if he calls, I'll answer," Violet said. "Has he called?"

I shook my head. "He won't. The divorce papers said it all. And anyway, I left my cell in England, along with the key to his apartment."

"How will you get your stuff back?"

I shrugged. "I was so focused on leaving him I never

thought about it. I just wanted to step back through the wardrobe and for him to have been a figment of my imagination."

"Oh well, we'll figure it out. I can collect your things. And knee him in the balls," she said, making a jerking motion with her legs that wouldn't scare a nervous Chihuahua. I didn't like her chances where Ryder was concerned, but I liked the sentiment.

After all, why should I be the only one hurting?

"God, it's so good to have you back in New York," Cecily said as she opened the door to my office with a dramatic swoosh. "You should have said you'd be here and I would have cleared my diary this morning."

I shook my head. "No need. I had a ton of things to get through." I smiled up at her as she sat on the corner of my desk.

"We have so much to catch up on," she said, her hands clasped as if she were holding herself together. "I just got a meeting with the beauty buyer for Saks."

She didn't sound very excited. "Are you kidding?"

She leaned across the table. "Can you believe it? I've been trying to hold it in all week. I wanted to wait to tell you face-to-face." Her eyes were beaming and her smile was wide.

"Oh, my God." I sat back in my chair, my arms flopping on the metal. "That is amazing. Well done, you."

"Well done us, you mean. You were the one who told me it was possible. And the one who told me to get back to them even though they said no like four times already. If it hadn't been for you, I would have given up."

I grinned up at her. "We're a good team."

"We're the best. We need to celebrate. Can you spend an evening away from that gorgeous husband of yours and sample some champagne with me?"

I held my smile in place despite the darkness that seemed to drift over me at the mention of Ryder.

"Sure." My phone buzzed, reception lighting up the line, and I put it on speaker.

"Your hot-as-hell husband is on his way to see you. Did I mention how lucky—"

I hung up and jumped to my feet.

"What are you so jumpy about?" Cecily asked.

"Cecily, I don't want to—" I couldn't think. I looked out through the glass of my office to see Ryder coming toward me. What the hell was he doing here? Shouldn't he be in England still?

"I'd love a man who brought me lunch, or even one who picked up the check." I could just make out Cecily's muttering under the booming in my ears.

"Fuck," I managed to spit out as I stood, bracing myself for impact.

Cecily narrowed her eyes. "What's the matter? Did you two have an argument?"

I didn't have time to answer before he had his hand on the door to my office. Our eyes met through the glass, but I looked away and stared at Cecily as if she was going to be able to tell me what to do. The last thing I wanted was to add to my humiliation by having to come face-to-face with the man who had discarded me as if I were an old pair of sneakers.

"Hello," he said as he walked through the door. The heat

of his stare burned me. Why was he here? "Cecily, please, can you leave us?" he asked.

Jesus, he thought he owned the whole world. What an arrogant asshole.

Cecily looked at me apologetically but slid off the desk and left us, closing the glass door behind her. I watched her go, only turning away when Ryder said, "Scarlett."

"Ryder," I replied, sitting down and flicking through some papers, trying to do anything other than focus on the embarrassment cloaking me.

"Is that all you're going to say to me? You leave England without so much as a goodbye and '*Ryder's*' the best you've got?" He said his name in a sing-song voice as if he were a nine-year-old boy pulling his sister's pigtails.

"Why are you here?" I asked, looking him square in the eye. I had nothing to be embarrassed about. He was the one who'd been a jerk.

He rubbed his thumb and forefinger over his brow as if he were confused. "Why didn't you wait for me?" he asked. His voice had softened and I felt my shoulders drop, just a little.

"What?" I asked.

He tilted his head. "You didn't even say goodbye, Scarlett. You just left." He spoke as if he was half mad, half frustrated. Like he was the one who'd been wronged. Unbelievable.

"Are you seriously going to pretend that you're the wronged party here? When you didn't have the balls to ask me for a divorce in person rather than having me served?" Shit, I hadn't wanted to let him know that it bothered me. That it had hurt.

He slumped in the chair opposite my desk as if I'd shot him. The same chair he used to sit in when he brought me lunch three times a week. Goddamn it. How had I let him in enough to hurt me like he had?

"Darcy was right," he muttered.

I didn't quite know what to do. He was sitting in front of me not saying anything. "I have a lot to get through this morning. Surely, anything you need to discuss, you can handle through your lawyer." I began to scroll aimlessly through the customer research that I had open on my computer screen, doing my best to ignore his strong, hard jaw and mussed hair. I missed touching him.

"I didn't know that Giles had drawn up the divorce papers," he said and my heart surged in my chest. That couldn't possibly be true. "And I certainly didn't know that he'd had them delivered to you."

I turned to him, clenching my fists under my desk. "Lawyers don't just draft divorce papers."

He leaned toward me. "Honestly, Giles thought he was being helpful. I had no idea he was even thinking about drafting those papers, let alone had delivered them to you."

He should have known. "We were staying in the same house. In the same bed," I replied.

"I know. You must think I'm a total bastard."

I raised my eyebrows. That was an understatement.

"But I don't get why you would think I would. I mean, that's not who I am and you know that," he said, his brows drawn together. "I care too much about you to do something so callous."

I closed my eyes, wanting to shut out everything he was saying. I didn't want to hear how much he cared about me. I had to focus on how getting those papers had ripped the Band-Aid off. At least the inevitable breakup hadn't been prolonged. It hurt, but I was clear on where I stood. I refocused on my screen, keeping silent.

"Why didn't you say anything? How could you just walk out?"

I slammed my palms down on my desk. "Are you freaking kidding me? How is this my fault? Your grandfather died and my services were no longer required. Fine. I took the hint. Don't you dare turn this around to try to make me feel bad about a situation I feel bad enough about."

He reached across the desk, covering my hand with his, but I snatched it away.

"You better go," I said.

"Scarlett, seriously, I'm sorry. But you have to believe me, I didn't send you those papers. Divorce was the last thing I wanted." He leaned close, reaching for me again.

"Sure it was. You can get back to screwing anything and everything. You are officially a free man." I jiggled my mouse, but my cursor was frozen.

"What happens if I don't want to be a free man? I don't want a divorce."

My stomach swooped at his words. I wanted him to be telling the truth. And a huge part of me believed him. It made sense that his lawyer had sent the papers without him knowing. It fit into the picture of him that I knew.

But having had some time apart, I understood that it was better that things finished now than wait until I fell any deeper and harder. He could never feel the way I felt about him, and he'd leave me eventually. If I ended it now, at least I had a chance to survive it.

"I'd say it's impossible. I'm not a good wife," I replied.

"You're the best wife." Ryder's voice was softer now, and I wanted to sink in against his chest. Have him hold me tight.

"I was a fake wife with you, don't you get it? I'm not good in real relationships." One day Ryder would realize that, and I would prefer it if our worlds weren't entangled further when he did. I knew I wouldn't survive losing him if we were together any longer. It was best to walk away now. I tried to swallow down the lump in my throat.

He leaned back. "That's just not true. I've never opened up to anyone other than my family the way I've opened up to you. You know me in a way that no one else has. Can we talk about this? About . . ."

I glanced up and his brow was furrowed as if he were trying to find the right words. "About what, Ryder? There's no point. It's better this way. You'll be better without me. And I'm better on my own." I needed to go back to my life before Ryder.

"I want to talk about us, Scarlett," he said, his tone clipped. "I want to have a conversation about our relationship, our marriage and the fact that for the first time in my life, I'm in love with a woman. My wife, in fact."

In love?

I hadn't expected that.

I closed my eyes, trying to shut out his words. I needed to hold on to what was left of my heart. "You can't love me."

"How can you say that? We've shared our lives, our bodies, our everything these past months—I love you. And I think you feel the same about me."

"Look, I accept that you didn't mean for the divorce

papers to be sent to me at that time. But it doesn't change anything."

"Surely that changes everything."

I wanted it to, but at the same time, I hated hurting this much. No one, not even my ex-husband, made me feel so used and thrown away. Even if it was a misunderstanding, it was proof that Ryder had the power to hurt me. I couldn't risk him settling deeper in my heart only to rip it open when things eventually fell apart. "It changes nothing. We always knew our time was limited. It's up now, and we need to get on with our lives."

"I don't want to get on with my life without you." He drew his brows together and ran his hands through his hair. I'd never seen him look so frustrated and out of control.

"I'm sure you'll do just fine. I bet by the end of the month, you won't be able to remember my name."

"How can you say that? I just told you I'm in love with you. Doesn't that mean anything to you?"

It should mean everything, but I knew by now that a man loving me didn't mean he wasn't capable of breaking my heart. "It doesn't mean enough. It doesn't mean forever."

I couldn't fight him much longer. I couldn't hear how he loved me. It was too much, too painful. And I had to get away—get back to a life no one had the power to destroy. I couldn't have another man explode my happiness. I wouldn't let it happen again.

I stood and took the jacket off the back of my chair and slid it on. "I have a meeting." I glanced at him as I strode toward the door. His face was drawn but still impossibly handsome. His arms hung hopelessly at his sides, his shoulders hunched. I shook my head. "See you around,

Ryder," I said, and I slipped out of the door, leaving him in my office.

It was better like this. My heart was safe.

Chapter Twenty-Eight
Ryder

"You're a mess," John said, glancing around my flat. I'd not been in to the office all week. Next thing I knew, John was standing in my living room under the pretense of dropping by paperwork we both knew he could have emailed.

"The maid comes tomorrow."

"I don't just mean your apartment. Look at you. You're wearing track pants for crying out loud."

I glanced down. I may have gone to bed in them. Twice. I wasn't really sure. "I was just about to go to the gym."

"You're a shitty fucking liar. It looks like you slept in those clothes." He brushed past me and into the living space. "And since when do you eat pizza and drink beer? I thought your body was a temple."

"What are you, my mother? Give me whatever it is you brought and fuck off."

He ignored me and plonked himself onto the sofa. "Where's Scarlett?" he asked.

I groaned. "I have no idea. At work, I presume."

"You presume? Aren't you two joined at the hip?"

"My grandfather died. She has her money. I have my company. End of story."

"Oh, so that's what we're dealing with." John stretched

his arm along the back of the big sofa, as if settling in. I glanced at the time on the oven. I wanted him gone. *The Young and the Restless* was about to come on and I wanted to know whether or not the woman with the blonde hair managed to escape from the woman who'd kidnapped her.

"I don't have time for this. Why are you here?"

He grinned, but otherwise ignored me. "It all makes sense now, my friend. The pizza boxes. The elasticized pants. The clear aversion to showering."

I was pretty sure it had been a couple of days since I stood in the shower, but who was counting?

"You can't just not come to work because you and Scarlett broke up," he said. "Pick up a sport, go buy a Bugatti, bang some other chick, hell, have a threesome. But get your shit together. We've got a business to run."

"I'm sick. I must have picked it up on the plane—" The thought of *banging some other chick*, as he put it, churned my stomach.

"You fly private, you dick. People who fly private don't pick up germs on a plane."

"Well, I'm not a doctor. I don't know where I caught it." I rubbed the back of my neck. "My muscles are wound tighter than a corkscrew, and I've got a wicked headache."

"More like a bad case of heartache."

"Don't be ridiculous."

"You might not recognize it, and who could blame you? The only organ you've been using around women all these years is your tiny dick—"

"Hey, now that's a step too far. My dick is plenty big enough, thank you. You're just jealous."

He rolled his eyes. "Sort your shit out. You're never

going to get back in the game looking like that." He waved his hand up and down my body as he winced. "This is New-York-Fucking-City. Women have standards."

I collapsed on the sofa opposite him and pulled the furry blanket that Scarlett had left over me. All her stuff was still here, which gave me some hope that I'd see her again. It had been part of the reason I'd stayed home the day after I'd seen her at her office. In case she came for her things—and gave me the opportunity to convince her to give us a second chance. Now, I couldn't face going out. I didn't want to speak to or look at anyone who wasn't her.

"What the fuck are you doing with that blanket? Have you reverted to your five-year-old self?"

"I'm cold." Her scent lingered on the fabric, letting me imagine she hadn't really left.

"Then do some exercise or put on a sweater. My God. Did Scarlett take your balls when she moved out?"

When she moved out. I hated those words. I leaned forward, and put my head in my hands. "What do I do, man? I can't sleep. I can't eat. I think about her all the time." There was no point in denying it to John anymore. My defenses were crumbling.

"Aww, shit," he said. "I'm sorry. I can see you're really cut up about it. I thought you were just sulking."

I sighed. "I've never been in this situation before. Women don't leave me." I'd made sure they never got an opportunity.

"So now you care about someone and you just give up? Just like that?"

"What else can I do? I can't force her to want to be with me." I didn't need shit from John on top of everything else.

"All I know is that this hurts like a bitch."

"I know. Unlike you, I've had my heart broken before. But you'll get it. But first, I'm going to burn all your sweat pants."

I chuckled and grabbed my stomach. I couldn't remember the last time I laughed.

"Why don't you get cleaned up and we'll go hit some bars, talk to a few girls—you know you'll feel better when you have some hot, naked woman in your bed."

My stomach hurt for a different reason now. "The only hot, naked girl I want in my bed is Scarlett."

"Then make it happen," he said.

"I told you, I can't *make* her come back to me."

He paused and took a deep breath. "You're Ryder-fucking-Westbury. You want her back, then you get her back."

"It's not that simple. I really hurt her. And now she doesn't want me back. Says she's bad at relationships."

He jumped to his feet. "That's good. Don't you see?" He stared at me, grinning.

"That you're being a callous bastard? Yeah, that's clear."

"Jesus, you're touchy. I meant, obviously if she was that upset, then she cares . . . and it's not too late."

"She walked out. Told me it was over—that we were better off apart. I was an idiot. I served her with divorce papers. Well, I didn't serve her, my law—"

"Look, I don't care. If you want her back, get off your ass and go get her back."

I shook my head. "You make it sound simple."

He sighed as if I were the dumbest bastard on the planet,

261

then took out his cell and dialed. All I could do was sit and watch. I knew the situation was hopeless.

"I need two flipcharts, some Sharpies and a lot of Post-its."

"What are you doing?" I asked as he hung up the phone.

"*We* are making a plan."

"A plan?"

"To get Scarlett back—assuming that's what you want?"

"Of course that's what I want. I love her, man."

"Have I ever steered you wrong?"

He'd always been the most fantastic friend to me. "Well, there was that one time in Vegas—"

"Not funny," he said, shooting me a glare that promised painful retribution. "So, the plan. Step one—get your smelly ass in the shower then dressed in pants that have a fly. Then we'll get started."

CHAPTER TWENTY-NINE
SCARLETT

"Thanks, just put it on the counter," I told the UPS guy, pointing to the maple cupboard on the far wall of my office. He set his delivery down and held out his electronic pad to sign. Again. It was his fifth visit to Cecily Fragrance this week, and it was only Wednesday.

"Who sends a basket of DVDs?" Violet asked, poking through the cellophane.

"It's better than the kale that arrived yesterday."

"Someone sent you a basket of kale? That's sick. Aren't you meant to get champagne and truffles? Or dim sum? Has New York changed so much since *Working Girl*?" Violet sighed dramatically.

"You weren't even born when *Working Girl* released. It's not like the eighties were your glory days."

"No, they were New York's glory days. Now this place is all kale smoothies and working nineteen hours a day."

I shut the door behind the courier and turned to find Violet tearing through the wrapper and taking out the movies. "Speaking of classic movies, these are good," Violet said.

I knew what the movies would be. *Casablanca*, *North by Northwest*, *An Affair to Remember*. Our Friday night movies.

I'd even managed to make him watch *The King and I* once.

"Who are they from?" Violet asked.

"Ryder," I said, sitting back down at my desk. I hadn't heard from him since I'd left him standing in my office almost two weeks ago.

She turned and I felt her glare on my back.

"Ryder? To say sorry?"

I shrugged. "I have no idea. I'm not interested."

"Have you seen him?" she asked, wandering toward my desk.

"Yes, I told you that he came by and said he didn't know the divorce papers had been sent to me."

"But, I thought you hadn't heard from him since?" She sat down opposite me, tapping the card she'd pulled from the basket against her knee.

"Yeah. That lasted for about a week, then I got an email. Then these deliveries started to arrive twice a day like clockwork."

"Twice a day?" She held out the card to me. "What does that say?"

I didn't want to open it. Every time I read one of the cards, I missed him a little bit more. "I don't know."

"Then I'll open it if you don't." She snatched the envelope back and tore it open.

I tilted my head back and looked up at the ceiling.

"*I miss Friday night movie night. I miss you. I love you. Your husband, Ryder,*" she read. "Scarlett. Wow—you can't just ignore this. What are you going to do?"

"Nothing, of course," I said, turning back to my desk. "It's over. He'll get bored eventually."

"Scarlett. He's wooing you." She splayed her fingers

wide, holding out the card. "It's like a movie or something. Why don't you want him to?"

"It's better this way. We're both free." I couldn't spend the rest of my life waiting for him to leave, worried that he'd stop loving me.

"Hey, when did you get so cynical? He's saying he loves you. And I imagine a lot of women have waited to hear those words from him."

"Thanks for that, Violet." But she was right. He'd soon be back to dating a million women.

"I'm just saying, this isn't a man who needs to work for it, but he is. I think he really cares about you."

"So? Honestly, Violet, why prolong the inevitable? If I was to call him up now and say, okay, let's go back to how things were—or whatever he thinks he wants to do—eventually it's going to end. It's always going to end. I'm just skipping to the good part here." I was saving myself heartache further down the line. If we didn't last then I didn't stand a chance. "There's no point in going through a breakup twice."

"You don't know that. Maybe it will work out and you'll grow old. Have babies." She tossed me the card and it skidded across the desk.

"Life doesn't work out like that."

"Mom and Dad worked out like that. Harper and Max are doing a good impression of a happy couple. Love finds a way."

I turned to her and looked her in the eye. "Not for me."

"Then, my gorgeous sister, tell me why you accept these deliveries? If you're so convinced you and Ryder aren't meant to be, why don't you reject them?"

Part of me didn't want to let go. Not yet. I wasn't quite ready. I shrugged. "I don't know. I don't want to make a scene." I needed to wean myself off him slowly, rather than go cold turkey.

"Well if you say so. Did you go back and get your stuff?"

"No. I asked him to box it up and send it to me."

"What did he say?"

"No." His response had been ridiculous. He'd replied to my email with a statement about how I'd need everything when I moved back in. The man was delusional. "Look, there's no point in talking about it. It's over."

Violet sighed. "I don't think even you believe that. And I certainly don't."

I snapped my head up at the tap on my glass door. It was the courier again. Violet scrambled to the door. "Sorry, dude, I forgot this," he said as he handed Violet a padded envelope.

"More gifts," she said. "If you don't like it and it's expensive, can I keep it?" she asked, handing me the delivery.

"Don't be a brat." It was Ryder's handwriting. Curiosity overtook my desire to cut off Violet's commentary and I turned the envelope over, opened it and reached inside.

I pulled out a small box with a note on top of it. The blue ink definitely wasn't Ryder's handwriting. Perhaps it was his lawyer. My stomach twisted.

Dearest Scarlett,

You are now Duchess of Fairfax. I can imagine that might seem a little strange for you, but please be assured, I've never met anyone so up to the task apart from my beautiful wife. Your good heart will guide you in life. Just make sure you quiet the voices that may try to drown out what it's telling you. I know you've been married before and someone has made the mistake of letting you go, but don't become cynical about the direction your heart leads you. Don't let the past prevent you from having a beautiful future.

My dear wife's necklace no doubt looked beautiful on you, and I want you to have these earrings that are to be worn with it. They were an apology to my love after behaving very badly toward her. I never deserved her, but after she accepted this gift, I spent my life trying to be a man she could be proud of.

Men are silly creatures. Often we don't realize what we have when we are lucky enough to find it. And we don't cherish the best things in our lives as we should. Ryder is a good man, but he's still a man.

I'm giving you these earrings as a sorry in advance of all the mistakes he'll no doubt make. There is no malice in his actions. He may be stupid, but he loves you. And you love him. Don't waste a moment in argument for the sake of pride or principle—or just because things get difficult.

Make sure he knows what you'll stand for and what you won't. But ultimately, forgive him and yourself. I know you make him happy—I've seen it in his eyes since he first met you. And I believe I saw it in yours, too.

Indulge an old duke. Be happy.

All my love,

The Duke of Fairfax (Your grandfather-in-law)

I couldn't hold the tears that blurred my vision as I folded up the letter and leaned forward on my desk, covering my eyes.

CHAPTER THIRTY
SCARLETT

My heels made satisfying clicks down the sidewalk as I headed north, carrying a large, white paper bag of Thai food. I'd never been to Ryder's office. I had no idea what his routine was, or what he normally did for lunch when he wasn't sitting across from me in my office. But he'd once issued an open invitation and today I'd decided to take him up on it.

He might not want to see me here at his place of business. He might send me away, unprepared to interrupt his day for a conversation with me. But I understood, finally, that time with Ryder was worth the risk of rejection.

About four o'clock this morning, I'd decided we needed to talk, and lunch seemed like a good time.

I'd spent the night awake. After two hours of tossing and turning, I got up and read and re-read Ryder's grandfather's letter.

Then I opened my laptop and scrolled through hundreds of photographs of my first husband and me, flicked through pictures of a life that seemed to belong to someone else. I smiled at some, cried at others. I finally finished mourning my first marriage. Sometime in the time since our divorce and the duke's death, I'd moved on. I didn't want him back. And I didn't want my old life back anymore.

I wanted Ryder.

A life with Ryder.

And that was worth risking my pride for. That I'd received the divorce papers without ceremony or introduction wasn't Ryder's fault. And he wasn't guilty of not sharing his feelings for me any more than I was guilty of not sharing my feelings for him.

I'd rejected him because I'd been hurt—prideful. And I didn't want to be hurt again. But a life with him was worth risking my heart for. I understood that now.

I signed in at the front desk and rode the elevator up to the eleventh floor. As I stepped out into the lobby, I took a deep breath before pushing on the chrome handle of one of the double glass doors.

I was doing this.

I smiled at the receptionist. "Scarlett King for Ryder Westbury."

I turned my head to the right to find Ryder staring at me through a glass partition in a conference room. The door to the room was open, and I heard someone call his name.

I tilted my head and held up the paper bag containing our lunch.

I saw his lips move but his eyes never left mine. Murmurings grew louder from the meeting room and people started filing out.

The last person to fill the door frame was Ryder himself. "Lyndsey, please make sure I'm not interrupted," he said, his eyes still fixed on mine. "I'm having lunch with my wife."

I couldn't stop the corners of my mouth from curling up.

I was careful not to touch him as he held the door open for me and I went inside the conference room. My knees were weak. My heart was weak. Neither could withstand physical contact, and we needed to talk.

I sat and began to unpack the containers of food I'd brought as he poured water into two glasses on the other side of the table from me.

I passed him his plastic knife and fork. "Thanks," he said, smiling carefully, like he was holding back.

"You're welcome," I replied, tapping my finger against the carton of food in my hand. The last thing I wanted to do was eat.

"I'm sorry," he said, but I shook my head.

"We did that," I said. "You apologized and explained. That's not where we are."

The crease between Ryder's eyebrows deepened. "Where are we then?"

"In your office, having lunch."

He laughed tentatively and leaned back. "You're funny."

"I know." I smiled and my body relaxed into the chair. This was who we were. This easiness between us—the immediate intimacy—it wasn't born out of a contract. It was just who we were together.

"Are we husband and wife?" he asked.

"I'm scared," I admitted, poking the noodles in front of me with my fork. It wasn't what I'd planned to say, but no less true.

"Whatever it is that you're afraid of, I'll stand between you and it my whole life," he said.

"But I'm scared of us. Of me. Of my choices. Of losing you."

"You'll never lose me," he said. "I just want to make this right between us. Tell me how."

Oh God. Was it really as simple as he made it sound?

"You can't promise that I'll never lose you. No one can. And that's what's so terrifying. My first divorce . . ." I closed my eyes as I remembered the pain. But it was a memory of the pain that I felt, not the pain itself. "It was like pouring bleach over everything I ever wanted. I had to start again. And I'm not sure I know if I could ever do that again. We were never the beginning of anything—just a means to an end, an adventure." It was so different with Ryder and I didn't know if that was good or bad.

"But isn't that always how the best beginnings start? When you don't know what to expect?"

"Maybe." Silence stretched between us. "I know I can't just walk away. You mean too much to me."

He sucked in a breath. "Scarlett, we can make this work."

The surety in his voice wound through me, a comfort I'd missed. I dropped my fork and dabbed at the corners of my eyes with my fingertips. I didn't want to cry, but his words somehow released me of a burden—I believed him. His chair scraped against the floor, and before I knew it he was touching me, pulling me onto his lap. "I hate to see you cry."

"It's relief."

"What is?" he asked.

"That you didn't throw me out for being crazy. That it was more than a contract for you too. That . . . that I'm here with you."

"Nothing makes sense without you," he said. "I feel like the last few weeks I've been treading water until I got you back. All these years without parents, I'm so used to being independent, self-reliant and you come along and within months, I need you just to function."

I turned into his chest, pressing my cheek against his shirt. I knew exactly what he meant. I felt more myself when I was in his arms.

"We went into this marriage as strangers and now— you're my lover, my teammate, my soulmate. The woman I love. You're my *wife*."

"So, where do we go from here?" I asked.

"I want to be married to you," he said.

I looked up at him. "We are married already unless . . ." Had he processed the papers?

"I know, and I burned the papers you signed. I meant that I want to be with you. Stay married to you—share a life with you."

I lifted my head and kissed his jaw. "I want that, too. I just need to know that you'll always let me in here," I said, scraping my fingers through his hair. "I accept that people change and maybe feelings do, too, but not out of the blue. I need you to share your feelings with me. I was blindsided by my first husband. That can't happen to me again. Not with you."

"I can do that. I love you."

"I love you, too. More than I thought I could love a person."

The corners of his mouth twitched but he resisted a grin. Instead he dipped his head and pressed his lips gently against mine.

"Does the door lock in this conference room?" I asked as I placed my hand against his chest. "This wife wants to fuck her husband."

"Well, my duchess, I'm going to insist I take you home

for that. I'm not willing to share your screams with everyone waiting in reception."

"Well, the car better be ready. Because I've waited long enough."

CHAPTER THIRTY-ONE
RYDER

I slammed the door shut and pressed her against the walnut surface with my hip as I cupped her head, tipping it up slightly as I slid my tongue through her lips. How I'd held out from fucking her in the car I had no idea.

Relief had given way to desire. I'd been prepared to do anything to get her back, but the fact she'd walked through the door to my office and laid it all out—her fears, her need for me—gave me a hard-on the size of Africa. The balls on this woman. She was so brave, so perfect. And I was a lucky fucking bastard to be married to her.

I turned the heavy metal lock to the side of her head. "I won't let anything disturb this," I said. Now I knew I had her back, I needed to make up for lost time.

I grabbed the bottom of her dress with both hands and pulled it up, my fingernails scraping against her skin. I wanted my naked body pressed against hers for hours. Raw instinct echoed within me, urging me to cover her body with mine. My fingers found her lace underwear and I yanked them down, kneeling as I did.

"Ryder," she whispered, threading her hands through my hair. She gasped as I dragged my tongue over her slit and deep into her folds. She tasted like mine, and I wanted to swallow every last drop. Her clit throbbed against my mouth and her hips bucked off the door. I grabbed her thighs, forcing them wider and then pushed her hips back. I'd never have a problem kneeling before my duchess, but there'd never be a time when I wasn't in charge when it came to her orgasm.

As her head fell forward, her silky black hair provided a curtain around her pulsing, wet pussy, her moans growing louder and louder. "It's been so long—I can't stop—Ryder." I dug my tongue in deeper, pressing my thumbs into the sensitive flesh just above her pubic bone. My dick pressed against my zipper at the thought of being able to bring her to climax with just my mouth. It was as if there was so much connection between us, the emotional and mental brought us to a point where we were constantly on the brink with each other.

Her hands tightened in my hair as she cried out my name. Her body began to shudder and I stilled. Slowly, I licked up to her clit, soothing her pulsing sex as she came down from her orgasm.

Her body sagged and I jumped to my feet to catch her before she fell. Because that was my job—to catch her before she fell. Now and forever.

"Someone needs to lie down," I said, scooping her up and taking her into our bedroom.

"I'd forgotten how good you were at that," she said, grinning up at me from where she was lying on the bed, watching me as I unbuttoned my shirt.

"You forgot?" I asked.

She laughed. "I have a bad memory. You're going to

have to remind me of those other things you used to do to me as well."

I shrugged off my shirt and as quickly as I could, stepped out of my shoes and trousers. "Other things?"

"Yeah, you know. Naked things."

I groaned at her words, fisting my cock as I neared her. "I'd be very happy to remind you of it all. I want it etched on your brain."

I climbed onto the bed, over her, my weight to one side of her. I stroked her side, under her arm, next to her breast that was always my favorite part of her.

She gasped. "Stop," she said, pushing me to my back and sitting up. "We've not thought this through."

I was done thinking; I needed to be inside her. "Hey, I've done nothing but think this through." I tried to focus on what she was saying and ignore the throbbing of my cock.

"We should talk practicalities before we—I mean I don't want to think everything is fine and—"

"What practicalities?" I grabbed her and pulled her back against me. "I have a condom if that's what you mean, but—"

Her hands lay chastely on my chest and it took serious effort not to push them down to my cock.

"I'm not kidding, we haven't discussed a prenup, whether or not we want kids, where we're going to live . . . Do you see yourself going back to England?"

I groaned. I didn't care about any of this shit. I just wanted her—whatever that looked like. "Scarlett, I don't need a prenup because we're never getting divorced. And I want as many kids as you do, and I don't care where we live as long as we're together."

"What if I said I want twelve kids?" she asked, circling her finger on my chest. My dick jumped in response.

"Then we'll have twelve kids, and I'll enjoy making them with you." I rolled her to her back and dipped to kiss her.

"I don't want twelve kids. Maybe three. But I don't want to live in your apartment."

"Three is good. And pick a home. You want to move back to Connecticut?"

She shook her head. "My life in Connecticut is over. I'm ready for a new life with you. I want to be in Manhattan, but I like England and Woolton."

"We can visit a lot. I'll contact some real estate agents tomorrow and we'll start looking for a new place together. Three kids are going to require a yard."

She grinned. "You're thinking ahead."

"To our life together," I said. Her hands skirted around to my back.

"I like that," she said, her legs parting wider and I nudged at her entrance. "No condom?" she asked.

"You want three kids, remember? And we *are* married."

Her eyes fluttered as I began to push into her. I couldn't wait to get her pregnant. Again and again.

"Oh Ryder," she whispered as I filled her to the hilt. "I love you so much."

"You mean you love my dick," I said, dipping to lick the hollow just above her collarbone.

"That is for sure," she said with a grin.

"Works for me," I replied. I blinked as I pulled out of her, that delicious tightness of hers pressing all around and shooting sensation down every limb. Christ, what had I done to deserve a woman like this?

I pressed my cock, coated in her wetness, in again, quicker

this time, and she cried out as if she was surprised by how good it made her feel. I hoped I'd *always* make her feel that way.

My skin slid against hers, our sweat mixing together and becoming one. I gathered pace, unable to hold myself back. We were together, both where we should be. Her fingernails dug into my shoulder and the twitch in her hips told me she was close. Seeing what I could do to her always pushed me over the edge. Her stomach arched up and I thrust again, gasping as I filled her—our climaxes perfectly in time.

"I never want you to forget how I can make you feel," I panted into her ear. "How I'll always make you feel. You're never to forget that you're mine, Duchess. That's just how it is and how it will always be."

Epilogue
Ryder

The gravel under my feet was confirmation we were back at Woolton. Before I'd shut the car door, Darcy sped past Lane and me to hug my wife, who was only half out of the car. "It's so good to see you," Darcy said. "Was the flight terrible?"

Despite my sister's show of affection, I hadn't let go of Scarlett's hand. Since we'd huddled over the pregnancy test, holding each other, waiting for that double blue line to appear, I'd been able to stomach being away from her even less than usual. I'd be very happy for her to move Cecily Fragrance into our building. We could even share an office. My suggestion had been refused with an eye roll. I'd bring it up again when Scarlett had the baby. The three of us could hang out all day. We could put a playpen in one corner, my desk in another, Scarlett's by the window. It seemed like a perfect solution.

"The flight was fine. Except no champagne," Scarlett said.

"Urgh," Darcy replied. "That's the worst."

"I had champagne," Violet called from where she was clambering out of the car.

"You're going to need it to get through dinner," Darcy mumbled. "Nobody have a cow," she said, as she took Scarlett's purse, studiously avoiding eye contact with me.

"Tell me you didn't," I said. Had she invited Frederick and Victoria to dinner?

She sighed and turned to walk back into the house as Lane unpacked the car. "It wasn't my choice. They invited themselves over."

"Who?" Violet asked.

I squeezed Scarlett's hand. "My cousin and his wife."

Violet groaned. "Fred and Vi," she said and Scarlett began to giggle. God, there was nothing more beautiful to me than her happiness.

Pregnant and happy.

"Honestly, they seem to be making an effort," Darcy said. "I guess what's done is done. And you have a few hours to sleep a little before they arrive at seven."

I checked my watch. Not long enough.

As I stepped inside, Scarlett squealed. "You did it." She dropped my hand. "It's perfect."

"Lane and Mrs. MacBee don't approve, of course," Violet replied.

"It looks great. Good for you," Scarlett said.

I tried to work out what was going on as I glanced from one of them to the other but they were just staring at the floor. "What are you two shrieking about?" I asked.

"The carpet, silly," Scarlett replied. "Do you like it? Darcy wondered if she should ask you but I said you trusted her."

"The carpet?" I asked, staring at the floor.

"Oh, good lord, Ryder," my sister said. "I've replaced

the worn, fraying carpet that had been down a half century. You didn't even notice?"

I guess it seemed cleaner. "Sure. Looks good," I said, hoping I was saying the right thing.

"You don't mind that I didn't ask? I know it's your house."

"It's just as much your house as mine, Darce." I slung my arm around her shoulder. Was she really worried? "You can do what you like with it. The carpet is great. I know you love this place, and you're not going to do anything but look after it," I said. "Things can't stay the same forever. Grandfather wouldn't have wanted that. He'd want you to do what made you happy."

"And about that . . . I know Grandfather ran everything on a skeleton staff, but I really think we need some admin personnel. I know it's indulgent. It's just that—"

"I think that's a great idea. I don't want you tied to this place. You need to go out and have a life, too."

Darcy snaked her hand around my waist and squeezed. "Thank you."

"Come to New York," Scarlett said. "We can find you a man."

"I prefer horses," Darcy said.

"Men smell better," Violet replied. She cocked her head. "Well, not all of them. But you should come to New York. I hate being the only single girl at dinner. Sometimes I feel like I'm going to be asked to sit at the kids' table."

I chuckled. I'd never had that feeling when I was single. I'd always been happy with life as it was until Scarlett walked in and turned it upside down. I wouldn't have it any other way.

"You never know, I might make it stateside when the baby's born."

"I'm going to hold you to that. For now, I'm going to take my wife upstairs and make sure she's well rested before dinner." I'd have to share Scarlett for the next few days, but right now I wanted it to be just the two of us.

"It feels good to be back." She smiled over her shoulder at me as we walked into our bedroom. She kicked off her shoes and padded across the room. "Oh look, someone's changed things around." Her eyebrows twitched in confusion as she took in the changes I'd requested to the room.

I'd called Lane earlier this week to ask him to move the two velvet chairs from the summer suite into my room and to put them opposite each other under the window, overlooking the croquet pitch. I didn't even need to ask her to take a seat—she naturally gravitated to the view of the Woolton gardens.

Despite it being early, the sun streamed through the windows and lit up my already glowing wife. The setting wouldn't get any more perfect. "You look beautiful," I said as I followed her across the room and stood beside her as she sat, my heartbeat growing louder with every step.

"You have to say that. I'm pregnant with your child."

"I have to say that because it's true."

She tilted her head to one side, the way she did when I was being a cheeseball. "Do you think we can play a little croquet while we're here?"

"Yes," I said, the words forcing their way from my dry throat. She leaned forward and poured out two glasses of cucumber water from the jug on the table in front of her.

"Need a drink?" she asked, offering me a glass as I stood over her.

I shook my head and she took a sip.

"Do *you* need anything?" I asked, rounding her chair, bracing myself for the moment I was about to make.

"Just you," she replied.

I took her hand and dipped to one knee.

She narrowed her eyes. "What are you—"

"Scarlett Westbury, when I invited you home the first night I met you, I could never have known how you would change my life. Change me. And when I suggested our arrangement, it was hardly the proposal you deserved." I fumbled in my pocket and pulled out the navy-blue ring box I'd been carrying since leaving our brownstone yesterday. I squeezed it tight, trying to steady my hands. My wife was the only person in the world who could make me shake.

"It was here at Woolton that I fell in love with you. So I wanted to wait until we were back, overlooking the lawn where we had our first disagreement because that was the moment I realized you were the first person outside my family whose good opinion I desired. In this house that you helped me secure and in this room where I first made love to you as my wife." The lid creaked as I opened the box, revealing my grandmother's engagement ring. "I want to ask you to do me the honor of wearing this ring, as my wife, for the rest of our lives."

She didn't reply straight away and I shifted slightly, lowering the ring before she caught my hand in hers. "Ryder, I would be as honored to wear that ring as I am to be your wife."

I captured her face in my hand and stroked her cheekbone with my thumb. "What did I do to deserve you?"

She shrugged. "Well, I've had a lot of nice jewelry since

I got married to you, so there's that." She wiggled the fingers of her right hand in front of me.

I chuckled and took the ring out of its box.

"And you know—you've got a *huge* penis."

I slid the ring onto her finger, the fit perfect. "You're so romantic," I replied.

"And there's your big heart and the way you love me. You'd stand between me and a bullet, and I know that."

There was no doubt I would.

"The way you do whatever it takes to make me happy, even if it just means bringing me lunch."

"You've thought about this," I said as I dipped to kiss the hand now adorned with my family's ring.

"Every day I think about how lucky I am," she said. "I'll never take what we have for grant—" She gasped and her eyes went wide. Grabbing my hand, she placed it on her slightly rounded belly. "Did you feel that?"

A little ripple passed under my hands. "Scarlett?"

"That's our baby joining in this moment. It's the first time I've felt kicking."

"That's unbelievable." I had the urge to scoop her up and wrap her in a duvet and not let her leave this room for the next four months. Scarlett didn't like me fussing, but what did she expect? "You're unbelievable."

I felt like the luckiest man alive. Scarlett had given me everything I never knew I wanted.

SCARLETT

"What are you two talking about?" I asked my brother and husband as I walked toward them carrying Gwendoline on my hip. The sun spilled out of the Connecticut sky and it was only the slight breeze that stopped the river bank from being too hot. They claimed to be fishing, but that was what they always said when the two of them disappeared within thirty minutes of us arriving in Connecticut. I was pretty sure it was just an excuse to gossip.

"Kids," Max said. "Ryder wants more."

I tipped our daughter onto my husband's lap and kissed him on the forehead. "It's Gwendoline's first birthday tomorrow. Give my body a break; we have time." My cheeks pinched as Gwendoline squirmed under her father's tickles. I hadn't said anything to Ryder but I was three days late. I'd picked up a pregnancy test at the grocery store and tomorrow morning we could take the test together like we had with Gwendoline.

"This one needs a little brother to take care of her," Ryder said.

"God, please, we need some more testosterone around here," Max said.

"Are you having another girl?" I asked.

"We don't know yet, but seriously, if it's another girl, you can have it."

I smacked my brother on the arm as Ryder chuckled. "You don't mean that," I said.

"I don't. But I'd really like a son."

"I don't mind what we have as long as all twelve of them are healthy," Ryder said.

"Twelve?" Max gasped. "Well, when you've had three daughters, tell me again that you don't want a son. All that pink. It gets to be too much."

Ryder shrugged. I really wasn't sure whether he would

ever mind having all daughters. "I'm not committing to anything more than two at the moment," I said.

"Two what?"

I turned to find Grace and Sam approaching.

"I'm so pleased you made it; how's the house?" Max asked.

"Oh my God, we're buried in boxes and contractors. Who knew a nineteenth century farmhouse would be so much work?" Grace sank to the grass on a sigh. "I'm so glad I hired people to decorate. We turned up with our suitcases last night. I can't take any credit. Apart from the art. We have the most beautiful Chagall in the dining room."

"It's colorful, that's for sure," Sam said with a grimace.

Grace started to laugh. "It will grow on you, my love. I promise."

"It better, Grace Astor," he replied as he kissed her on the head.

"Lauren loves her bedroom but insisted that I put Miles's cot in her room so he doesn't get lonely," Sam said and Grace shook her head.

"Something tells me it's not her baby brother she's worried about. But she'll be fine." Grace beamed. "And we're only up here on weekends. You're next," she said, lifting her chin toward Ryder and me.

"I love it up here," Ryder said.

I turned to him as Gwendoline clambered up his chest. "Really?"

"Of course. It's nice to get out of the city without having to fly to England."

"Yes, the trip's shorter."

"What trip?" Harper called out as she joined us and Max

pulled her onto his lap. "You know we have a thousand square feet of patio to socialize on with enough chairs for everyone, right?"

"We're trying to convince Ryder and Scarlett to buy a place up here," Max said. "You interrupted our sales pitch." He stood, wrapping his arms around her. "Now that we're all here, let's go get some beers."

I glanced up at Ryder as he slid his arm around my waist and we headed back to the house behind everyone else. "You want a place in Connecticut?"

He blew a raspberry on Gwendoline's neck and she covered his lips with her chubby fingers as she giggled. "Yeah, I think it would be nice to have a place up here with your family. But I know that it's maybe not what you want."

I'd been dead set against a place in Connecticut after my divorce—there were too many memories and broken promises—but now all that felt redundant. Life before Ryder was forgotten. I wanted what was best for my family and my future.

"I think it would be great," I said. The way Ryder's lips started to twitch at the edges gave away how happy he was. "You don't mind not going back to Britain so often?"

"My life is here with you and our family. We'll still visit and Darcy can come over and stay. I actually saw a plot of land a couple of weeks ago that might be perfect."

"Land?" How long had he been thinking about this?

"About a mile from here. Maybe we can go and take a look tomorrow."

"Okay. But there's something we have to do before that. And we have to be home to prepare for the party."

"What?"

I shrugged. "Just a pregnancy test."

Ryder stopped with a jolt and turned toward me, our baby in his arms between us. "You're pregnant?" he whispered, his head dipping to take in my face.

"I don't know. That's why we need to take a test."

"You're pregnant," he said. "Gwendoline, did you hear that? You're going to have a baby brother."

"Shhh," I said as he kissed my forehead and then our daughter's crown. "We don't know anything and we certainly don't know if it's going to be a boy."

"I know," he said. "I know because I'm the luckiest guy on earth. I've done nothing to deserve it, but the best things keep on happening to me."

What he didn't realize was I was the luckiest woman on earth. I had everything I'd ever thought possible and more. He might be British aristocracy, a duke and one of the most powerful men in Manhattan—what was more important was he was the best man I knew, my lover and my best friend.

The most incredible things kept on happening to us and, pregnant or not, I had everything I'd ever dared wish for.

Sign up to the Louise Bay mailing list

www.louisebay.com/newsletter

King of Wall Street

THE KING OF WALL STREET IS BROUGHT TO HIS KNEES BY AN AMBITIOUS BOMBSHELL.

I keep my two worlds separate.

At work, I'm King of Wall Street. The heaviest hitters in Manhattan come to me to make money. They do whatever I say because I'm always right. I'm shrewd. Exacting. Some say ruthless.

At home, I'm a single dad trying to keep his fourteen year old daughter a kid for as long as possible. If my daughter does what I say, somewhere there's a snowball surviving in hell. And nothing I say is ever right.

When Harper Jayne starts as a junior researcher at my firm, the barriers between my worlds begin to dissolve. She's the most infuriating woman I've ever worked with.

I don't like the way she bends over the photocopier—it makes my mouth water.

I hate the way she's so eager to do a good job—it makes my dick twitch.

And I can't stand the way she wears her hair up exposing her long neck. It makes me want to strip her naked, bend her over my desk and trail my tongue all over her body.

If my two worlds are going to collide, Harper Jayne will have to learn that I don't just rule the boardroom. I'm in charge of the bedroom, too.

the
NIGHTS
series

(A series of three, full length, stand-alone novels)

Parisian
NIGHTS

The moment I laid eyes on the new photographer at work, I had his number. Cocky, arrogant and super wealthy—women were eating out of his hand as soon as his tight ass crossed the threshold of our office.

When we were forced to go to Paris together for an assignment, I wasn't interested in his seductive smile, his sexy accent or his dirty laugh. I wasn't falling for his charms.

Until I did.

Until Paris.

Until he was kissing me and I was wondering how it happened. Until he was dragging his lips across my skin and I was hoping for more. Paris does funny things to a girl and he might have gotten me naked.

But Paris couldn't last forever.

Previously called What the Lightning Sees

promised
NIGHTS

I've been in love with Luke Daniels since, well, forever. As his sister's best friend, I've spent over a decade living in the friend zone, watching from the sidelines hoping he would notice me, pick me, love me.

I want the fairy tale and Luke is my Prince Charming. He's tall, with shoulders so broad he blocks out the sun. He's kind with a smile so dazzling he makes me forget everything that's wrong in the world. And he's the only man that can make me laugh until my cheeks hurt and my stomach cramps.

But he'll never be mine.

So I've decided to get on with my life and find the next best thing.

Until a Wonder Woman costume, a bottle of tequila and a game of truth or dare happened.

Then Luke's licking salt from my wrist and telling me I'm beautiful.

Then he's peeling off my clothes and pressing his lips against mine.

Then what? Is this the start of my happily ever after or the beginning of a tragedy?

Previously called Calling Me

indigo
NIGHTS

The only thing better than cake is cake with a side of orgasms.

Dylan James has no expectations when it comes to relationships. He uses women for sex and they use him for his money and power. It's quid pro quo and he's good with that. It works.

Beth Harrison has been burned. She's tired of the lies and the game playing that men bring and has buried herself in her passion—baking which keeps her out of the reach of heartbreak. As she begins her career as a TV baker, a new world opens up to her.

Dylan and Beth both know that casual sex is all about giving what you need to get what you want.

Except that sometimes you give more than you need to and get everything you ever wanted.

The Empire State Series

Anna Kirby is sick of dating. She's tired of heartbreak. Despite being smart, sexy, and funny, she's a magnet for men who don't deserve her.

A week's vacation in New York is the ultimate distraction from her most recent break-up, as well as a great place to meet a stranger and have some summer fun. But to protect her still-bruised heart, fun comes with rules. There will be no sharing stories, no swapping numbers, and no real names. Just one night of uncomplicated fun.

Super-successful serial seducer Ethan Scott has some rules of his own. He doesn't date, he doesn't stay the night, and he doesn't make any promises.

It should be a match made in heaven. But rules are made to be broken.

The Empire State Series is a series of three novellas.

HOPEFUL

Guys like Joel Wentworth weren't supposed to fall in love with girls like me. He could have had his pick of girls, but somehow the laws of nature were defied and we fell crazy in love.

After graduation, Joel left for New York. And, despite him wanting me to go with him, I'd refused, unwilling to disappoint my parents and risk the judgment of my friends. I hadn't seen him again. Never even spoken to him.

I've spent the last eight years working hard to put my career front and center in my life, dodging any personal complications. I have a strict no-dating policy. I've managed to piece together a reality that works for me.

Until now.

Now, Joel's coming back to London.

And I need to get over him before he gets over here.

Hopeful is a stand-alone novel.

love
unexpected

When the fierce redhead with the beautiful ass walks into the local bar, I can tell she's passing through. And I'm looking for distraction while I'm in town—a hot hook-up and nothing more before I head back to the city.

If she has secrets, I don't want to know them.

If she feels good underneath me, I don't want to think about it too hard.

If she's my future, I don't want to see it.

I'm Blake McKenna and I'm about to teach this Boston socialite how to forget every man who came before me.

When the future I had always imagined crumbles before my very eyes. I grab my two best friends and take a much needed vacation to the country.

My plan of swearing off men gets railroaded when on my first night of my vacation, I meet the hottest guy on the planet.

I'm not going to consider that he could be a gorgeous distraction.

I'm certainly not going to reveal my deepest secrets to him as we steal away each night hoping no one will notice.

And the last thing I'm going to do is fall in love for the first time in my life.

My name is Mackenzie Locke and I haven't got a handle on men. Not even a little bit.

Not until Blake.

Love Unexpected is a stand-alone novel.

AITHFUL

Leah Thompson's life in London is everything she's supposed to want: a successful career, the best girlfriends a bottle of sauvignon blanc can buy, and a wealthy boyfriend who has just proposed. But something doesn't feel right. Is it simply a case of 'be careful what you wish for'?

Uncertain about her future, Leah looks to her past, where she finds her high school crush, Daniel Armitage, online. Daniel is one of London's most eligible bachelors. He knows what and who he wants, and he wants Leah. Leah resists Daniel's advances as she concentrates on being the perfect fiancé.

She soon finds that she should have trusted her instincts when she realises she's been betrayed by the men and women in her life.

Leah's heart has been crushed. Will ever be able to trust again? And will Daniel be there when she is?

Faithful is a stand-alone novel.

⚜ LET'S CONNECT ⚜

Sign up for my mailing list to get the latest news and gossip.
www.louisebay.com/newsletter

I love hearing from readers – get in touch!

Website   www.louisebay.com

Twitter: twitter.com/louisesbay (@louisesbay)

Facebook: www.facebook.com/louiseSbay

               www.facebook.com/authorlouisebay

Instagram: @louiseSbay

Pinterest: www.pinterest.com/Louisebay

Goodreads: w w w . g o o d r e a d s . c o m / a u t h o r / s h o w /
8056592.Louise_Bay

Google+:   https://plus.google.com/u/0/+LouiseBayauthor

❦ Acknowledgments ❦

I've loved the characters in this series. The epilogue was particularly lovely to write as a goodbye—either a temporary or a permanent one. Maybe I'll tell Violet or Darcy's story one day. There's plenty to tell. Thank you all for reading. I know I say it all the time but being a part of your world, even in the smallest of ways, is such an honour. Thank you.

Elizabeth – Thank you for saving me from my own asshole. I think that's what you told me to write wasn't it? And as you know, I always do as I'm told. As ever, thank you!

Nina – Thank you for all that you do and for all your support. Let's kick some ass!

Karen Booth—Thank you for being in my world and for your help with blurb, again. I swear it's the worst part of the whole process.

To all the incredible authors that constantly give me help and support as well as amazing stories—I love this community and I'm so proud to be a member.

Najla Qamber – Everytime I think you can't get better, you do! You're amazing.

Jules Rapley Collins—Thank you for your support babycakes. Megan Fields I'm so pleased you like Ryder. And to my proofreading team – Sally, Charity and Peggy - I'm delighted you enjoyed Ryder as much as I did!

Thank you mummy for pushing me, for supporting me, for telling me how proud you are. Thank you for showing me what bravery is. I'm off to go and earn money for shoes. I love you.

Thank you to all of you who blog, tweet, share, like and help spread the word about my books. I couldn't do it without you!

Made in the USA
Middletown, DE
04 January 2019